Escape to Freedom

Book one of the FreedomRedux series

AJ Reissig

Enjoy!
AJ Reissig

Published in the United States by Freedom Notes Press, LLC.

Printed by CreateSpace www.createspace.com

Printed in the United States of America

ISBN: 1939489040
ISBN-13: 978-1-939489-04-3

DEDICATION

This book is dedicated to all of those who have fought for the ideas of freedom and liberty. May we never forget what they stood for.

CONTENTS

AJ Reissig

PREFACE

The United States Constitution is the blueprint for the government of our nation. More than anything else, it places limitations on our national government's powers. The first ten amendments, collectively known as the Bill of Rights, guarantee personal freedoms and judicial protections, as well as reserve certain powers to the people and the states. Of particular interest is the Tenth Amendment, which states, "*The powers not delegated to the United States by the Constitution, nor prohibited to it by the states, are reserved to the States respectively, or to the people.*" To put it quite simply, the federal government only has the powers that the Constitution specifically grants to it.

From early on, politicians increased and concentrated power in Washington DC. Lincoln intensified this effort during the Civil War; however, this paled in comparison to the expansion of the federal government by FDR. Beginning with his new deal and continuing through the Second World War, the government of the United States grew by leaps and bound. This continued after the war, albeit at a slower pace.

In the past twenty-five years, I have watched the acceleration of the pace of government growth. We have now reached a point where you can buy no product that is not regulated by the government, and government's burdensome regulations are becoming a massive drag on our economy. As well, we are now living in an era where the government is attempting to micromanage all aspects of our lives. Government run healthcare, retirement, welfare...all things that the government tells us are for our benefit...take away the individual liberties and freedoms of the American citizens.

As our liberties are eroded, citizens are becoming less productive and dependent on the government...just the opposite of what the Founding Fathers would have wanted.

I wrote *Escape to Freedom* as a fictional novel that illustrates where we are headed as a nation. More and more power concentrated in the hands of a few will lead us down a path of tyranny. We have seen this happen many times throughout history. I ask that you heed my warning, and let us make sure this does not happen to our nation.

ACKNOWLEDGMENTS

I would like to say thank you to all of the people who helped make this book possible. To all of the people who volunteered to act as beta readers, your assistance in the refining of this book is greatly appreciated. To my editor, Todd Barselow, thank you for the time spent editing this novel. I would like to say thanks to my children who have had to deal with all of my late nights and early mornings while I wrote this novel. Most of all, I would like to say thanks to my wife Christina. Not only have you had to deal with my eccentricities, but you have also supported and encouraged me through the past year of writing this book. Thank you.

All tyranny needs to gain a foothold is for people of good conscience to remain silent.

Thomas Jefferson

CHAPTER ONE

"I don't think you understand me, Mr. Dillon."

"Apparently I don't. While I realize that in the year 2049 this school is far different from when I went here as a teenager, I don't see what the problem is. Why don't you try to explain it to me like I'm a moron? Maybe you should use small words and speak slowly so I can grasp your meaning."

Kirk Dillon's voice was full of sarcasm as he glared intently at the high school principal.

Mrs. Rosenthal appeared to be in her late-40s. Her hair, which was the color of espresso streaked with silver, was pulled back tightly…Too tightly in fact, as the crow's feet around her eyes had been nearly stretched out of existence. In true Granny style, her oversized glasses were sliding down her very large, parrot-beak shaped nose.

Like the entire high school faculty, she wore the standard gray twill suit mandated by the Department of Education.

However, unlike the teachers, she had a small pin displayed prominently on the lapel of her suit. About an inch and a half in diameter with the image of a gold eagle embossed over a red, white, and blue circle, this was the symbol of a respected member of the Freedom Party and given only to those who showed extreme loyalty.

There were a few seconds of unnerving quiet as Mrs. Rosenthal began tapping her middle finger on her desk.

"I get enough lip from the students without having to take it from the parents; I can do without the sarcasm, Mr. Dillon. As principal of this school, it is my duty to the state to ensure that all students in this school meet the mandated education requirements. Furthermore…."

Kirk's eyes opened wide as he cut her off. "My son Sebastian has a 3.95 grade point average. That hardly sounds like he's not meeting the mandated educational requirements."

Mrs. Rosenthal squinted as she looked Kirk in the eyes but she continued without skipping a beat. "Furthermore, I have an obligation to be sure that the students that graduate from the school are ready to meet the challenges of college and career."

"Once again, GPA of 3.95," Kirk countered. "He scored a 35 on the ACT, and a 2345 on the SAT. Academically, he is ranked as number one in his class. It appears that he has been properly prepared for college. What is the freakin' problem?"

Straightening her posture and jutting her chin slightly, Mrs. Rosenthal continued. "Let me be blunt, Mr. Dillon. In American history class, Sebastian recently had an assignment to explain the historical significance of a famous figure from

American history. Sebastian chose to write his paper on Patrick Henry. Moreover, Sebastian's main argument for the significance of Patrick Henry was the 'give me liberty or give me death' speech."

Kirk blinked twice and then said, "I don't get it. What's your point?"

Leaning her head forward and looking over the top of her glasses, Mrs. Rosenthal gasped, "Don't you realize how dangerous an idea that is? He is idolizing treason! That is exactly the kind of thinking that we are trying to avoid in the school system!"

Kirk leaned back in his chair and thought, *"I can't believe what I'm hearing."* Kirk turned his head slowly to look behind him. Sebastian was sitting on a bench in the back of the principal's office, and had remained silent during the entire conversation. As Kirk's eyes met his son's, a small grin eased from the corner of Sebastian's mouth. Kirk absently began rubbing his West Point Academy class ring with his thumb, and then turned his head slowly to look at Mrs. Rosenthal.

"The 'give me liberty or give me death' speech is an important part of our American heritage," he said. "During the American Revolution, the great orators of the day, which included Thomas Payne, Thomas Jefferson, and Patrick Henry, gave voice to our grievances with Great Britain. Their words were inspiration not only for the soldiers who fought during the American Revolution, but also for the countless generations who followed."

Mrs. Rosenthal leaned over her desk and folded her hands. "And how many people died in the American Revolution? If it were not for the fire branders of the time, there may never have been an American revolution at all. How many lives would've been saved? And how many lives were wrecked by the war?"

Tilting his head first to the left, then to the right, Kirk could feel the sweat running down his back and his face began to flush. He unfastened the top button of his polo shirt, and then took a deep breath. He continued to speak as calmly as he could.

"And we'd still be a British colony!" he replied slowly.

"And that's a bad thing?" she replied. "So many lives would've been saved. And your so-called great orators were nothing more than robber barons who didn't want to pay their fair share of taxes…taxes that supported the very nation that protected the American colonies. Were it not for the American Revolution, we would be so much closer to the One World Government today. Once the entire world is united under a single government, the whole planet can live in peace and harmony working together for the collective good and ending the evils of capitalism."

Kirk stared directly into her eyes and said, "I served during peacetime and during combat for more than 20 years in the service of my nation, and I have spilled blood on three different continents. I will tell you this: I hope that neither I nor my son sees the day when we live under a One World Government."

Kirk took a deep breath, and then continued. "The ideas of liberty and free market capitalism are what made this country great. During the 19th and 20th centuries, the great booms in our economy were due to free-market ideas and the growth of free market capitalism. As a nation that is who we are…a capitalist society."

"Yes, Mr. Dillon, as a nation that is who we are, or rather who we were. It is also a past that our government wants us to forget. That is why there is such an effort in our history classes to show the errors of the past and why ideas such as capitalism and free markets lead to nothing but income inequities in the creation of robber barons."

Mrs. Rosenthal then reached into her desk and pulled out a very old book. The book's brown cover was extremely worn, and the spine was beginning to break down. She then continued to speak. "Had the history class incident been a solitary infraction, I may have let it pass. After all, teenagers are prone to hasty and unwise acts. However, there was another incident. Sebastian was found reading this book in study hall. Not only do we have a policy against books on printed paper, the subject matter is totally inappropriate."

Mrs. Rosenthal handed the book to Kirk Dillon. He took the book, looked at it for a moment, and then began to speak. "Mrs. Rosenthal, this book belongs to me; I gave it to Sebastian to read."

"You *what?*"

"Yes, the book is mine. Ever read it? It was written by…."

"I know who wrote it, Mr. Dillon," she interrupted.

Kirk continued, "Anyway, the book was written to warn of the dangers that result from government central planning. Since schools today glorify socialism and cast capitalism as wicked industrialists exploiting the poor masses, I have seen the need to teach my child about the benefits of living in a society that believes in free market principals, capitalism, and individual rights. Sebastian has been required to read books on the Austrian school of economic thought, as well as books that warned of the dangers of socialism. Oh, and The Bible…I'm sure you know who wrote that one."

Kirk Dillon pointed his index finger at Mrs. Rosenthal. "There was a time, not that long ago, when some of those books would have been required reading at this high school."

"You have no right to force that child to read those books!" she protested.

"I'm his father!" Kirk bellowed. "It's my job to see that he is prepared for the real world!"

"No! That's my job, the job of every teacher at this school, and the job of the Department of Education!" Mrs. Rosenthal shouted. Deep furrows formed on her forehead as she squinted her eyes. "You have no business trying to educate a child. Do you have a degree in education? I think not. You are not qualified to teach a child."

The pounding of his heart could be felt all the way to his ears and Kirk's face felt as if it were on fire. He squeezed the arms of his chair in an attempt to regain control.

"Well, apparently you and your teachers aren't qualified either. If you people weren't doing such a half-assed job, I wouldn't be spending as much time teaching Sebastian things that he needs to know. Do you have any idea how much time I have spent re-teaching him because of the socialist crap you people are forcing down his throat? Whatever happened to focusing on reading, writing and arithmetic? Instead, he gets to hear about social justice, and how capitalism isn't fair to the poor, and how the evil rich guys just want to make more money on the backs of the little guy. Maybe you people should focus on teaching skills and get out of the brainwashing business!"

Mrs. Rosenthal blinked, stood up straight and crossed her arms. "I was of the belief that Sebastian had come upon these ideas through a poor choice in friends. I now see that I was wrong; it is you who are the bad influence. You are not fit to be a parent. I must tell you now Mr. Dillon, that hearing talk such as this makes me consider contacting child services."

As the pressure inside Kirk continued to build, his grip on the chair tightened. As his fingers and knuckles turned white from the lack of blood flow, he took a deep breath and tried to calm himself.

"Back in 2025 when they passed the American Child Protection Act, the bill was sold to the public as a way to get children out of the hands of abusive or criminally prone parents," Kirk said. "It was *not* intended as a way for the government to silence those who spoke their minds–like we have seen in this town recently. And it most certainly was not intended for high school principals to take children from people who have opposing political views."

"It depends on what those views are, Mr. Dillon," Mrs. Rosenthal said as she crossed her arms. "In a government boarding school, a child is not exposed to radical ideas that would endanger him or the nation. I'm sure you have read the stellar reviews of some of the schools."

"Yes, I have," Kirk replied. "And since every one of those news outlets are censored by the government, they would lose their license if they didn't give an impressive review. Of course they're not going to report or follow up on the stories of brainwashing and turning those kids into state robots who can't think for themselves."

"You couldn't mean that!" Mrs. Rosenthal gasped. "Everything the government does is for the people's benefit. The president has said so!"

Kirk stood and leaned over Mrs. Rosenthal's desk, looking her in the eyes with an icy stare. "Eight years ago, when you were assigned here, I was irritated because you were a Department of Education appointed stooge rather than an employee hired by a local school board."

"The Department of Education knows better than to give average citizens, with no experience in education, the important task of selecting a high school principal," Mrs. Rosenthal interjected.

Ignoring Mrs. Rosenthal's interruption, Kirk continued.

"I now realize that is not why I despise you. I now realize that *you* are one of the government's mindless robots. You are one damned piece of work."

Kirk straightened up and put his hands in his pockets as he said, "We're done here."

He quickly turned around and looked at Sebastian. "Let's go, son." Sebastian grinned and immediately leapt out of his seat, grabbed his backpack, and quickly proceeded to exit the principal's office without saying a word.

Mrs. Rosenthal put her hands on her hips and said, "The two of you are not to leave this office until we finish this. This is a serious issue and it must be resolved and resolved right now!"

Not even bothering to turn his head and face her, Kirk calmly said, "As far as I'm concerned this issue is resolved.

Good day to you, ma'am."

Neither Kirk nor Sebastian said a word as they crossed the parking lot. Kirk was unlocking the door when he heard a voice call, "Hey Sebastian!"

They both turned toward the voice to see a student walking from the track to the school.

"How's it going, Ted?" Sebastian said.

"Alright," he replied." Hey, is that the old truck your dad restored?"

"Yep," Sebastian replied with a broad smile. "1985 Ford Bronco. Took Dad seven years to restore it…it was a real heap when he got it. I helped build the diesel engine he swapped in."

"Very nice," Ted said. "Don't they have a top or something that covers the rear end?"

"Dad likes to drive with the top off when the weather is warm," Sebastian replied.

Ted nodded, and then said, "It's a real sweet ride, Mr. Dillon."

"Thanks," Kirk replied. He looked at Sebastian and said in a huff, "Hop in so we can get going. I don't want to hang around here."

Without a word, Sebastian threw his backpack into the open cargo area of the truck and then made a beeline for the passenger's side door. As he took his seat, Sebastian said, "I don't know why you lock the doors when the top is off. Anyone who wanted to get in would just climb in through the back."

"Just a habit," Kirk replied.

Sebastian looked at Kirk and said, "You may have said a little too much to the principal, Dad."

Kirk quickly turned toward Sebastian and said, "That woman has me fuming right now; I really don't want to talk about this." Sebastian knew his father well enough to know that this was the time to keep quiet and let him burn off a little steam.

Kirk put the key in the ignition and turned it with a quick flip of the wrist. The transplanted turbo diesel roared to life, settling into the slow, loopy idle common to diesel engines of the early 21st century. He stepped on the accelerator, revving the engine to about 4000 RPM's, and then held it there for nearly thirty seconds. The loud growl of the engine drew stares from others in the parking lot, but Kirk paid them no mind. He closed his eyes, and thought back to his days of following the NASCAR circuit, thinking about the races at Talladega and Daytona. *"They should have never made racing illegal, no matter what the environmental impact,"* Kirk said to himself. He opened his eyes and looked at Sebastian, who was wearing a broad grin. There was no doubt in Kirk's mind that Sebastian shared his love for racing. As he shifted the transmission into reverse, he said, "Sebastian, I'm taking the long way home."

"Gotcha."

As Kirk drove the country roads toward home, it seemed like he was traveling down a tunnel of colored leaves. The leaves were at the peak of their color, and the fall showing of 2049 was no disappointment. Firebrick red, gold, blazing orange, bright yellow, all mixed with touches of brown and various shades of green. Intermixed with the trees were fields of corn and soybeans, which had reached their harvest-time color of golden brown. To Kirk, scenery was intoxicating; he had almost forgotten the problems of the day when Sebastian's voice snapped him back to reality.

"Dad, I'm really sorry about all of this. And I know this is a tough day for you anyway."

At first, Kirk said nothing. Finally, he said in a raspy voice, "Nine years. It's been nine years since your mother was killed in that car crash."

"That was a rough year," Kirk thought. Not only had his wife of twenty-one years died, but his father had died of cancer earlier that spring. After the loss of his wife and father, he had fallen into a state of depression, which had led to a drinking problem. Writing novels…novels about his military exploits during the Middle Eastern Wars…that is what ultimately snapped him out of his state of depression and ended his alcoholism.

After what seemed like an eternity of silence, Kirk spoke again. "Son, what happened at school was none of your doing. You were in the right; not them."

"Then why was I the only one who was sent to the principal's office?" Sebastian asked. "If the school is in the wrong there should've been a whole slew of us who had to visit the Beak."

"The who?" Kirk asked.

"The Beak," Sebastian replied. "That's what everybody calls Mrs. Rosenthal because of that nose."

Kirk chuckled. "Now that you mention it, it was rather large and looked like a parrot's beak." He sighed. "Maybe you were the only one in the Principal's office because you were the only one who stood up for what you know is right. Since you were a little boy, I have always tried to teach you to think for yourself and stand up for what you believe in. I've also spent a lot of time teaching you the things the school system either refuses to teach or is incapable of teaching."

"The school teaches stuff that is so radically different from what you have taught me," Sebastian said. "They say that people who own businesses are evil and greedy; you like and respect them. They say capitalism nearly destroyed America; you say it is what made us a great nation."

"It's because I am what was once called a libertarian. I believe in free markets and limited government. I am all for freedom and liberty. Many teachers are what used to be called liberals."

"Are all teachers liberals?" Sebastian asked.

"No," Kirk replied. "However, the education system has always been a haven for liberals; it's just the nature of the beast. And that's not a big deal if educators stick with facts and figures; in the nineteenth century, they spoke of teaching the "three Rs"…reading, writing, and arithmetic. But no teacher, liberal, libertarian, or otherwise, should be trying to sway kids to their political beliefs, and that is exactly what is going on at your high school…and at other high schools across the country. In the past twenty years or so, that practice has been put into overdrive. In an effort to mold everyone into their image, they are rewriting history, putting such a backward spin on our past that I don't even recognize what they're teaching as American history these days. What makes it worse is the politicians of today not only allow this to happen but they promote it. You see, the liberal idea of government dependence is what keeps those politicians in power. When everyone in our country has been brainwashed into believing that they can't do anything on their own they will never, ever elect any politician who even hints at personal responsibility. Want to stay in power? Just keep the gravy train a rolling. "

"You don't like the Bea…I mean, the principal, do you, Dad?" Sebastian asked.

"There are good teachers and bad teachers, just as there are good Principals and bad Principals. You've had some good teachers at this school, people who really want to see kids get a top notch education. Unfortunately, they are shackled to a system that is more interested in spreading socialism than teaching kids the skills they need to become productive members of society."

Sebastian looked at Kirk and said, "Dad, you didn't answer my question."

"Sorry." He took a deep breath and replied, "I despise that woman. She represents everything that is wrong with the education system today. She doesn't see it as her job to merely give students the tools to become successful; in fact, that isn't much of a priority to her. Her priority, and the priority of her superiors within the Department of Education, is to crank out graduates that are all cut from the same mold, spouting the same political beliefs and the same social values. I believe in individual freedom, the right to succeed or fail on your own, with no government input. That doesn't sit well with most government bureaucrats."

Sebastian looked at his father. This lecture was beginning to sound familiar, and his father was beginning to preach again. Sebastian decided to try and change the subject.

"You've made me read a lot of books that we haven't read in school. And a lot of them are printed on paper. I think that's cool; it's almost like…. I don't know… like touching history."

"Well, as convenient as it is to be able to store millions of books on my e-reader, there's just something about the tactile feel of having a book in your hand and reading off of real paper. Back when I was a student at your high school, about half of what is now the cafeteria was the school library. At one end of the room there were a few small tables where you could sit and read, but the rest of the room was completely filled with shelf after shelf of books; shelves that went all the way to the ceiling and required a ladder to reach the top."

Sebastian began to laugh and said, "Yeah, you told me about when the brakes went out on the school bus and it crashed through the wall of the library."

"That was back in your Grandpa's day," Kirk said with a smile. "He said that crash was pretty spectacular."

"Are there any companies that make books on paper anymore?" Sebastian asked.

"No," Kirk said quickly. "At least not in the United States. The government has seen to that."

"You mean it's illegal?" Sebastian asked.

"Not exactly. While it's not illegal to print the book, the government has regulated the industry to the point where no company, large or small, could print an affordable book."

"Is it all environmental regulations?" Sebastian asked.

"Most, but not all," Kirk replied. "The Fairness Doctrine of 2031 created tons of new regulations that apply to all forms of media… print, audio, video…all of it. They were especially hard on anything printed on paper…hard copy, we used to call it. However there was what seemed to be at the time a loophole for digital print."

Sebastian looked puzzled. "What do you mean by seemed?"

"I don't think it was a loophole," Kirk replied. "I think it was put there for a specific reason. I think the government wanted all paper books to be gone. Once the physical libraries were gone, the only way to either borrow or buy a book was electronically. Since the government controls the Internet, it can now not only monitor every sale and borrowing of a book, but it can also control what goes into print. One of the key principles to controlling a population is to prevent the spread of subversive ideas."

Sebastian leaned his head back and look straight ahead not saying a word. His father was once again beginning to preach about freedom and liberty and how this country was just a shell of its former self. While Sebastian agreed wholeheartedly with his father, he had heard the speech so many times that he couldn't wait to get home.

CHAPTER TWO

Senator Jack Spearman paced about the West Wing lobby of the White House. He looked at Congresswoman Mavis Young, who was reading from her computer tablet while seated on a black couch on the other side of the lobby.

"What the hell is going on?" he snapped in his strong Texas accent. "Son of a bitch had us here an hour ago; we're still waitin'!"

Mavis looked up from her tablet and said calmly, "Blackjack, he's the President of the United States. I'm sure he's busy."

"And I'm not?" he replied angrily. "Son of a bitch never had a real job. What's he ever produced…besides debt? What does he know about busy? All he knows how to do is steal money from businesses to put in the hands of union thugs and his pet projects. And we still don't know Jack about him."

"He is a bit of a mystery," Mavis said as she continued to

read from her tablet.

"Damn right he's a mystery," Jack said. "Here he comes, an unknown professor from up north, and takes the '44 election by storm. And how does he win? By promisin' more handouts to people who are already at the government feedin' trough. All he did was slop the hogs. Won by a landslide…same thing this last election."

Mavis looked over the top of her tablet and said, "Don't forget how popular he was when he said he would stop the political stalemate in Washington by reforming campaign finance and merging the Republican and Democrat parties."

"How could I forget?" Jack exclaimed as he continued to pace.

"Well," Mavis continued, "It resonated well with the people, who were tired of watching billions of dollars being spent on political campaigns, with no real difference between the candidates."

"I agree with you on that," Jack replied. "Towards the end, there wasn't much difference between the two parties. But look what we have now. We have only one party, and the president's best buddy, Adolph Brooks, is the chair of the party. And with that campaign finance law, all donations have to flow through the party."

"Which means all political funding has to be approved by Adolph Brooks," Mavis added. "Which may as well mean the president controls who gets into politics."

"Damn right," Jack said.

"Unless of course, you're very wealthy," Mavis said with a

coy smile.

Jack stopped pacing for a moment and looked at Mavis. "And I earned every dollar. I never went to no college. Mom and Dad were East Texas farmers who were dirt poor. I went to work on the oil rigs as soon as I was old enough."

"I'm not being critical, Blackjack," Mavis said. "Your parents instilled in you the drive you have today, and had you not gone to work on the oil rigs at such a young age, you many have never invented your own rig design. Your parents and those experiences are what made you a billionaire."

Jack took off his Stetson, looked at the floor, and ran his fingers through his hair. Putting his hat back on, he looked at Mavis and said, "Just glad my parents lived long enough to see the start of Spearman Offshore. If only they could see my little company today."

"There's nothing little about your company Jack," Mavis said with a smile.

Jack returned her smile and said, "So even with no outside funding, how is it you keep gettin' elected? We both know you're on the president's shit list."

Mavis shrugged her shoulders and said, "Most popular teacher in school, I guess."

Chuckling, Jack said, "Come on Little Sister, there's more to it than that. Your opponents always outspend you by a huge margin, but every election you come out on top."

"I guess the people in my district still believe in what I'm fighting for," Mavis replied. "As a teacher, I became increasingly disgusted with the education system. As the years passed, federal regulations took more and more control away from the states. At the same time, the education system placed less emphasis on the core subjects - reading, writing, math, and science - and more time was spent on political and ideological indoctrination. Parents had less of a say in the education of their children, and were constantly told by the government that it was the duty of educators to teach moral values. That's just not right."

"What was the tippin' point?" Jack asked. "When you finally said the hell with it?"

"When the school systems were nationalized in 2040," Mavis replied. "By that time, schools had become little more than political training camps. Home schooling became illegal. Private schools remained but they were forced to adopt the same curriculum as the public system, as well as employ Department of Education approved Principals and staff. That's when I decided to run for Congress. Been here ever since."

"One woman and a cause," Jack said. He smiled and then added, "Of course, being the product of Texas education must have helped, too."

Mavis grinned as she looked at Jack and said, "Texas A&M, class of 2025…and don't you forget it."

"Yes ma'am," Jack said as he laughed. "Anyway, to get back to the president…I don't trust him."

Mavis placed her tablet on the black couch and looked the Senator in the eyes. "Blackjack, he is not like you or I; he is a career politician who spends his time kissing babies and then stealing from their parents. Of course he's not to be trusted."

Mavis was about to speak again when she heard the sound of someone walking toward them. Looking to the left, she saw a young, blond haired woman approaching. Like all White House and Capitol building staff, she wore the standard gray twill suit.

"Senator Spearman, Congresswoman Young...President White will see you now," the woman said. "If the two of you will follow me, I will take you to the Oval Office."

Jack adjusted his suit jacket, and looked at the presidential assistant. "Thank you ma'am," he said. Looking to his left, he said to Mavis Young, "Well Little Sister, should we get this over with? Son of a bitch only had us waitin' an hour."

Mavis nodded, and stood up. "Let's go. But try to mind your temper, Blackjack. No matter what you may think of him, he is the President of the United States."

"President or dictator?" the senator shot back quickly. "There was a time when that title belonged to the leader of the free world. Now that title goes to the person who wants to become the king of the entire world."

"Let's just get this over with," Mavis replied.

The senator and congresswoman followed the presidential assistant from the West Wing lobby to the Oval Office. The entire West Wing seemed to be devoid of sound, except for the clickety-clack of the women's shoes and Jack's cowboy boots on the walnut and cherry hardwood floor. Upon reaching the main entrance to the Oval Office, the presidential assistant knocked loudly on the door. "You may enter," a voice called from within.

The assistant quickly threw open the door to the Oval Office and bowed deeply; so deep in fact, that her long blonde hair nearly touched the floor. "With your indulgence, sir, may I present Texas Senator Jack Spearman and Texas Congresswoman Mavis Young."

"Son of a bitch thinks he's a king," Jack whispered out of the corner of his mouth. Mavis fought back her laughter; only a faint smile was visible.

President Conrad White sat at the Resolute Desk in the center of the room, apparently reading. He looked up, and stroked his thick black and gray mustache with two fingers, almost as if out of habit.

"I see. Very well, close the door on your way out, Jessica." The president went back to reading, completely ignoring the congresswoman and senator. Jack looked at Mavis; she could see the building anger in his eyes. After about a minute, the president, without looking up, said "I'll be with you in a minute; have a seat."

The congresswoman and senator sat down in identical antique chairs that were very beautiful but very uncomfortable. Mavis began to rub her thumb and forefinger together nervously, as if trying to break the tension of the moment through any action possible. Jack began tapping his boot heel, creating a ting-ting-ting sound as the metal heel cap of his boot struck the hardwood floor. The congresswoman glanced sideways at him; she could see from his face this was not nerves; this was anger. Jack was not a patient man; he was a man of action, and was not used to waiting on anyone. "Time is money," was his favorite saying.

Finally, after what seemed like an eternity, the president rose and walked toward the pair from Texas. He was fairly short, approximately five foot five, and of husky build. He had a thick mop of black and gray hair, and a long, thick mustache that covered his upper lip. As always, he was wearing a sparkling white suit.

Looking at the senator he said coldly, "The next time you come to the White House, take those metal things off of your shoes. I will not tolerate anyone scratching up my floors. And you take that hat off! You are in the White House, *not* in a barn. Don't they teach manners in Texas?"

The senator leapt to his feet. Standing toe to toe with the president, the Senator was at least a foot taller than the president. Looking down at the president, Jack said, "You're one to talk about manners! The metal toe and heel caps are in honor of the Texan's cowboy past. And I wear boots, not shoes. Shoes are for women and East Coast sissies. The hat ain't comin' off; the only time a man from Texas takes off his ten gallon hat is when he's in the shower or in bed for a romp with his wife. "

"Mr. President," Mavis spoke quickly and nervously, hoping to stop a confrontation before one started. "Perhaps you could tell us why you asked us to the Oval Office."

"Yes. Yes. The pair from Texas. Yes. Yes."

It took the president a moment to stop staring Jack, but he finally turned his head and walked back to his desk. Standing behind the desk, he crossed his arms and looked at the congresswoman and senator. "As you know, I signed the National Public Safety act into law three months ago. As part of the act, all owners of firearms are required to turn their firearms into national police, or register their firearms with the national police. Unfortu…."

"At a cost of fifteen million per firearm!" Jack burst out.

The president continued speaking as if had not heard the senator's outburst. "Unfortunately, in many of the southern states, the firearm turn-ins have been extremely low; far, far lower than the estimated level of gun ownership. Now, we expected there to be some lawbreakers but this level of un-cooperation is totally unacceptable. I am charging you, as representatives of the state of Texas, with the task of getting the people of your state in line. They need to comply with the law."

"Mr. President," Mavis began. "I'm sure that you are aware of the protests springing up all over the country. They exist because of this particular bill. The consensus of the people is that certain senators and congressmen were offered deals…bribes…to get the bill passed."

"Don't worry about the protesters. The national police will take care of them, if necessary. Disobedience of federal law will not be tolerated." The president shook his head. "It's so sad these people don't know what is good for them."

Mavis stood up. "Mr. President, with all due respect, many people in this country…. a majority in fact…. believe that that this act is unconstitutional. They are waiting for a ruling by the Supreme Court, which should take place any day now."

President White smiled. "Oh, I wouldn't worry about that. I already thought about that little wrinkle; it won't be an issue."

Jack glared at the president with an icy stare. "How's that? Did you buy off the Supreme Court justices, just like you bought the members of the House and Senate? Or are you just confident that your court packing idea will pay off?"

The president's smile broadened. "All good rulers know how to get legislation passed. I have ensured not only that my act was passed, but that there would be no challenges that could not be overcome. Please," he said in a very sarcastic tone. "Do you really think the people who disagree with me on this act, who are generally nothing more than country bumpkins, could outsmart me? For Pete's sake I have a PhD from Harvard; most of these protestors can barely write their own name. They should be thankful there's someone so educated looking out for their well being."

Jack began walking towards the president's desk. "I don't care whether a man has letters after his name or not. It doesn't take a genius to figure out if your rights are being violated. Most folks just want to be left alone, to succeed or fail on their own. Most Texans, at least. And I bet a good number of folks across the country would agree with me. And they definitely don't want their guns stolen from them by the very government that should be protecting their rights!"

Mavis began walking towards the desk as well. "After all Mr. President, we are talking about a right that is guaranteed in the U.S. Constitution Bill of Rights."

The president began to laugh, and then waved his hand in front of his face. "What does that matter? It is an 18th century document, which belongs in the 18th century. The year is 2049; we need to stop worrying about old-fashioned ideas such as what is in the Constitution. How will we make any progress if we don't make laws as we need them? I'll tell you, we won't make any progress at all. But times are changing; fewer and fewer people worry about such old-fashioned notions. In fact, for the most part this nation has forgotten about the Constitution. Except for those in the southern states. It's really difficult to get those inbred, uneducated hillbillies to stop clinging to guns, God and the Constitution. Well, no matter."

He looked Jack in the eyes and said, "Let me make this perfectly clear. If the gun turn-ins don't increase by the end of next week, I'm ordering the national police to go door to door looking for those guns. If I need to take the guns by force, then that's what I'll do."

Jack's nostrils flared as his face began to turn red. "Don't you even think of searching the homes of my people…it will be the biggest mistake of your career."

"Then get those redneck hicks to obey the law!" the president shouted. "Don't you people understand this is a necessary step in improving the lives of everyone in this country and eventually the world? Once we control the population, we will have a much easier time in the redistribution of wealth, goods and services throughout this country. Once we've provided an example for the entire world, it will be much easier for the United Nations to implement the One World Government. Everything and everybody will be equal. There will be no rich; there will be no poor. Every need will be taken care of."

"And who provides those goods and services?" Jack asked angrily.

The president looked at him as if he did not understand. "What do you mean?"

"What's gonna be the motivation to provide a good or service if there's no chance of gettin' rich?" Jack asked. "Or not even rich, just improvin' your living standard. What's the motivation to work? Where's the motivation for someone to take the risk in startin' a business to provide somethin'.... Anythin'?"

Mavis injected herself into the conversation. "What the senator is trying to say, Mr. President, is that without a chance, just a chance mind you, of improving one's condition, there is no motivation to take risk. Nor is there any sort of motivation to go above and beyond and achieve greatness."

The president looked at the two Texans as if he was looking at two children that needed to be taught a lesson. "You mean the private sector? The private sector is yesterday's news, the arena of greedy industrialists and capitalists. Their day is over. In case the two of you haven't noticed, government jobs now make up 85% of the workforce. And of the remaining 15%, more than 14% work for multinational corporations that are completely unionized, which means they might as well be working for the government. In a few more years, those corporations will be nationalized as well."

The president continued, "Achieve greatness? Ha! What a joke that is. All capitalism ever did was allow the rich to take advantage of the poor so they could become even richer. Poverty, famine, poor education, lousy healthcare.... That is the legacy of capitalism. The sooner it is put to rest the better. The government will take from industry its goods and services and distribute them to the people of this nation with impartiality. Everyone will be paid a fair wage, everyone will receive equal healthcare, and everyone will be taken care of in their golden years."

Mavis stared at the president and crossed her arms. "Who do you think you are, Fidel Castro? You're talking about communism. Communism has failed everywhere it's been tried. Without an incentive people don't work as hard.... or they don't work at all. The system goes against everything in human nature."

The president raised his hands and touched his temples, closed his eyes, and took a deep breath. After a moment, he opened his eyes and said "Look, I think we have gotten off to a bad start. Maybe I can make things a little clearer for you. I can make sure that you…" at this, he looked back and forth between the congresswoman and the senator, "both of you…have certain…assurances."

"What do you mean?" Jack asked.

President White folded his hands on his desk. "My meaning is simple. I can guarantee you remain in office as long as you desire. Political donors? I can deliver. Your office would have virtually limitless funds. Enough that not a soul would notice if a little was…unaccounted for."

Jack's forehead wrinkled and his eyes narrowed as he stared daggers at President White. "Someone needs to bitch slap you. That's what I came to Washington to fight. You and every other career politician who has leached the nation dry. You're nothin' more than a grubby little parasite."

Looking at Mavis Young, the president said, "I take it, Congresswoman Young, that is how you feel as well?"

Mavis nodded.

President White sighed, and then said, "That's pretty much what I expected. I'd heard that about the two of you; that's why I didn't bother trying to...persuade you when the National Public Safety Act was before Congress. I didn't want to waste my time, when there were so many willing to make deals."

The president looked at the congresswoman, then the senator, and then back to the congresswoman. He pointed a short, stubby finger at the congresswoman. "You, and your pious friend over there, go back to your state and get those inbred, uneducated hillbillies to take their guns to the police station. Now, get out of my office."

Mavis' dark eyebrows lifted; she was appalled at how the president was talking to her. Before she could say anything, Jack said, "Little sister, let's skedaddle; no use beatin' a dead horse." Looking at the president he said, "Don't bother callin' your honey, we can find the door."

Unexpectedly, President White smiled and said, "Don't forget, I'm addressing a joint session of Congress tomorrow at 11am. No press. You won't want to miss this."

Jack and Mavis walked quickly to the main entrance of the Oval Office. Jack opened the door and motioned for Mavis to walk through ahead of him. He was about to follow when he stopped suddenly, turned, and said, "You ever read *Atlas Shrugged*?"

The president looked up from his desk and said, "No, although I have read other works by Ayn Rand. I do not enjoy reading books that glorify individual achievement. Her works suggested that society can benefit from people who are motivated to better themselves, which is preposterous." The president's eyes narrowed slightly, and then he added, "Why?"

The senator shook his head. "I thought you would say somethin' like that," he said, and then walked through the office door. After closing the door behind him, Jack looked at Mavis and said, "So?"

Mavis Young rubbed her chin, and was quiet for a moment. Finally, she said, "I'm going to call Levi Walker and let him know what happened here today."

Jack nodded. "He'll wanna know."

"What was the deal with his reminder?" Mavis asked. "Or that stupid grin? It's almost as if he was boasting about something he's about to do. What's his speech about?"

Jack scratched his head. "Don't know. It's usually all over the news about his addresses to Congress, but not a peep on this one. And no press? That's not like him. Somethin' *is* up. Well, let's get a move on. We both have lots to do."

CHAPTER THREE

As the Bronco pulled into the driveway of the Dillon home, Sebastian breathed a sigh of relief. Ever since leaving the high school, his father had been talking about how the president had merged the Republican and Democrat parties into the Freedom party for his own personal gain, the spread of socialism, and the loss of freedom in the United States. Sebastian needed a break from the lecture. As soon as the Bronco came to a stop at the end of the long gravel driveway, he leaped out of the passenger seat. "Don't forget your backpack," his father told him.

"I've got it," Sebastian sighed.

"Hey kid, what's a matter? Is doom and gloom preachin' about the decline of America again?" The voice spoke slowly, with a very strong Tennessee accent.

Both Kirk and Sebastian turned towards the voice. Standing there was Kirk's longtime friend, Matt Pickett. He was leaning on a shovel while standing at the fence between their two yards.

Matt Pickett was medium height, about five foot nine, with a stocky, muscular build. Now in his mid sixties, he still had a physique that men half his age would be envious of. The bulging biceps and triceps of his upper arms pushed the sleeves of his t-shirt nearly to his shoulders, while his massive barrel chest made him look as if he wore an armored vest. Only his bushy, gray eyebrows, bald head and wrinkled, weathered face betrayed his true age.

"Like always," Sebastian replied. Matt began to laugh.

Kirk glared at Sebastian, then his neighbor, and then finally smiled. He remembered back to the time he and Matt had first met. It was 2019 and they were on a combat tour in the Middle East. Kirk Dillon was Second Lieutenant Dillon of the US Army's 173rd Airborne Brigade. Matt Pickett was his platoon sergeant, who took it upon himself to turn the green Lieutenant Dillon into an exceptional combat officer. Sergeant Pickett was already something of a legend within the Army. Having already served several combat tours in both Iraq and Afghanistan, he was a graduate of the Army's Ranger school and had a reputation as an utterly fearless soldier. There were even rumors that the Taliban had put a bounty on Pickett's head, although both Pickett and the Department of Defense denied it.

In March of 2020, Lt. Dillon was part of a convoy that was ambushed by the Taliban. Lt. Dillon, the sole survivor, was captured and taken hostage. Sgt. Pickett, against orders, mounted a one man assault and rescue mission. While the rescue was successful, Pickett was injured so badly that Dillon had to carry him to safety and radio for the helicopter exfiltration.

The Taliban caught up with them while waiting for their

extraction. By this point, Sgt. Pickett was so weak from his injuries that he was unable to shoulder his rifle. Lt. Dillon fought of the attackers single handedly, protecting his injured friend until a friendly chopper arrived. The two men were lifelong friends from that day forward.

After returning from the Middle East, they saw very little of each other, but stayed in contact. As chance would have it, fifteen years later the men would be working together again. They were now Sergeant Major Pickett and Lieutenant Colonel Dillon, and both men would spend their few remaining years of service at the Pentagon. The two men retired within days of each other and Pickett, having no surviving relatives in his home state of Tennessee, decided to follow Dillon to Southwest Ohio.

"What have you been up to today?" Kirk asked Matt.

"Same as every day," Matt replied. "Up at five for an hour of PT. Breakfast. Worked in the garden most of the day. Gettin' ready to put her to bed for the winter." He paused for a second as he wiped the sweat from forehead. "Still got a good crop of cabbage, kale and chard. Carrots, too. Best time of the year for carrots…cool weather makes 'em sweet." Matt looked at Sebastian and said, "Whatchadoin' home so early kid? It's only 2:30."

Before Sebastian had a chance to reply, Kirk jumped in. "Just a little trouble at the high school that needed my attention. I had to straighten that principal out."

"Dad called her a God damned piece of work," Sebastian blurted out.

Matt shook his head, and then began to speak in his usual slow manner. "Colonel, all these years and you still can't keep your mouth shut. Can't always speak your mind. Been your problem for years. Had you learned to zip it you might've been a General. Sometimes a man's got to be what they call diplomatic. You need to start thinkin' before you open your mouth. Years ago in Tennessee, you run your mouth the way you sometimes do, you'd a met with a stiff rope and a short drop."

Kirk looked at Matt and said, "A speech like that and I am the one who needs to keep his mouth shut?" Kirk shook his head. "And another thing: both you and I have been retired for more than a decade. You don't have to keep calling me Colonel. You could call me Kirk, you could call me Dillon, you could even call me Mr. Dillon, but I think it is about time for you to stop calling me Colonel."

Matt shrugged. "Old habits are hard to break, I guess. And you still slip up now and again when you call me Sergeant. We still doin' dinner tonight?"

Kirk laughed. "Yeah, still doing Italian tonight. Is that all right with you?"

"Sure thing," Matt replied. "Was plannin' on it. Got a couple of big Italian loaves I'm gonna make into garlic bread. I'm headed back to the house to work on that now."

Sebastian butted himself between the two men. "Hey Dad, before he goes home, maybe he could help us put the top back on the Bronco? They're predicting some cold rainy weather for the next few days."

Kirk scratched his head. "I guess it's about that time; there won't be much warm weather left this year. And I've got to drive to Cincinnati tomorrow morning. That would be one long cold drive without the top."

"Whatchadoin' in Cincy tomorrow?" Pickett asked.

"I have to meet with my publisher," Kirk replied. "They just finished reviewing my latest book, and they have a contract offer for publication. I have to be there at eight in the morning."

"I didn't know those business types got started that early," Pickett replied.

Kirk smiled. "Most don't. But I'm meeting with Byron Reynolds, the CEO of the company. He always likes to meet personally with the writers that bring in the big bucks. He's actually quite an interesting guy. He's very old and very old-fashioned, but he's still a real go-getter. Eighty-five years old and still start his work day at 7 AM, Monday through Friday."

Sebastian's eyes perked up. "Is he the guy that has the smoking hot chick for a secretary?" He asked eagerly.

"Yes, that's him," Kirk replied.

Matt looked at Sebastian. "Pretty easy on the eyes, kid?" He asked with a smile.

Sebastian began to talk quickly and excitedly. "Like you would not believe. She is so hot! She has got the goods, and knows how to use them. One time, I was at the publishing office with Dad and she knew I was watching her, so she leaned way forward over her desk, I think she knew I was watching her because she had a smile on her face when she bent over, and I could see all the way…."

"Whoa! Easy!" Kirk said as he began to laugh. "Okay, hormone factory, that's enough. Let's head over to the barn and get the Bronco top."

Sebastian's eyebrows raised and his eyes widened. "Are you sure I couldn't come with you tomorrow?" His voice was almost pleading.

"Let's get a move on kid," Matt injected. "We're burnin' daylight."

The trio had just begun to walk toward the barn when they heard the crunching sound of a car coming down the gravel driveway. As they stood watching, a sleek, dark limousine slowly snaked its way down Kirk's long gravel driveway. The body of the car was high gloss black, with tinted glass and blacked out headlights. Oddly, the limousine didn't have the usual Ohio license plates. Instead, the metal tags were plain white with the markings "UNPRP-LX1" in large black letters.

The car finally slowed to a halt, and the back door swung open. Out stepped a tall, lanky man. His long blonde hair had been slicked back and tied off in a small ponytail at the back of his head. His pinstripe suit sported two pins on the lapels. Kirk recognized one of the pins as that of a loyal Freedom Party member; the other pin he had never seen before.

The man looked at the three of them through mirrored sunglasses and said with a strong Chicago accent, "I'm looking for Mr. Kirk Dillon."

"That would be me," Kirk said.

The man smiled. "Mr. Dillon, my name is Richard Boyle and I represent the International Brotherhood of Writers. We have been attempting to contact you for some time to give you the privilege...and protection...of joining the brotherhood. I'm assuming that none of our messages got through to you because we've not heard from you. Obviously, the e-mail addresses and phone numbers we were provided with were incorrect. So I am here, in person, to allow you to sign this union card today."

Kirk squinted his eyes and said, "Mr. Boyle, I'm afraid you've made a wasted trip. I have no desire or intention of joining a union today, or any other day, for that matter. So if you'll excuse me, we have some work to get done before the sun goes down."

Richard Boyle took a couple of steps closer to Kirk Dillon. "Come now, Mr. Dillon. I don't think you understand the protection the brotherhood can provide. We know that tomorrow you're negotiating a contract with Byron Reynolds. Just think how much better off you would be if you went into those contract negotiations with one of our highly skilled, highly trained contract negotiators."

Kirk took a deep breath and said, "Byron Reynolds is an old friend of mine; his company has published every one of my books. Every time in the past, he has been very generous with his contracts and his company provides me with very nice royalties. I've always been happy with his publishing contracts and see no need for representation. And to be quite honest, I have no desire to hand part of my royalties over to any union. So, no sir, I will not join your union. Please, leave me alone."

Richard Boyle's smile broadened to the point of showing his teeth. "But Mr. Dillon, the paltry 20% you would pay in union dues would be more than made up for by the much larger contracts that our highly skilled negotiators could get for you."

Kirk's complexion began to take on a crimson hue as the blood vessels in his neck began to stand out. "That's neither here nor there. I don't care how much larger a contract you get for me, I don't want to join the union, end of story."

"Come now, Mr. Dillon," Boyle replied. "This is 2049, and everyone belongs to unions these days. That's just how it is. Going it alone is so unwise, so unsafe, and so old fashioned. Going solo…that kind of idea went away with the 20th century. Now let's get you…."

"I'm not joining any damn union!" Kirk shouted.

For the first time, the smile disappeared from Richard Boyle's face. He sighed deeply and shook his head. "Okay, I've tried to be nice, but I guess I have to put it lightly to you. I didn't come here to ask you to join the brotherhood; I am telling you that you will join."

"Get out of here you bastard!" Kirk yelled.

Richard Boyle shook his head again, saying "I had hoped it wouldn't come to this, but you leave me no choice." Looking back at the limousine, he nodded his head. The back door of the car opened again and another man stepped out. While this man was slightly shorter than Boyle, he probably outweighed him by 150 pounds. This man had the solid look of a pro bodybuilder.

Looking as if he were in his mid twenties, he was wearing dark blue jeans, and a black T-shirt that was so tight on his huge, muscular body that it looked like it had been spray-painted on. Boyle continued to talk. "Jimmy, I've tried to explain things to Mr. Dillon and have had no success.

Perhaps you can explain things a little better than I?"

Jimmy quickly stepped up to Kirk. "Look," he said, shaking his huge hand at Kirk Dillon. "You're joining the brotherhood today; you can do it with or without a trip to the hospital. Your choice; what's it going to be." Kirk backed up a few steps; Sebastian looked nervously at the big man and stepped back as well.

"Son, you're entering a world of pain that you cannot imagine. Get in your car and get the hell out of here." Jimmy whirled around to face the voice, only to find Matt Pickett. Matt was once again leaning on his shovel, looking as calm and cool as if he were discussing the weather or the latest town gossip.

"A world of pain," Matt repeated.

"Go tend your garden Grandpa, or you'll be next," Jimmy said to Matt. He turned to face Kirk again, and took a few steps forward. "So you going to sign or not?"

"I'm not joining any union," Kirk reiterated.

Jimmy shook his head and took a deep breath. He raised his arm as if he was about to throw a punch. Kirk prepared to duck: his hope was that he was fast enough to avoid the punch. If he successfully evaded the initial attack, he planned to land a swift kick to Jimmy's crotch and then grab something...anything…to use as a weapon against the much larger and younger foe.

Just that instant, Matt Pickett, still standing behind Jimmy, clubbed him on top of the head with the blade of his shovel. Jimmy shrieked in pain and fell to his knees. Without pause, Pickett took another swing at the kneeling giant, this time hitting him between the shoulder blades. Jimmy collapsed to the ground, withering in pain. Matt's face was cold and emotionless; it was quite apparent that his thirty years of combat training had not been forgotten.

Both Kirk and Sebastian stood perfectly still, almost like statues, not quite able to believe what they were seeing. Richard Boyle's mouth was wide open in disbelief and he was gawping like a fish.

Tossing the shovel to the ground, Pickett walked around toward the front of Jimmy's body. He then proceeded to kick the fallen adversary in the stomach. Jimmy tried to protect himself by curling into the fetal position, but it was no defense against Matt's steel toed boots. Matt kicked again. Then twice. Then three times. Each time Pickett kicked him, Jimmy cried out, and which each kick, the scream became feebler. Another kick, this time to Jimmy's face. Dark red blood began to gush from Jimmy's nose, and he was gasping for air.

Standing at Jimmy's head, Pickett knelt down on one knee. He grabbed Jimmy's chin with one hand, and turned his face so that they could look eye to eye. Pickett's face was cold and showed no emotion. "Ya know, the Colonel and I served our first tour in the Middle East before you were born. Picked up a lot of fightin' skill over there. Now I know that the Colonel and I aren't as young as springtime no more, but that doesn't mean we're willin' to let ya'll walk all over us. Now, the Colonel told you he's not joining. He ain't goin' to tell you again. You and your boss better get." At this, Pickett let go of Jimmy's chin, stood, and backed up a few steps. Looking at Boyle he said, "You best collect him up and get."

Boyle was standing a few feet away, still in disbelief at how a sixty-five year old man has so quickly and effectively subdued one of his best enforcers. At first, he was speechless. "The police will hear of this," Boyle finally said angrily.

Kirk shot back quickly. "Well when they arrive, we'll explain to them about your union intimidation and trying to force me to join a union through violence. I'm sure that will go over well with the police officers."

Richard Boyle smirked and said, "You two don't get it, do you? We're here on union business; we can't be touched." His smirk disappeared and he pointed two fingers at Matt, as if he were holding an imaginary gun. "I could've put a bullet to your head today, and the law protects me because I'm doing the union's business. You think about that; I'll be in touch. Jimmy, let's go."

By this point, Jimmy had regained enough strength to get to his feet. Slowly, slightly hunched over and with great effort, he lurched toward the limousine, one hand covering his bloody nose, nearly collapsing on the back seat once the door was open. Richard Boyle shook his head, mumbling something about Jimmy being a disgrace, and then followed Jimmy into the car.

As the car pulled away, Kirk turned to Matt and said with a smile, "What were you saying about being diplomatic?"

Matt Pickett's face was still emotionless. "Couldn't be helped. You and the kid's all the family I got. Come on; we're burnin' daylight. Gotta get the top on your truck." Matt headed off to the barn, acting as if the previous events had not occurred.

Sebastian looked dumbfounded. "Did–did-did you see that?" he exclaimed.

Kirk Dillon nodded. "I suspect there will be Hell to pay for this incident. Let's catch up with Matt and get the cap on the Bronco. My guess is that we'll receive a visit from the law not too long from now. Let's hope it's the locals and not the national police. Come on."

Sebastian nodded, and followed his father toward the barn.

"Look Levi, I know you're trying, but I've got a business to run. And if we can't drill, I can't make a profit."

Levi James Walker, Governor of Texas, reclined in his chair and sighed heavily. He was in the middle of a video conference with Karl Stuart, the owner of an independent oil platform off the Texas coast. "Karl, I understand your situation. Had it been up to me, that oil cleanup bill would've never been passed. You and I both know that it was passed for the sole purpose of ending oil drilling in the United States. Those greenies up north still have this wild idea that we can run this whole nation on solar cells and windmills."

"I know that Levi," Karl replied. "And I know that the oil rig disaster in Louisiana was from somebody either working for the government or working with government. Course, since the government controls TV, radio, and Internet, the real story never got out. But that's beside the point. I'm a fairly small company…one of the few independents left…and I don't want to see any of my boys without a job. I can't afford to pay them to sit on their ass."

Levi Walker scratched his head. "I know; the situation stinks. I just want you to know that we are trying to fix this. Senators and congressmen from all over the southern coast are working to try to get this bill repealed…or at least changed. Your old buddy Blackjack Spearman is working on it himself."

Karl shook his head. "I owe a lot to Blackjack; he got me started in the business, and my rig uses his design. But with this bill getting passed, I don't have much choice. There's a new oil discovery off the coast of China, and the Chinese want that oil bad. Right now, I'm sitting on offers from three different Chinese companies. They're willing to cover my moving expenses, as well as offer me a great deal for the oil. Also, the Chinese government is sweetening the deal with no corporate tax for the next five years. That's a deal I just can't pass up."

Levi Walker sighed. "I understand. You have to do what's right for your company."

Karl rubbed his hands together; he looked as if he was in pain. "Look Levi, we've been friends for a lot of years. This isn't easy for me. It takes some time to get an oil platform ready to move. If something changes between now and our move date, I'll keep the rig here. Otherwise, I'm going to start brushing up on my Chinese."

"I can't ask for anything more, Karl," Levi replied. I hope things do turn around." With that, Levi Walker turned off the video screen. "There goes another one," he said to himself.

Ever since the Oil Cleanup Act had been passed three months ago, drilling platforms all along the US coast had been leaving the nation in search of friendlier waters. The bill itself didn't make oil drilling illegal; what it did was levy a heavy tax not only on oil drilling, but also on oil refineries. While the government controlled media hailed this as a victory for the environment, those who lived along the southern coast of the country knew a different story. The oil industry was big business, and the loss of that business cost thousands of jobs. The combined loss of the oil industry and the huge spike in unemployment was destroying the economies of those southern coastal states.

Levi Walker closed his eyes, sighed heavily, and leaned back in his office chair. He felt as if the entire Federal Government were out to destroy him and his state. This new act was destroying the oil industry in the United States. The Oil Cleanup Act had been sold to the public as a way to create a fund which would be used to cover the cost of oil spills. However, the tax revenue collected would go directly into the general treasury of the United States, just like all other tax revenue. And if an oil spill did occur, Congress had the authority to assign both blame and fines…without recourse in the court system. In essence, this was nothing more than a huge tax on the oil industry and since a Congressional Committee had passed it behind closed doors, the true details of the act were unknown to the vast majority of the public.

As Levi reflected on the situation created by the Federal Government, the phone on his desk began to beep; it was his office assistant's direct line. Pressing the button to put the phone on speaker, he said, "What do you have for me, Sarah?"

"Mr. Walker, you have a call from Congresswoman Mavis Young. She says it's urgent."

"Put her through on video," he replied. "And how many more times do I have to ask you to call me Levi?"

"Several more, at least," Sarah replied."I have my reputation as a professional to think about."

Levi Walker chuckled. "I see. Well, put her through."

"Yes, sir."

The video screen came to life, revealing Mavis Young sitting at her office desk in Washington, D.C. She had a worried look on her face.

"Hello Levi," she said.

"How are you Mavis?" Levi replied. "I hope you have some good news for me. I just got off the phone with Karl Stuart; he's moving his rig if we don't get something done about this oil legislation. How was the meeting with the president?"

Mavis Young shook her head. "I wish I had some good news for you Levi, but I don't. The Speaker won't allow me to bring my amendments to the floor for debate. That's the part that infuriates me; how can we have a debate if I can't bring my ideas to the floor?"

"I think that's her point," Levi said.

"I guess so," Mavis replied. "After all, she's the one who wrote the bill, and the one who assigned the committee that created the bill. But we have more important matters. Blackjack and I did meet with the president today, and I am really worried now. He claims he's going to use the national police to enforce his gun ban. He is of the opinion that the State of Texas has not been doing enough to get people to turn in their firearms."

"We're not doing jack shit," Levi replied. "Unless someone is a felon, it is his God-given right to own a firearm and I won't be a part of taking away someone's Second Amendment right."

"He says the police will begin door to door searches if that's what's needed to collect the firearms," Mavis said.

"Do you believe him?" Levi asked.

"I've never known him to bluff, so I will take him at his word." Mavis rubbed her chin, as if in thought. "There's something else, though. That joint session of Congress tomorrow; he reminded us to be there. He was almost gloating about it. It was as if he wanted to tell us what he had planned, but couldn't."

Levi's forehead wrinkled as he frowned. "That doesn't sound good. I don't trust him. Any ideas on what he's up to?"

Mavis shook her head."None, and honestly that's what bothers me the most. Usually, he wants full press coverage when he addresses Congress. This time…not a peep. None of the other Congressmen and Senators seem to know, either. Or, if they do, they're not talking."

Levi was quiet for a few seconds, and he drummed his forefinger on his desk as he thought. Finally, he said, "I'm going to make a few calls; see what I can dig up from some of the other governors…at least ones I trust. Let me know if you find out anything else."

Mavis nodded her head. "Will do, Levi. Talk to you soon."

"Take care Mavis. Be especially careful tomorrow." As soon as he ended the call, Levi made another call to his assistant. "Sarah, I need to talk to the governors of Mississippi, Alabama, and Louisiana…and I need them ASAP."

"Right away, Mr. Walker."

CHAPTER FOUR

Installing the hardtop on the Bronco took less than an hour. As predicted, law enforcement arrived before they had finished their work. Fortunately, things were as Kirk had hoped and the local police responded. The two police officers, upon hearing what had happened, were sympathetic to the situation, and more than willing to find a way to write this off.

"Chuck," one officer said the other. "Here's what I'm thinking; let me know your thoughts. I say we write this up as a case of PTSD gone badly; he is, after all, a combat vet with over thirty years in. With the number of cases of vets with PTSD, that's not too unbelievable. We can say that Mr. Pickett has agreed to go to counseling, and this issue is closed, from a law enforcement perspective."

"That sounds alright to me Pat," Chuck said. He turned to Matt and said, "And I don't want to know if you go to counseling or not; as far as we're concerned this issue is resolved."

Matt nodded. The officer continued, "Were it up to me, I would try to charge the union thugs with something… anything. Unfortunately, the law completely protects them when they're doing union business. There's not a thing we can do. In fact, me and my partner could get in real big trouble if our union knew what really happened here today."

"I do appreciate the two of you taking care of the situation. I'm not sure what we can do to say thank you," said Kirk.

Pat smiled and said, "Well, Chuck and I hear that Matt Pickett is the best damn vegetable gardener north of the Ohio River. I'd sure like to sample a few things from that garden…you know, just to confirm the rumors."

"That would make the extra paperwork worth our while," Chuck added.

Matt laughed and said, "Always happy to share the harvest."

He turned to Sebastian and said, "Kid, run over to my house and grab two cardboard boxes; there's a few in the garage." He then motioned for the officers to follow him. "Come on back to the garden and we'll get you some fixin's that are really fresh…not like that store bought crap. Don't have a big variety still in the ground, but what I got there's plenty of."

As Sebastian ran off to his garage, Matt led everyone else to the garden. Surrounded by a split rail fence backed by wire mesh, the garden was large enough to pass for a small farm. It was laid out in a grid-like pattern of raised beds, each bed four feet wide by about thirty feet long. Many had nothing growing in them and were covered with a thick layer of mulched grass and leaves. There were beds here and there, however, that still had fresh green vegetables.

"You must spend a fortune on seeds," Chuck said.

Matt's face beamed as he said, "Not a dime. I save seeds from the previous year's plantings."

"I thought the seed companies engineered the seeds so you can't do that?" Kirk said.

"Nothing growing in this garden is genetically modified; they're all heirloom types," Matt replied proudly.

"I thought it was illegal to sell those kinds of seeds," Pat said.

"Sure is," Matt replied. "Big seed companies pushed for that years ago, and they greased the hands of enough politicians to get it passed. But it's not illegal to trade seeds with friends. There's a group of us in town that trade back and forth to get what we want."

"I did not know that…I'll have to tell my wife about that," Chuck said. "How do you keep things growing this late in the year?"

"Row covers mostly," Matt replied. Pointing to a stack of white cloth he continued, "See the white tarps? They let in sun, water and air but hold the heat. I cover the beds on cold nights. Course, everything I got left can take the cold. Taters and carrots are good 'till the ground freezes; kale and chard can handle a little frost."

"Looks like you put a lot of time into your garden," Chuck said.

Matt looked at the officer and laughed as he said, "Son, I'm retired. I've got all day to work back here."

Sebastian soon returned with two boxes, and the five men went to work filling the boxes with vegetables from the garden. In minutes, the boxes were full, and after thanking Matt, the police officers were on their way.

Kirk turned to Matt and asked, "Dinner at six?"

"Works for me. Soon as I get my bread done, I'll be over." Matt turned and began walking toward his house. Kirk and Sebastian likewise began walking toward their home.

As they walked toward the house, Kirk asked, "Any homework tonight, son?"

"Most of it's done," Sebastian replied. "I have two physics problems to finish, and I need to read for moral and political ideas."

As they walked up the stone steps to the front porch, Kirk said, "Why don't you work on that when we get in the house? I want to flip on the news while I work on dinner; see what I missed out on while at the school. Besides, you know that whenever we have dinner with Matt, we end up talking or playing games all night."

"Oh, you can bet that I'll be taking on Mr. Pickett in *Street Boxing 2050*. He is going down!" Sebastian exclaimed.

Kirk laughed. "I'm surprised that you would want to play that virtual boxing game with him again; he gave you a serious ass-whipping the last time. But if you want to try again, I suggest you get the homework done first."

"Alright," Sebastian replied.

"How far did you get before the book was nabbed by the

study hall teacher?" Kirk asked as he unlocked the front door.

"Page 201," Sebastian replied.

"Try to get a little more done after the homework," Kirk said. "The Austrian school of economic thought is important to understand."

"Ok, dad."

Kirk arched his left eyebrow and said, "Be sure to read; you may be quizzed on this subject at dinner tonight."

Sebastian sighed, "Why am I not surprised?"

As Kirk and Sebastian entered the house, Kirk's cell phone began to beep. He pulled the phone out of his pocket and glanced at the display. Then he looked at Sebastian and said, "It looks like I have a call from your brother."

Sebastian's eyes grew wide and he smiled. "Put it on the big screen so I can talk, too," he said.

Kirk pressed a button on his cell phone and the large LCD screen in the living room came to life. The screen showed a man in his early twenties wearing a military uniform. He was of medium height and lean with chiseled features. In most ways, he looked as Kirk did twenty-five years earlier; only the bronze colored eyes gave away his mother's genetics.

"Hi Dad," the figure on the screen said.

"Michael, how are things at Fort Sam Houston?" Kirk asked.

"Doing just fine," Michael replied. "Just a few more weeks

of training and this cycle is done."

Michael looked at Sebastian and said, "Damn, you're getting tall. Has Dad been putting you on the rack and stretching you at night?"

"No," Sebastian replied. "He just gets me in trouble at school."

Michael got a puzzled look on his face, and looked as if he were about to speak when Kirk said, "I had a discussion with his Principal today. Apparently, books about freedom and the free market are blacklisted these days."

"How did that discussion go?"Michael asked.

Kirk was about to speak when Sebastian said, "Dad told her she was one God damned piece of work."

"Do you mind if I get a word in?" Kirk said to Sebastian.

"Sorry," Sebastian said with a grin.

"I see you're still as diplomatic as ever," Michael said with a smile. The smile quickly disappeared and Michael cleared his throat before saying, "You weren't drinking again, were you?"

"The last time I had a drop was when I started on my first book," Kirk replied. "I know it is my Achilles heel, so I avoid it like the plague."

"That's good," Michael replied. "I guess General McRain was right about you."

"How's that?" Kirk asked.

"He said you would have been a General if you had learned to play nice and keep your mouth shut."

"Everyone knows that's not me," Kirk replied with a broad grin.

Michael laughed and nodded, then said, "He also said that's what he always liked about you; you could always be depended on to speak your mind, even when the Pentagon didn't want to hear the truth."

"You still going to be in town for Thanksgiving?" Sebastian asked.

"I'm planning on it," Michael replied. "I am scheduled for leave starting the Tuesday before, and I will be in town for a week."

"Cool," Sebastian said.

Michael looked at his watch, and then said, "I hate to cut this short, but I need to get off the phone. I just wanted to check in with you two before we head out into the field for the next two weeks."

"Okay," Kirk replied. Give us a call when you get back to base. Take care out there."

Michael nodded and said, "You bet, Dad. Sebastian, be good and try to not piss off the teachers at school."

"Right," Sebastian said with a grin. "See you, bro."

As the screen went blank, Sebastian turned to Kirk and said, "I'm heading up to my room to get my homework done before dinner."

"That's fine," Kirk replied.

Kirk was putting water on the stove to boil when he remembered his intention to watch the news while working on dinner. He paused momentarily to flip on the television, and then returned to the preparations. The two newscasters were debating how some event would affect the US economy when Kirk read across the bottom of the television screen, "*…Germany leaves European Union and reinstates the Deutsche Mark; global markets plunge on news.*"

"That is big news," Kirk thought. Leaders in both the European Union and North America had been pushing hard for what they called a "One World Government." Essentially, the idea was to unify the governments and economies of Europe and North America to compete with China. While government bureaucrats were enthusiastic about the proposed union, the people of many of the member nations had been much less so. The One World Government would transfer power from national governments to an international parliament, headed by an international prime minister. Naturally, there were many people in both Europe and North America that did not want to see the sovereignty of their nation taken away.

From the beginning of the project, the German government had been skeptical of the plan. As Europe's largest economy, Germany had the most to lose in the plan; as a member of the European Union, it had already bailed out other nations within the Union. While the German government had tightened its belt and had become very frugal because of the bailouts, the nations it had saved were unwilling to make sacrifices themselves.

"*I wonder when that's going to happen in the US?*" Kirk said to himself. "*Someone is eventually going to say 'this far and no farther'. But when…and who?*"

As he continued his combined tasks of watching the news broadcast and cooking dinner, there was a knock at the front door. Before Kirk could stop what he was doing and answer the door, Sebastian came bounding down the stairs toward the front door.

"I've got it!" he shouted.

Kirk arched his left eyebrow and said, "I see."

Sebastian opened the front door to reveal Matt Pickett. In one hand, Matt was carrying a package wrapped in aluminum foil; in his other hand he was carrying a very worn and tattered book. Handing the foil wrapped package to Sebastian, he said "Take this to the kitchen, boy." He then looked at Kirk and said, "All cooked; just needs to stay warm."

"Ok," Kirk replied. "Sebastian, put that in the oven on warm."

As Sebastian took the foil package and placed it in the oven, Kirk looked at Matt and said, "You're a little early; I just started the spaghetti water. Meat sauce is done though; made it this morning."

Matt shrugged. "No big thang. Bread was done, so I came on over. Oh, and I wanted to give this back." At this, he handed the book to Kirk. "All finished. Good book; really long though. Really, really long."

Kirk Dillon laughed. "That book *was* pretty long winded. However, I think it was necessary to get her point across."

“I thought the book was kinda’ creepy,” Sebastian blurted out.

“In what way?” Kirk asked.

“Well, that book was written in the 1950’s, right?” Sebastian said.

“Yes.”

Sebastian continued, “One hundred years ago, she wrote about a future that is like our own present day. How is it she could see the future like that?”

“I was thinkin’ about that myself,” Matt said.

“It’s pretty simple, really. Ayn Rand was born in Russia, and saw the rise of communism.” Kirk spoke slowly and deliberately, as if he were teaching a class.

“She was a young girl at the time of the October Revolution. As a teen and a young adult, she saw what happened to people when they depended on the government for everything. She saw people starving, individuals sacrificed for ‘the good of the people’. Once you see what the effect of an all powerful government has on the people, it’s not hard to connect the dots and see what it will lead to.”

“What about all them business types goin’ on strike?” Matt asked

Kirk looked at Matt. “In a lot of ways, I think that has already happened. When was the last time you heard about a major technological innovation? Twenty years ago or more? Without something to gain, what’s the motivation to invent something new? And even if someone wanted to invent, who's going to pay for the research?"

"The government gives tons of money to Universities for research," Sebastian said as he tried to fight his way into the conversation.

Kirk looked at Sebastian and said, "And what have the taxpayers received for all of their money? Not much. Getting a handout from the government is not the same as a company or individual with a research budget. With public funding, there is no incentive to produce results, nor is there any drive to focus research on something productive or profitable. That's how we end up spending millions on researching how cows fart or the effect of Goth culture on the city of Lexington. When's the last time government funded University research produced something of value?"

"Colonel, your spaghetti is a boilin'," Matt said.

Kirk quickly turned down the heat of the stove to prevent the pot from boiling over. As he added the spaghetti to the water, he continued to talk.

"It's eerie how well Rand predicted the future. Tons of examples of government overreaching its legal power. Look at the protests in the South over the gun confiscation. When is someone going to say enough?" Kirk paused momentarily in thought, and then continued. "At least in Europe, someone has finally said enough. I just saw on the news that Germany has withdrawn from the European Union."

"Really?" Matt asked.

"Just saw it right before you came in," Kirk replied.

"They've been threatenin' to do it for years," Matt said.

"They seem to be the only ones over there who know how to handle money, or at least not waste it. Wonder what that'll do to the world government nonsense?"

"My guess is it will have to be scrapped," Kirk replied. "There's no way it will work without them. Let's face it, they are the only ones in Western Europe who manufacture anything, and the leaders of the other European nations were planning to leach off them."

"I never liked the idea of our enemies, either current or former, havin' a say in how we run this country. Don't even like our allies tellin' us how to run this place. Course, lota people were countin' on that to compete with China," Matt said.

Kirk stirred the boiling pot of spaghetti as he talked. "The thing is, it's the government's fault that we aren't able to compete with the Chinese. It is too incredibly expensive to manufacture anything in this country due to the government regulation. Energy is a problem, too. We sit on the largest natural gas, shale oil, and coal reserves in the world, yet we are not permitted to use those resources. At least not in large enough quantities, anyway. There hasn't been a permit issued for a new nuclear power plant in over 30 years."

"Wind and solar are much cleaner," Sebastian added.

Kirk shrugged. "Every method for creating electricity has its positive and negative points. While wind turbines produce no emissions, over one million birds are killed every year by those damn things."

"Bet they didn't talk about that in school," Matt added, grinning.

"Nope," Sebastian said.

"Of course not," Kirk replied. "Fish and Wildlife service used to track the numbers until Congress ordered them not to; it was making the wind farms look bad. Anyway, to get back to the green energy issue, the biggest drawback of green energy is the low output of electricity. Even with tons of homes having solar panels on the roof and mountains full of wind farms, we still can't meet the demands for residential power. And the one type of green power that did produce tons of energy, hydroelectric, has been banned because the fish couldn't get past the dams on the rivers."

"I guess the fish are more important than the birds," Matt joked.

Kirk smiled, and then continued. "Well, I guess it's a good thing there's no longer a large manufacturing base, because we couldn't supply the power it would need."

"But isn't that the reason we have the rolling blackouts?" Sebastian asked. "So that industry has the power it needs?"

"Yes, but my point is that there is not enough power to go around; at one time there was. You're too young to remember, but I never heard of a rolling blackout until about twenty-five years ago."

"Except California," Matt added.

Kirk nodded. "Yes, except California. Those nut jobs were just ahead of the curve, I guess." Kirk chuckled slightly. "Anyway, there was plenty of power provided by the nukes, natural gas and coal plants. Yes, the coal plants were pretty dirty early on, but as time passed, technological advances allowed them to become cleaner and generate more power on less coal. When the government forced them closed, power output in this country dropped dramatically, and electricity became very expensive."

"Lota people lost jobs, too," Matt said.

"Why?" Sebastian asked. "Why couldn't the people that worked for the coal plants go to work building solar panels and windmills?"

"It ain't that simple kid," Matt replied.

"Agreed. Even if you discount the fact that a person would have to be completely retrained…not an easy task when someone is close to retirement…you have to realize that we don't make anything in this country anymore. At least not much. Most solar panels are made in China; Germany if you want the good ones. Most of the wind turbines are made in China, too. Plus, the coal mining industry employed a huge number of people. When the coal mines went away, there was no way for any industry to hire all of those people."

Matt rubbed his chin in thought. "That wiped out West Virginia and a good deal of Kentucky," he said.

"Absolutely," Kirk replied. Well, enough of that for now. Spaghetti is done. Sebastian, while I drain the spaghetti, pour some drinks. Iced tea for me. And get the parmesan out of the fridge. Matt, there's a pair of mitts by the oven so you can get your bread out."

Matt looked at Sebastian and said, "Water for me kid. Lots of ice; can't have too much ice."

"Ok."

As they prepared for dinner, Kirk couldn't help but think about the news of Germany and the European Union. In a way, he was relieved. "*There's no way they can pull off this One World Government without the Germans,*" he thought. Now if the leaders of this nation could be made to realize what they were doing to the nation, there may be hope. There has to be a few good politicians left. But where are they? And how would they combat the politicians who represented the status quo? And would that be enough to fix the damage already done? All of these questions swirled about in his head as they sat down to dinner.

"Ralph, you need to pick up the pace. The president is not a patient man."

Ralph Marco, the presidential speech writer, and James Duncan, the president's chief of staff, were on their way to the oval office for an emergency meeting. The president's assistant had phoned them just moments earlier, saying it was important that they get to the oval office as soon as possible. While James was rushing to get there as fast as possible, Ralph proceeded with his usual, more leisurely pace, as if everything would be put on hold until he arrived.

Ralph looked at James with indifference. "Jimmy, if you're in such a hurry to get your ass chewed, you go ahead. I run for no man."

James stopped walking momentarily and pointed an index finger at Ralph. "Ralph, I am the Chief of Staff," he said with indignation. "Everything that happens is my fault…even stuff that I don't know about. And quit calling me Jimmy!"

"Whatever," Ralph replied. "You need to lighten up or you'll have a heart attack by age fifty."

James shook his head and once again began walking at his usual brisk pace. "Not everyone can be the president's favorite speech writer," he said angrily.

"Damn right," Ralph replied with a snicker.

As the two men approached the door to the Oval Office, they could hear the president shouting from within the room. As usual, the two national police officers who worked as the president's personal bodyguards were standing outside the large oak doors that led to the Oval Office.

"You may want to get in there quick," one of the officers said to James.

"Or maybe not," the other officer said. "He's really pissed."

"Any idea what's up?" James asked.

"Germany has withdrawn from the European Union," the officer replied.

James shook his head with skepticism. "I knew about that; he and I talked about it earlier. Some of the European leaders were going to try to work with Germany to get them to reconsider."

"Well," the officer continued, "I guess none of them can change the German's mind. They say we and the European Union are just trying to boost our economies on their backside."

"Which would be true," Ralph chimed in.

James glared at Ralph with contempt and disgust clearly visible on his face. "You're a lot of help, you are."

"Well it's true, and you know it yourself," Ralph replied.

"Let's just get in there and see what's going on," James said with a sigh.

"Lead the way, oh wise one," Ralph replied sarcastically.

The two men entered the Oval Office to see President White standing behind the Resolute Desk with his assistant directly in front of him. The president's face had turned a bright crimson and his eyes, which were normally wide open, were narrowed to thin slits that glittered with rage as he barked at his assistant. As Ralph and James entered the room, his attention turned to them.

"About damn time!" the president snarled. "When I say I want to see you, I mean now! Everything is falling apart, and you two can't be found!"

"I'm sorry Mr. President," James replied. "I got here as soon as I could, but I was halfway across the compound when your assistant called me."

The president pounded his fist on the Resolute Desk. "I have had conversations with the leaders of almost every European Nation. Nobody can convince the Germans to change their minds. Half of those bastards blamed me for Germany dropping out of the Union in the first place. Me!"

"I'm sure they're just venting their frustration, Mr. President," James replied.

"Shut up and listen!" the president said angrily. "Do you know what this means? No One World Government! We can't pull it off without the German economic machine. Not a chance in hell. This destroys my chance. I was poised to become the first Prime Minister of the World!"

James shook his head. "Mr. President, there is still a chance that this can be fixed. Let's keep negotiating with the Germans. Maybe the British can apply a little pressure for us and we can still get this worked out. Even if they are not a member of the European Union, it might still be possible to get them to join the One World Government. You know how much they hate the Chinese; that might be the leverage we need to get them to join."

The president stroked his mustache as he reflected on what James had said. Finally, he responded, "You may be right. Have Filburn keep the negotiations going. Do whatever is needed to get them to join."

"Yes, Mr. President," James replied.

The president continued, "Also, I want to begin the gun seizures in the Northeast. All of our intelligence is telling us that a majority of the people who owned firearms in those states have turned them in already. Let's go in and finish the job."

"But if most of them have been turned in already, why bother with what is left?" James asked.

The president shook his head. "You don't know your history, do you? Back in World War Two, there were certain officials within the Japanese government who wanted to invade the United States. However, a certain general…I can't remember his name…said the losses would be huge because the average American citizen is armed. I plan to heed his advice."

"So you're planning to invade Boston?" Ralph asked sarcastically.

"No!" the president protested. "Look, when the One World Government is instituted, there are going to be a lot of changes. The people of this country are going to have to get used to the idea that they will only have a small voice in how they are governed. There are a lot of people that may not like that. It will be much easier to control the population if they are unarmed."

"Yes, Mr. President," James said.

The president turned toward Ralph, who was standing with his hands in his pockets and swaying back and forth."Ralph, the speech for tomorrow is great…as usual. So is Speaker Ravana's."

"Any changes you want to see?" Ralph asked.

"No, I like it as is." The president shook his head and then said, "Don't know what I would do without a writer like you."

"You'd still be teaching at Harvard," Ralph replied.

The president looked at Ralph and said, "You are the only person around here who could get away with saying something like that to me."

"I know," Ralph replied. "That's because you need me more than I need you."

"I could have you fired," the president replied. "Or worse."

“Go ahead and fire me, imprison me, or kill me; it would hurt you more than me. The speeches you come up with on your own suck. Without me, you go back to being a school teacher, and not a very good one at that.” Ralph began to sway back and forth again, knowing that he had the upper hand. “No matter if I write speeches for the President of the United States or for the President of the Teamsters, I am a highly paid bullshit artist and I am in high demand.”

“I guess I can’t argue with that,” the president said matter-of-factly.

No, you can’t,” Ralph retorted. “And as far as tomorrow goes, I would suggest you…and the speaker…practice those speeches a lot before the assembly. You have quite a show to pull off.”

“I agree,” the president replied. “Everything is riding on tomorrow. We can’t, no we mustn’t fail.”

CHAPTER FIVE

Kirk Dillon knelt behind the crumbled remains of a wall on top of a sandy knoll. Looking toward the west, he could see the Taliban soldiers rushing towards him from a distance. He was on the last magazine from his stolen AK-47. He fired two short bursts, and another enemy fell. He fired again, hitting his opponent in the shoulder, knocking the soldier onto his backside.

"Behind you," a weak voice said.

Kirk spun around and looked down at Matt Pickett. Matt had three bullets in his left arm, two in his left leg, and one in his abdominal area. He was covered in blood, and was drifting in and out of consciousness from blood loss. He was already too weak to walk and was fading fast. With a blood soaked arm, he shakily pointed to the Southwest.

"Four of 'em," he said. "Tryin' to be stealthy."

Raising the AK-47 to his shoulder, Kirk fired at the closest enemy, dropping him instantly. Keeping the rifle at his shoulder, Kirk turned toward the next enemy. Bullets were coming from west of his position;

they sounded like an angry swarm of bees flying over his head. He dropped to one knee and fired. Only one round fired; he was out of ammunition. Throwing the AK to the ground, he grabbed the handgun that Matt Pickett was holding; Matt was too weak to use it anyway.

"Last mag," Pickett gasped.

"Where's that damn Blackhawk!" Kirk yelled. He reasoned they had only minutes to live without help. He fired the handgun at an approaching soldier, hitting him in the neck. Just then, Kirk heard a loud cracking sound, and then felt an incredible pain in his upper left leg; it was as if he had been stung by a giant wasp. The pain brought him down on his backside. Instinctively, he rolled over and fired the handgun in the direction from which he had been hit. Another Taliban soldier went down.

Kirk pulled the magazine out of the pistol. Four shots left. Save two, he told himself. If an evac chopper didn't arrive in time, he would use the second to last shot on Matt Pickett, and then shoot himself with the last one. That was far better than a death at the hands of the Taliban. Another enemy soldier came within range, and Kirk dropped him with one shot. Then another. Is this how it ends, he thought? Looking at Matt Pickett, Kirk said, "I'm sorry," and raised the pistol to fire….

Kirk leapt out of bed in a cold sweat, heart racing, body shaking. After almost thirty years, he was still having the same nightmare about the ordeal in the Middle East. Every time, he woke up in the state he was in now. He sat down on the side of the bed and tried to bring his breathing and heart rate under control. As he began to calm down, he reached down and rubbed the backside of his left leg. He could still feel a slight depression where the bullet went into his leg so many years ago.

Kirk looked at the alarm clock on the nightstand; it was 4:15am. Realizing he would never fall back asleep, Kirk decided it was a good time for a morning workout. Pulling on a pair of sweatpants and a t-shirt, he headed to the basement to pound on his punching bag. Reaching the bottom of the basement stairs, he picked up his bag gloves, pulled them on, and with a deep breath, went to work on the punching bag.

Kirk began with slow, light punches to warm up. Gradually he began hitting the bag with greater force and speed. He could feel his heart rate begin to rise; his body was warming up. Feeling much looser, Kirk fell into a rhythm of slow, heavy, underhanded hits to the bag, switching from left to right between each punch. As he did so, he began to reflect on the events and news of the previous day.

The news of Germany leaving the European Union had not been a complete surprise, as they had been threatening to leave for over thirty years. But they had always been persuaded to stay. *"What had changed?"* he wondered. The only logical conclusion he could come up with was the One World Government unification plan. That must be it. It was likely that the German government saw the unification as nothing more than a way to bailout the nations who were deep in debt; the Chancellor of Germany, Felix Hoffman, had expressed that opinion on several occasions. Could he have persuaded Germany to take a different course, one where an independent Germany would no longer be held back by the non-productive western powers?

"If Germany can do it, why can't we?" Kirk asked himself. Not the nation itself, he thought, but the productive people of the nation. For far too long, hard working individuals have allowed the fruits of their labor to be taken from them. Why? Why do the entrepreneurs allow the less motivated to walk all over them? Why is hard work such a dirty word?

By now, Kirk was breathing heavily and dripping with sweat; while he was in good condition for a man in his 50's, he found it difficult to put in the workouts that were routine thirty years earlier. Pulling off his gloves, he settled down on the floor to do some sit-ups while his heart rate slowed down.

"Someone needs to hit the reset button," he said to himself. The original thirteen colonies were founded by people with the spirit of entrepreneurship, people willing to put it all on the line to try to make something of themselves. These were people who knew they had much to risk. Indeed, in the early days of North America, failure meant more than a loss of a fortune; it meant starvation and perhaps death. "One meal away from starvation must be an incredible motivation," he thought.

"*Where is that spirit today*?" he wondered. While he knew some very hard working individuals, they were a rarity these days. With government providing nearly all of one's basic needs, there wasn't much motivation to work hard. In fact, many government laws and policies discouraged it. The seven hour work day, mandated vacation time, laws against firing employees, unions preventing members from manual labor…all of these contributed to an unmotivated, unproductive work force. "*Just plain lazy*," he concluded.

Kirk stood and stretched the pain from his lower back; he decided he'd had enough of a workout for the morning. Besides, he still needed to get ready for his meeting, and he always enjoyed watching some of the morning news programs before starting his day. As he walked up the basement stairs, he pondered the idea of hitting the reset button in America. *"How would it be done?"* he mused. A revolt? What if the productive people of the nation went on strike as they did in the book *Atlas Shrugged*? Civil war? There were rumors of Southern businessmen and politicians meeting in secret, waiting for just the right time for a new American Revolution. "*What where they called again*?" he struggled to remember. *"That's right…The Sons of Liberty."* The name had already been used several times in American history. The United States government classified them as a terrorist group; in fact the government had already put a great deal of effort into trying to convince the general public that the group's members were terrorists. *"One man's terrorist is another man's patriot,"* he thought.

"But what would be the event that flipped the switch; what would be their Lexington and Concord?" he asked himself. There would need to be some cataclysmic event that set the Sons of Liberty into motion. During the American Revolution, the Tea Act had been the spark for the Boston Tea Party. But what would be the spark that infuriated this group? Shaking his head, he headed off to the shower.

Levi Walker was sitting in his favorite chair, drinking Jack Daniels over ice, unable to sleep. A little after four, he had decided to give up trying to sleep. He had a bad feeling. Something big was about to happen…he could feel it in his bones.

After speaking with Mavis Young the previous afternoon, he'd made calls to the Governors of eight southern states. All reported the same thing; members of Congress receiving bribes and threats from the president. But what did it all mean? Whatever was on the horizon, it was definitely not good.

Levi's cell phone began to vibrate. "*Who is calling me at this hour?*" he thought. Levi pulled the phone from his pocket and checked the screen, only to find a text message full of gibberish. He knew what this meant…someone from the Sons of Liberty was trying to contact him.

He went to his desk and retrieved an antique laptop computer from one of the drawers. Placing the laptop on top of the desk, he opened it, and then powered it up. As the old beast of a computer began the slow, laborious process of booting the operating system, Levi sat back down in his favorite chair, once again sipping his Jack.

He laughed to himself as he thought about how the Sons of Liberty had a communications network across the entire nation which the Federal Government had yet to crack. "*All the feds need is Windows 98*," he thought to himself.

After what seemed like an eternity, the laptop was ready to go, and Levi keyed up the instant messaging program that the Sons of Liberty used to contact each other. Once the program was running, a message popped up at once.

"T. State legislature to meet in secret session. Subject: unchecked federal power must be stopped."

Levi knew that this message must be from one of the Texas Legislature members who belonged to the Sons of Liberty; very likely, it was Jason Stratton, the Speaker of the House. *"Amazing how many of us have become members of the Sons,"* he thought, and began typing on the laptop. "*Ideas on the table?*"

"Secession."

Levi's face turned pale. For generations, there had been a strong secession movement in Texas, and supporters of the idea had become more numerous and vocal in the past few years. But to hear a member of the state legislature bring it up…even one who was a member of the Sons of Liberty…it was just unbelievable. Levi tossed his head back and drank the remaining Tennessee sour mash in one gulp. He then leaned forward over the laptop and began to type quickly. "*Do you realize the consequences?*"

"Yes."

"Civil War?"

There was a long pause, and then a new message popped up on Levi's computer screen. "*I would rather die on my feet as a free man than live on my knees as a slave.*"

"Sebastian, time to get moving!" As he buttoned his suit jacket, Kirk was shouting up the staircase toward Sebastian's bedroom.

"I've been ready," came Sebastian's voice from behind him. Kirk whirled around to see Sebastian standing behind him, backpack on one shoulder, eating an apple. He had a wide grin on his face. "You don't have to shout."

Kirk laughed."I thought you were still upstairs. How did you get behind me?"

Sebastian threw out his chest and in his best impression of Matt Pickett's voice said, "Just tryin' to be stealthy."

Kirk laughed again. "If you are going to try and impersonate Matt, you need to hit the bench press more often…a lot more often." Kirk's face became more serious. "Let's get going. I need to drop you off early today so I can make my appointment at the publisher's."

"I'll just ride the school bus today," Sebastian replied. "I really don't feel like hanging out at school any earlier than I have to."

"I thought you didn't like riding the bus?" Kirk asked.

"I don't," Sebastian replied, "but it's better than hanging out at school."

Kirk checked the time on his cell phone. "Ok, that's fine but you had better get to the end of the driveway to wait for the bus. It should be coming around in the next few minutes."

"Ok," Sebastian replied. He began to walk toward the front door, and then stopped and turned around."You know, if you let me drive to school, this wouldn't be an issue."

Kirk shook his head. "Cars are extremely expensive these days. It's not like back when I was your age and the average family could afford to buy a beat up old car for their teenager. The licensing and federal taxes make it too expensive for the average family to have a car for their teen."

"We can afford it," Sebastian countered.

"Yes, I know we can," Kirk replied, "but most can't. And I think it's wrong to flaunt wealth in front of people who are doing the best they can. Gives the wrong impression. Look, we can get into this later; we both need to get going."

"Ok," Sebastian said a bit sulkily. "I'll see you when I get home."

"See you this afternoon," Kirk replied as Sebastian headed out the door. He grabbed his car keys and headed for the Bronco. As he exited the front door, a crisp autumn breeze nipped at Kirk's face. It was still dark; looking toward the eastern horizon, one could just begin to see the first hints of light.

As Kirk got in the Bronco and headed down the driveway, he made sure to wave to Sebastian, who was stationed at the end of the driveway. As he began the drive down the street, Kirk could see headlights in the distance. "Must be the bus," he said to himself. "At least I know he didn't miss it."

After driving for about ten minutes, it had become light enough to make out the general shapes and figures of what Kirk passed along the road. He could see the fields of corn and soybean that would soon be harvested. He knew this farm well; it was owned by his friend, Leslie Smith, one of the few independent farmers left in this area.

In recent years, most of the small farms in Southern Ohio had been bought out by the huge corporations who controlled most of the agricultural production in the U.S. But Leslie Smith had refused to sell at any price; he said he owed it to his grandfather who started the family farm in the 1970's.

Up ahead, to the right side of the road, Kirk could make out a large area of lights. The lights had an eerie glow in the misty, early dawn light; it was almost like something out of a low-budget horror movie. Kirk slowed as he approached the lights. He soon realized that the lights were coming from an old combine near the side of the road. He could just make out a large, shadowy figure walking in front of the combine. "*That must be Leslie,*" he thought. Kirk pulled to the side of the road and rolled down the window, shouting, "Morning Leslie!"

A huge, hulking man wearing worn blue jeans and an Ohio State University sweatshirt stepped into the beam of Kirk's headlights. As the light gleamed off the man's dark skin, Kirk could see the man squint to see into the SUV.

"Kirk Dillon," the man said, extending his hand. "I thought that was you. Not many people around here drive an old Bronco. How have you been?"

Leslie was a big man. He was a dark-skinned African-American about six foot six in height and a tad over three hundred pounds; he was literally built like a mountain. He had a bald head and was wearing well-worn bib overalls.

"Not bad Leslie," Kirk said. How are things for an old OSU lineman?"

"That was a long time ago," Leslie said with a smile. "Although I must say, I was a force to be reckoned with on the field. If it hadn't been for that back injury, I might have gone pro."

"Well, you seem to have done pretty well in spite of it all," Kirk replied. "You managed to turn a profit on the family farm."

"Not many farmers with degrees in marketing," Leslie quipped. "Or even ones that understand how to market a small farm. You got to find a niche that eliminates the big boys' size advantage."

"Is it harvest time already?" Kirk asked.

Leslie nodded. "Yeah. I've been going over the grease fittings on this old girl while I'm waiting on the dawn. Looks like you aren't the only one around here who likes to work with antiques. I think this combine is older than your Bronco," he said with a grin.

Kirk smiled. "They just don't make 'em like they used to, eh boss?."

"No, they don't," Leslie replied. "I'll bet nobody's made a combine for small farms in eighty years. Everything is geared for those mega-farms out west. I guess there's not a big enough market for small combines anymore. Not that it really matters; I couldn't afford a new one anyway. At least not without going deep into debt. And I won't go that route; I won't live that way."

Kirk nodded his head. "I don't blame you, I won't either. My father always taught me that the only thing you go into debt for is a house. Remember in our younger days when there were people graduating from college deep in debt?"

"Sure do; my sister was one of them. And I remember when the government bailed them out and nationalized the public Universities." Leslie shook his head. "Remember back in the day when they bailed out the banks? And the car companies? Ha! That was nothing compared to the student loan fiasco. And now the government tries to brag that a college education is free. Free! Nothing in this life is free!"

"Instead people like you and I are paying for it," Kirk replied.

"And paying out the ass," Leslie said. "Problem is, there is no incentive to do well in school or to pick a major that can lead to a good job. My granddaughter just started college this fall. You know what her major is? Music History. I asked her what the hell you can do with a degree in Music History; I don't think any company would be in a rush to hire someone with such a useless degree. You know what she said? She told me that's what is interesting to her and that is why she chose that major. Then she said it doesn't matter if anyone wants to hire her or not because the government will take care of everyone's needs. That's the kind of commie crap they're teaching kids in schools these days."

"What's happening to this country?" Kirk asked.

"Damned if I know Kirk," Leslie replied.

He shook his head, and then continued, "No incentive to work, nobody wants to work, everyone wants a handout. Glad my grandfather didn't live to see this day. I'll bet he's turning over in his grave. Things are going to hell in a hand basket. Did you know that I had to join a union just so I can sell my harvest?"

"I didn't know about you joining a union," Kirk said.

"I had to," Leslie replied, "Or at least if I wanted to stay with farming. Because of the new laws, the big food conglomerates aren't allowed to buy from any company that isn't unionized. The Feds said the reason was to keep foreign food out of the country and keep American farmers working. The real effect has been to either eliminate or unionize all small farms. I think that was the plan all along. Damn union lobbyists."

"Is it working out for you?" Kirk asked. "The union I mean. Are you better off as a member of the union?"

Leslie rubbed his bald head. "I don't know. I can sell my

harvest, but the union keeps twenty percent of my profit. I really couldn't afford it, but I had no choice. For a while, I was specializing in local organics, which let me charge a premium price. People were willing to pay a little more, knowing it was locally produced and organically grown. But when the Food Equalization Bill passed, I was no longer allowed to charge a higher price than the industrial giants…even if I had a superior product. And on top of that, you had to be a licensed vendor to sell produce, but no permits are issued to growers. They said it was to protect the people; I say it was to make small roadside stands illegal."

Leslie shook his head. "The way I see it, the only people who benefit are the union bigwigs, corrupt politicians, and agribusiness CEO's."

"Sorry about that," Kirk replied. "Listen, I'd love to talk more, but I'm on my way to the publisher's for a meeting. I've got to get going."

Leslie smiled. "Another best-seller?"

"I hope so," Kirk replied. He reached out of the truck window and shook Leslie's hand. "Real good to see you Leslie. You take care of yourself."

"You too Kirk," Leslie replied. "I'll be looking forward to that new book."

After saying his goodbyes to Leslie, Kirk continued his drive toward Cincinnati. Not long after turning onto US 52, he spotted the abandoned power station. Streaks of reddish brown rust extended down from the tops of the smokestacks, in almost the same way that wax ran down from the top of a candle. Most of the windows in the main building were broken, and the grounds of the power station were littered with the rusty remains of trucks and heavy equipment.

The station had closed in 2015 when it could no longer meet the increasingly tough standards set by the EPA. The closing of the station has been a double blow to the local economy. Not only were over one hundred people left without work, the community then had to deal with the loss of millions of dollars in tax revenue; the area had never recovered.

Kirk continued his trip to Cincinnati via Interstate 471, which ran parallel to the Clermont-to-Cincinnati commuter train line. Soon he could see the city's skyline from the high point of the Interstate. The downtown skyscrapers, with their multiple glass windows shimmering in the morning light, the riverfront stadiums, the array of bridges over the Ohio River…..beautiful. While the skyline was nothing like that of New York or Chicago, it was still quite impressive. *"I know your secret though,"* Kirk thought. *"A very bad case of urban blight."*

Kirk pulled off the Interstate at the Liberty Street exit, entering the area of Cincinnati known as Over the Rhine. Built by German immigrants in the middle of the nineteenth century, Over the Rhine had become the poster child for poverty and unemployment at the end of the twentieth century. There had been an effort in the early part of the twenty-first century to revitalize the area, but by 2030 it was realized to be a doomed effort.

There was too much crime, too many abandoned buildings, and no local businesses. Vandalism was evident, as the majority of buildings had broken windows and absent doors. There were large numbers of people milling about and sitting idle on street corners and doorsteps. Kirk noticed the lack of ambition and purpose in the way they looked; it was if their life was just a matter of waiting for death.

"How can they live this way?" Kirk thought. *"They can't enjoy living like this; why don't they try to better themselves?"*

Kirk was now entering the downtown area, and he soon found himself at his publisher's office building. He parked in the lower level garage and then made his way to the front desk reception area. Upon checking in at the front desk, he was informed that Byron Reynolds would be meeting with him personally and he should take the elevator to the top floor. After thanking the desk clerk, Kirk found the elevator and began the slow ascent to the top floor. Upon stepping out of the elevator, he approached a desk with a receptionist, who pointed Kirk toward Byron Reynolds' office.

Seated at another desk just outside of Mr. Reynolds' office was a young woman, reading from a computer tablet. Kirk recognized her as Jenny, Byron's executive assistant. She looked up from the tablet as he approached, then smiled and stood up.

Sebastian had good reason to talk about Jenny's good looks; she could have been a supermodel if that sort of thing was still legal. Jenny was about five foot three and had a very athletic build. Her face displayed high, curving cheekbones and a pointed dimpled chin. Thin eyebrows arched gracefully over her viridian green eyes, which were hidden behind black framed glasses. She had ruby colored lips and long, wavy, chocolate brown hair that fell to her shoulders and partially covered one eye.

Jenny brushed the hair out of her eye and said, "Mr. Dillon, I don't know if you remember me; I'm Jenny Thelon, Mr. Reynolds' executive assistant." She extended her hand to shake his.

As he shook her hand, Kirk said, “How could I forget? Last time I was here, Sebastian was practically drooling over you.”

Jenny smiled, and laughed. “I remember. He’s not with you today?”

Kirk shook his head. “Nope. School.”

“He’s a senior now, isn’t he?” Jenny asked.

“Yep. And in a huge rush to get done and out of there,” Kirk replied.

“I remember being like that,” Jenny said with a smile. “Anyway, Mr. Reynolds told me to bring you in as soon as you arrived so if you will, follow me.”

“Lead the way,” Kirk replied.

Byron Reynolds was seated at his desk, reading from his computer screen when Kirk and Jenny entered the office. With the aid of his cane, Byron stood and said in his thin gravelly voice, “Kirk Dillon, so good to see you. How have you been?”

“I can’t complain,” Kirk replied.

“Excellent,” Byron said. He turned to Jenny and said, “Jenny, I don’t want any disturbances while I’m meeting with Kirk, understood?”

“Absolutely,” Jenny replied.

Byron continued, “Any of those pricks from the third floor give you any flack, you tell then they can kiss my ass.”

Jenny began to laugh. "Yes Mr. Reynolds." With that, she left his office.

Kirk looked at Byron. He was a very thin, withered old man who needed the assistance of a cane to walk. His head was nearly bald, and what little hair remained was pure white. His face narrow, with a rather long, straight nose; hollow cheeks and high cheekbones accentuated the thinness of his face. A thin goatee of white and gray highlighted rather than concealed his thin lips and slightly pointed chin. These features, combined with his somewhat large and slightly pointed ears gave him the appearance of an elf-like character from a fairytale. His steel-gray eyes were close set and framed by nearly white tufted eyebrows. Those steel-gray eyes, however, where what betrayed him for who he was…an experienced publishing tycoon. While this eighty-five year old man was frail, his mind was razor sharp, and he still had the motivation and drive of a man in his twenties.

"I'm glad to see you're still keeping yourself busy by running the show around here," Kirk said.

"It keeps me young. At my age, I need something to keep me young," Byron replied. "Of course, having kids like Jenny around helps keep me young, too. I can't count the number of assistants I've had since I got started in this business. Hell, when I got my first assistant, we were still allowed to call them secretaries without getting slapped with a sexual harassment suit. But of all of the assistants I have had, Jenny's the best in a long, long time."

With a smile Kirk said, "And that of course has nothing to do with her looks."

Byron raised his index finger to his lips as if he were to tell Kirk to be quiet, but then began to speak. "Listen kid, Jenny speaks four languages, knows the customs of just about every country on this planet, and knows the publishing business inside and out. She knows every government regulation regarding publishing, and knows the lobbyists in DC who can keep us in the black." Byron then smiled and said with a wink, "Of course, having an assistant sixty years younger than I, who looks like a super model, does help keep me young."

"I thought as much," Kirk replied.

"Jenny is driven like no other," Byron replied. "I never ask her to work late to finish a project; she just does it. She has the go-getter attitude that makes her a success at everything she does. Let me show you something kid."

With that, Byron took Kirk by the arm and directed him to the south wall of the office, which was glass from floor to ceiling; it offered a view of most of the downtown area. "What I see here is a city rotting at the core. Why? No motivation; no drive to improve one's self. Thousands of people out of work, but no drive to find a job or to be an entrepreneur."

"All facilitated by the government," Kirk said quietly as he gazed through the wall of glass.

"That's a big part of it," Byron replied. "I remember back in the 80's and 90's when government *wanted* you to start a new business, and they *wanted* you to be successful. Even though the politicians were just as crooked and slimy as today, at least they had the sense to understand that a successful business kept people employed and those employed people paid taxes. It provided the money the politicians needed to fund their pet projects." Byron shook his head. "Do you remember the streetcar fiasco?"

"I was pretty young at the time," Kirk replied, "and I was stationed overseas but I remember reading about it."

"Well, I remember it like it was yesterday," Byron replied. "City fathers came up with this grand plan to build a streetcar system in this city. Said it would bring tons of business and tourism to Cincinnati. But the city was already in the red; they were considering selling Music Hall because they couldn't afford the upkeep. Public employee pensions were underfunded, the streets were full of potholes, but they insisted on building that damn streetcar. They even tricked the people of this city into voting for it with that no means yes and yes means no crap on the ballot…and then claimed they had a mandate from the citizens to build the confounded thing. It's been a downward spiral in this city ever since. So sad…we have lost our way."

"I keep thinking the same thing…about losing our way," Kirk replied, still staring out the wall of glass. It was as if he were mesmerized by the view of the city.

Byron turned to Kirk and said with a smile, "But there are still people with spirit, kid. People like Jenny. People like you. Look at you; retired Army officer, you should be enjoying the good life, living off that government pension. Instead, you still work when you don't need to. You pay more in taxes than you receive in pension. What the hell for?"

Kirk shook his head and said quietly, "I can't stand to sit idle. I want to be productive. That's something my father taught me as a kid; something I have worked very hard to instill in my boys."

Byron slapped Kirk on the back and said, "That's exactly what I am talking about. Even with government treating you like shit because of hard work and a can-do attitude, you still bust your ass. Because you were raised right. The situation with the government is an effect, rather than a cause. Believe me, if everyone had attitudes like you, or I, or Jenny, the government would not be our worst enemy; it would be our best friend. The seeds for this were planted long ago. Do you know what caused this?"

Kirk looked at Byron and said, "When the people who vote for a living outnumbered the people who work for a living," Kirk replied.

Byron chuckled, and then continued, "No, it was before that. When we decided to start giving kids awards for participation. We created an entitlement society. These kids spent their entire childhoods being told that it didn't matter if you achieved and everyone was equal. Guess what? When they became adults they expected everything to be handed to them; they felt that they were entitled to success and didn't have to work for it. And once those attitudes took hold, it was a downhill run."

Byron continued, "You know, when I was a kid, a father would be walking with his son down the street, and if they saw a nice car drive by, the father would tell his son that that is Mr. Johnson. Mr. Johnson is someone to look up to, he would say. Mr. Johnson started with nothing and built an empire; look what he has now. Today, the people of this city would say why is he driving that car? Why should he have something I don't have? Mr. Johnson needs to share the wealth!"

Kirk looked at Byron and said, "Are we going to talk about the book deal, or all of the problems facing our society?"

Byron laughed and said, "That's what I like about you Kirk;

a businessman at heart. Not enough guys like you around. Have a seat and we'll talk about this contract."

Just as Kirk and Byron were about to have a seat, the door to the office opened and a man walked in with Jenny close behind. Kirk recognized the man as Richard Boyle, the union representative he met one day earlier. "I'm sorry Mr. Reynolds; I couldn't stop him," Jenny gasped.

Byron raised his hand and shook his head."It's all right, Jenny. Just call a security team." Jenny nodded and left the office; Byron looked at Richard Boyle and said, "It will be about two minutes before security arrives, so whatever you have to say, make it quick."

"Mr. Reynolds, my name is Rich…."

Byron cut him off. "I know who you are; your union represents many of the authors who are published through my publishing house. What do you want?"

"Let me get to the point then," Richard said. "The union has decided that you will not be permitted to produce this man's book."

"Nobody comes in to my office and tells me how to do business or run my company," Byron replied with fire in his eyes. "Get out of my office."

Richard pointed at Kirk and said, "If you attempt to publish this man's book, every union member at this company will go on strike." Richard straightened his tie and the front of his suit jacket, obviously feeling he had the upper hand.

"If that's the route you want to go," Byron replied, "that would be fine with me. I hope your union members like going without a job. I can produce Kirk Dillon's book at my division in Germany just as well as here in Cincinnati. Maybe I'll just close up shop here and publish exclusively from Germany. Maybe then you can explain to your union members why they are unemployed."

"You can't do that!" Richard shouted. "It is against the law to close a business and move to a non-union location! Businesses tried that all of the time back in the days of right-to-work states; the government would never allow it."

Byron looked Richard directly in the eyes. "If I close all of my US operations, who are you going to complain to? The US government will not have jurisdiction over me. And I'm sure the German government will have no qualms about the expansion of my facilities in Germany. What is your…or should I say, the union's…issue with Mr. Dillon?"

Before Richard could speak, Kirk said, "We've met before. He's not too happy that I have refused to become a member of his union."

"I see," Byron said as he slowly nodded his head. "And let me guess; the union isn't happy about not getting twenty percent of what Mr. Dillon earns. I could care less if he does or doesn't join a union. I have already decided what I will pay for the rights to this book; there will be no discount or bonus due to union or non-union status."

Richard pounded his fists on Byron's desk. "But it just isn't fair!" he shouted. "How can the union continue to function without member dues? You have no right to stop us from earning a living."

Byron looked at Richard and said, "Then I suggest you go out and earn a living and stop leaching off the productive people in society. You and people like you seem to have forgotten why unions existed in the first place. They were formed to protect the rights of the working man; to ensure he received good working conditions and a fair wage. Mr. Dillon already receives all of those things. He works from his home; a very nice home I might add. All of the terms of his contract are reasonable and are negotiable. I see nothing that the union can offer him that he does not already have. However," and at this he turned toward Kirk, "if Mr. Dillon wishes to join your union, he may do so with no threat or retaliation from me."

"I will never join a union," Kirk replied.

The door to Byron's office opened at about that time, and three security officers entered. It was two men and one woman; all dressed in black and carrying holstered handguns.

Byron looked at Richard and said, "I believe you have your answer, sir. Now let me tell you something else." He pointed a skinny, bony finger at Richard. "NOBODY comes into my office and tells me what to do or how to run my company. NOBODY." Turning toward the security team, Byron said, "Escort this man out of this building."

As the security team approached, Richard Boyle adjusted his suit jacket and tie. Looking at Kirk Dillon he said, "This isn't over. I've been nice up until now. I'll give you one last chance to accept membership into the union. If not, you will have to suffer the consequences."

"What does it take to get it through your thick skull?" Kirk replied. "I have said no, and that is final!"

The two men on the security team grabbed Richard by the arms. As Richard began to struggle, one of the security team said, "Easy way or hard way?" Richard threw off their grip and began walking toward the office door. As he exited the room, he turned his head and shouted, "This isn't over!"

After Richard and the security team left the room, Byron turned to Kirk and said, "Kid, I'll never understand the union mentality."

"You and me both," Kirk replied.

Bryon sat down at his desk chair, and motioned for Kirk to sit in a chair facing him. "You know," Byron began, "I'm a business man and not an unreasonable one at that. So I look at everything from a market perspective. Labor is just another commodity. If I have to pay a premium above market value, then I should get something in return. So if the union were to offer me something to improve my product, or offset production costs, I would be inclined to listen. If the union were to take over editing manuscripts for my authors, or increase distribution… But no; they offer nothing."

"They see the world through the prism of 'US versus THEM'," Kirk replied.

Byron nodded his head. "You read my mind, kid. I am going to warn you to watch your back. The union is not above extortion, assault, or blackmail."

"I'll be careful," was Kirk's reply.

"Good," Byron replied. "Now let's talk about this new book of yours…."

CHAPTER SIX

Jack Spearman and Mavis Young made their way into the House Chamber of the Capitol building for the president's speech. The House Chamber was packed; not only were both congressmen and senators milling about, but there were a huge number of national police officers.

Mavis looked at Jack and said, "I'm used to the police protection wherever the president goes, but this place is packed with police."

Jack nodded and said with a grin, "Maybe he knows how many of us would like to put him down."

"You had better mind your tongue, Blackjack," Mavis replied. "You know what the penalty is for making a threat against the president, and we both know how much he would like to see you gone."

Jack chuckled and said, "Little sister, I'll try to watch my language, just for you. Remember back when it was the

Secret Service and not the National Police that guarded the president?"

"That wasn't too long ago, Blackjack," Mavis replied. "That was part of Conrad White's election platform; streamlining all federal law enforcement to save on costs and eliminate duplicate duties. And look what we got."

"Yep," Jack said as he nodded his head. "FBI, CIA, Secret Service, Marshalls…all gone. And in its place, the national police, under the direct control of the president."

"His own private army," Mavis said with a sigh. "Well, no use dwelling on that now. Let's find our seats."

It was some time before all of the senators and congressmen made their way to their seats. Finally, Samantha Ravana, the Speaker of the House, made her way to the front of the room. She was an older woman who was very thin with graying hair. She moved slowly but deliberately, as if each step were painful but necessary. After reaching the rostrum, she looked around the crowd for a few moments, sometimes nodding to individuals she made eye contact with. Finally, she began to speak.

"Senators, Congresswomen, Congressmen…let us begin our business."

The noise in the room quickly dissipated; the Speaker continued. "At this point, I would like everyone to rise for the President of the United States!"

Mavis and Jack rose along with the rest of the members of Congress. As the president, surrounded by national police, began his walk down the central isle of the house chamber, people began to applaud. Soon the applause was deafening.

The president waved to various individuals as he walked down the aisle, occasionally nodding in approval at certain members. After reaching the rostrum, he shook hands with Samantha Ravana. After shaking hands with the president, the Speaker said, "Mr. President, both Houses of Congress are assembled and are waiting to hear you speak."

President White stroked his thick mustache with two fingers, as he was apt to do, and smiled briefly. After regaining a solemn composure, he stepped up to the microphone and began to speak.

"Senators, Representatives, we face grave economic times. The Chinese economy has overtaken that of our country; we find ourselves falling further and further behind. As the leaders and law makers of this great nation, it is our responsibility to regulate this economy. We do this not only to provide prosperity for our nation, but to ensure that wealth is distributed to all members of our society, each according to his needs."

"In recent years, the rich have become richer, the poor have become poorer, and the nation has gone deeper into debt. One must come to the obvious conclusion that the wealthy of this nation are not only preventing the poor from rising to the middle class, but they also do not pay their fair share in taxes. Their greed disgusts me; they complain about their tax rate, and yet they have so many deductions that they pay nearly nothing. This is not fair; not all Americans can afford high priced lawyers to get them out of paying taxes."

"The rich also prevent real tax reform because so many politicians are in their pocket. While there are good politicians who fight for the good of the poor and working class, far too many are in the pocketbook of greedy, wealthy business owners. That is going to stop, here and now."

"I have been working with the Speaker of the House as well as the Senate majority leader to create a bill that will be known as the American Prosperity Act. This bill will ensure the economic survival of this great nation. The first part of the bill states that no member of either house of Congress may be a business owner or former business owner. All current members of the House and Senate who are or were business owners must resign on passage of the bill. There is an exemption for private practice lawyers."

"The second part of the bill deals with the current economic emergency. Since all branches of government must pool resources and work together to battle this economic crisis, we can't be distracted by elections. Part two states that all national elections will be temporarily suspended for the next seven years. These seven years will give us an uninterrupted time frame to focus all of our energies on the economy."

The president looked at Samantha Ravana and nodded as he backed away from the microphone. Samantha stepped up to the microphone and began to speak.

"For two weeks, a special committee, hand selected by myself and the president, have hashed out the details of this bill. This bill was debated in secret in the interest of national security. At this time, both houses will vote on the bill."

Jack and Mavis looked at each other with mutual shock and disgust. "This can't be happening!" Mavis exclaimed.

"It is," Jack replied dryly. "But I guarantee that this has nothing to do with helping the poor. There's more to this."

Mavis nodded and said, "I guess we know why we were

called to the White House; he was feeling us out. He wanted to see if he could buy another two votes."

Jack nodded."Damn right, Little Sister, and with no national elections for seven years, he just added another four years to his term and he's already on his second term."

"The same goes for everyone in this room," Mavis replied."Money grubbers! Only after power! Of course, every bit of this bill is unconstitutional."

I don't think that really matters to President White," Jack replied, "or most of the others in this room. And now that the president has packed the Supreme Court, even if someone does challenge its constitutionality, the court will side with the president."

"He had it all planned out," Mavis said.

"Damn right," Jack said with a nod.

"Well," Mavis said, "we should vote, but I have a hunch that votes have been bought and paid for already. Otherwise, I don't think the bill would have been brought up."

"We still need to do our duty, even if this is my last act as a Senator," Jack replied. "Let's get it done."

Kirk Dillon was having a pretty good day. The morning had been beautiful, and save for the union interruption, the meeting with Byron Reynolds had gone extremely well. With the exception of his first book, all of Kirk's books had paid well, and his latest work was the highest paying yet. Byron had spent much of the meeting trying to convince Kirk to open an account in Switzerland or the Grand Caymans so that the top tier tax rate of 90% could be avoided. When Byron wouldn't take no for an answer, Kirk agreed to think it over in the next few days. *"Maybe Jenny can help me work around Byron on this,"* he thought.

Kirk turned the Bronco down the driveway to his home; over the fence line he could see Matt Pickett trimming the bushes in his front yard. *"That man is dedicated to everything he puts his mind too,"* Kirk thought. After reaching the end of his driveway, he got out of the SUV and walked to the fence line between his and Matt's yard. Looking at Matt he said, "You want to come over to my yard and take care of my roses too?"

"I should," Matt said with a grin. "You suck as a gardener. Only thing you can grow is weeds. How'd the meetin' go?"

"Not bad; I'm pretty happy with this book deal," Kirk replied. "This contract is the largest I've ever signed." Kirk chuckled lightly, and then continued. "Byron Reynolds kept trying to convince me to open an off shore account to put the money in; said he could have his people set it up for me."

"What'd you say?" Matt asked.

Kirk shook his head and said, "I tried to tell him no but he was very insistent. He was almost begging me to do it. So I told him I would think about it. I'll call his assistant later and tell her to quietly put me down as a no."

"You should do it," Matt said.

"It's illegal," Kirk replied.

Matt stood up and stretched his back. Looking at Kirk, he said, "There was a time in my life when that would've mattered to me. But no more. You make all that money on those books, then you get taxed out the wazoo. Bet you pay more than your pension's worth, don't you?" Kirk nodded, and Matt continued. "You had to give up your pension…which you're due…'cause you wanted to continue working. That ain't right. Twenty years of service to the nation, most of that time in combat, all thrown away."

Kirk smiled and said, "Are you waxing philosophical on me?"

"No," Matt replied. "I guess I've just opened my eyes to what's been goin' on." He hesitated slightly and then continued. "Look, I'm not a smart man; just an inbred hillbilly from Tennessee, but I know right from wrong and takin' ninety percent of what someone makes ain't right. That's stealin'."

"Or slavery," Kirk replied. "No, it's not right. But I never thought I would hear you advocate for breaking the law."

Matt smiled and said, "It's them books you let me read. While we're talkin' about em', you wanna let me borrow another?"

"Sure," Kirk replied. "Come on in the house and you can pick one out."

Matt followed Kirk into the house. When they reached the bookcase that separated the living and dining rooms, Matt reached into his pocket and pulled out a pair of reading glasses. "It's hell gettin' old," he said.

"I know what you mean," Kirk replied. "Why don't you get

the surgery? Or intraocular lenses? That's what I did."

Matt shook his head and said, "Can't stand the idea of someone diggin' around in my eyes. Bad enough havin' bullets pulled out of arms and legs. The eyes? Too creepy."

As the two men looked over the bookcase, Kirk's cell phone began to ring. Looking at the phone, Kirk said, "Sherry Powel, one of Sebastian's teachers. I hope nothing's wrong today. I'm going to put this on the big screen."

Pressing a button on his cell phone, the large LCD screen in the living room came to life with the picture of a woman's face. She looked to be in her late twenties, with red hair and a thin face. She had a very worried look on her face."Sherry, how are th…."

"Kirk!" she interrupted. "There's no time for that now. They've taken him! They didn't know I was there; I was around the corner from Rosenthal's office and they didn't see me, but they've taken him!" Kirk could hear the fear in her voice; she looked as a child does when she knows what she's done was wrong and she'll be punished for it.

"Slow down. What are you talking about?" Kirk asked. "Who has taken who?"

"The national police! They've taken Sebastian." Sherry looked to the left, and then the right, as if she we looking for someone. She continued, "They called him to Mrs. Rosenthal's office and the police were there for him. They said you were unfit to be a parent because you are anti-union and anti-union is un-American."

"This is Boyle's doin'," Matt said.

"Anyway," Sherry continued, "They wrote their own warrant right there, on the spot, and they said that if she or anyone at the school told anyone about what happened, they would be taken to jail! They can't do that!"

"Yes they can," Kirk replied quietly. "That's been the law ever since the Patriot Act was first passed."

"But he's not a terrorist!" Sherry protested.

"The government decides who or what a terrorist is," Matt replied.

"Where are they taking him?" Kirk asked. "Which camp?"

"I don't know, Kirk, I don't know," Sherry replied obviously very shaken. "They didn't say when I was listening, and I got out of there as fast as possible; I didn't want to be discovered. Look, I've got to get off of here. If I'm discovered, I will lose my job…or worse."

"Get off the phone, Sherry," Kirk replied. "You've already risked enough and I do appreciate it." Sherry nodded, and after looking to the left and right again, the screen went blank. Kirk continued staring at the blank screen; silently, motionless. A tear welled up in the corner of his eye and rolled down his cheek, ending at the outer corner of his gray mustache.

Matt looked at Kirk and asked, "What's the plan, Colonel?"

Kirk was silent for what seemed like an eternity. Finally, in a soft whisper he said, "I'm going to get my son." As tears rolled from the corners of his eyes, he said, "I don't know where they've taken him but I will find him if it's the last thing I do."

“Let’s go,” Matt said.

Kirk was still staring at the blank screen. “I can’t ask you to go with me.”

“Don’t need to ask,” Matt replied. “I’m volunteering.”

Kirk turned and faced Matt. “I can’t let you do this, Matt. You’ll be labeled a criminal, and could go to jail. Maybe even be killed. In even the best case scenario, you’ll lose your home and your pension...everything you own. I can’t ask you to do that.”

“You and the kid are the only family I got,” Matt replied. “We’ve known each other for most of our lives, and you saved my life once. About time I repaid the favor.”

“I only had to save your life because you came looking for me,” Kirk replied.

Matt shook his head and said, “That don’t matter. The way I see it, my house and pension are a small price to pay to rescue the kid.”

Kirk smiled and said, “That’s twice today you’ve surprised me. What happened to Sergeant Major Matt Pickett who obeyed every rule in the book?”

Matt scratched his head and said, “He finally realized that while he was away serving his country, his country abandoned every belief that it was founded on. I haven’t decided to become a criminal; my country decided to make me a criminal.” He crossed his arms and then continued, “Anyway, enough of that; we’re burnin’ daylight. What’s the plan?”

"Well," Kirk said, "I'm not sure how we find out where he's been taken."

"I know someone who may be able to help us with that," Matt replied. "But after we find him and get him, what then?"

Kirk was quiet for a moment and then said, "We head south, using the back roads through the Appalachian Mountains as cover." As he spoke, Kirk began to unbutton his suit jacket. "We might even find some people who are sympathetic and help us out. We've got a better chance of a fair trial in the South. Worst case scenario, we cross the border into Mexico."

Matt nodded his head and said, "Better get some supplies to load into your truck…sleeping bags, food, flashlight, and anything else you can think to grab. I'm going over to my place to get a few things; be back in a few."

After Matt left the house, Kirk slipped out of his suit jacket and then headed down the basement stairs. Along the north wall he had his camping gear stored in large plastic storage boxes. Hoisting one box onto his shoulder and dragging another behind him, he took them to the Bronco and loaded them through the rear window. Kirk then rushed to his bedroom to change his clothes. Off came the rest of his business suit; in its place went blue jeans, a green t-shirt, and boots.

Grabbing a duffle bag from his closet, he stuffed it with a few other pieces of clothing as well as the contents of the small safe under his bed. He then opened the drawer of his nightstand and grabbed the .45 pistol that he kept for protection. He slid the pistol into his waistband and then placed two extra magazines and two boxes of ammunition in the duffle. Picking up the bag, he headed outside, grabbing his old army field jacket along the way.

When Kirk emerged from the house, Matt Pickett was tossing his own faded green army duffle bag into the back of the SUV. Looking at Kirk, he said, "You ready to do this? I think we're as equipped as we can be. Threw in a few boxes of old MREs I had in the garage. Taste like shit, but don't go bad."

Seeing the handgun in Kirk's belt, he said, "Didn't know you still had the 1911; figured you'd turned it in."

"No," Kirk replied. "Besides, this thing has changed hands so many times that the government could never track it down. Let's get a move on, Sergeant."

Matt smiled and said, "It's been a long time since anyone called me that. It feels good." He climbed into the Bronco's passenger seat and said, "Course, if we don't pull this off, my new title might be inmate 2645."

Kirk climbed into the driver's seat and said, "Let's make sure that doesn't happen to either of us." Kirk turned the ignition key and the turbo-diesel engine roared to life; the sweet smell of diesel fumes permeated the air.

Turning to Matt, Kirk said, "Ok, so you said you knew someone who could help us find Sebastian. Who is it and how do we contact them?"

"Head to Big Indian road," Matt replied. "We're going to see Old Man Bottoms."

Levi Walker sat at his desk in the Texas Capitol, drumming his middle finger on the desktop as he impatiently waited for the instant messaging program on his ancient laptop to boot. About an hour earlier, he had received a disturbing call from Mavis Young, telling him that the president's American Prosperity Act had passed both the House and Senate, and was on its way to the president's desk for final approval. As a result of the act, Texas would be losing both of its senators and thirty-four of its thirty-six congressional seats and none of those seats could be refilled for seven years, as the act forbade elections for the vacated seats until 2056.

Mavis was one of the two remaining congressional members, and the only one Levi trusted; the other, Stetson Smith, was a first term congressmen who seemed to have come out of nowhere with the backing of an international energy company.

The instant messaging program was finally ready, and Levi began to type without delay.

"American Prosperity Act passes; Texas loses most representation."

Levi again drummed his middle finger impatiently as he waited for a reply.

"Understood. We can suffer the destruction of liberty no longer. It is time to meet."

"I need to know who I can trust," Levi messaged.

"We will send you our contacts in the south. Also, contact the governor of Alaska."

"Alaska?"

"He is a kindred spirit."

"When do we meet?"

"ASAP. Before the last flicker of the torch of freedom is extinguished."

CHAPTER SEVEN

"Are you sure Old Man Bottoms can help us?" Kirk Dillon asked as he drove his Bronco down the pothole laden gravel road. "That old hermit creeps me out."

"Yep," Matt Pickett replied, eyes fixed on the road ahead. "He's a strange one; paranoid, too. Thinks the government is out to get 'im. I hear he was a spec ops guy in the ol' days."

"How do you know him?" Kirk asked.

"I met him trading heirloom seeds. He's the guy that has all of the weird ones you never heard of," Matt replied.

The Bronco hit a pothole; the jolt was enough to send both men airborne for a moment, and the steering wheel was nearly jerked out of Kirk's hands. Kirk slowed the truck down as he regained control of the truck. He was traveling far faster than he would have liked under the circumstances.

"You really think this lunatic is going to be able to track down my son?" Kirk said.

"He's our best bet, so don't write him off just yet," Matt replied, "and I know he won't turn us in; he hates the government far too much. We just have to hope that he doesn't shoot us when we get there."

"Great," Kirk sighed.

The road was becoming rockier, and Kirk began to wonder if they were lost. Suddenly, Matt pointed down the road and said, "Pull in over there. About eighty meters."

"No driveway?" Kirk asked.

"No," Matt replied. "Just a walkin' path from the road."

Kirk slowed and pulled over to the side of the road where Matt had pointed. After turning off the motor, he looked at Matt and said, "Ok, we're here. Lead the way."

As he opened the truck door, Matt looked at Kirk and said, "Leave your gun in the truck; don't wanna provoke 'im."

"What have you gotten me into?" Kirk replied.

The area was a thick forest with dense underbrush of honeysuckle and wild rose. The path that Matt and Kirk were walking on was very narrow, with many low hanging tree branches they had to duck under. Thorns from wild rose and blackberry brambles constantly tugged at arms and legs; it was as if Mother Nature did not want them down this path.

After about fifty yards, the forest thinned out, and Kirk could see a clearing directly ahead. Sitting on the back edge of the clearing was a small home. It looked like something out of a frontier movie. The house had a wide front porch, with a large stack of firewood near the front door. The board and batten siding, which was made of rough cut oak, was weathered to a dark gray.

Kirk followed Matt to the rough wooden door of the house. After reaching the front door, Matt turned to Kirk and said, "Let me do the talkin'." Matt began knocking on the door and then said in a loud voice, "Bottoms! It's Matt Pickett. I need to talk to ya. Bottoms! It's Matt Pickett!"

Kirk heard the lock on the door turning and the door opened a few inches. The smell of cigarette smoke permeated the air. A thin, gravelly voice called from within the house. "Pickett! Who's at whitcha?"

"Kirk Dillon," Matt replied. "We need your help."

"My help," the voice replied. "Doesn't seem likely."

"Can we come in so I can explain?" Matt asked.

"Ok, ok," the voice replied. "Do it quick."

The door opened fully and Matt walked in, with Kirk following close behind. The inside of the house was dimly lit, and reeked of cigarette smoke. The few pieces of furniture were very old and worn; they looked to be salvaged from the dump. The floor was made of dark, wide oak boards, and the walls were made of rough sawn wood instead of plaster or drywall.

Old Man Bottoms was perhaps only five foot two in height, partly due to his hunched over back. He was extremely thin, and was wearing bib overalls and a red plaid shirt. He had a thick, wiry beard of gray and white that nearly reached down to his waist. In his left hand, he held a lit cigarette between two fingers. After closing and locking the door behind Kirk, Bottoms whirled around quickly to face the pair. As he turned, Bottoms reached under the front flap of his overalls and pulled out a snub-nosed revolver. Pointing the revolver at Matt he sighed heavily and said, "Always knew the feds would send someone after me. Didn't expect it to be you."

Matt raised his hands to eye level and said, "Nobody's come to get you."

"Bullshit," Bottoms replied. He took a long drag on his cigarette. "You two pretended to be retired just to get close to me. DIDN'T WORK! I know the government tricks; can't fool me."

Matt shook his head and said, "Nobody's tryin' to get you; we need your help."

"Bullshit," Bottoms spat again. "Ain't nobody ever come to me for help. You two are government. Ronald Rambo Reagan said the most terrifying words are I'm from the government and I'm here to help."

"We said we need your help," Matt said.

"Same difference," Bottoms replied testily.

"They took my boy," Kirk said quickly.

Bottoms lowered his revolver slightly. "Who?" he asked.

"The national police," Kirk replied. "They're taking him to a re-education camp, but we don't know which one. We need to track him down."

Bottoms put the cigarette to his lips and took a long, slow drag. His eyes looked back and forth between Matt and Kirk, as if he were trying to decide if he could trust them. Finally, after what seemed like an eternity to Kirk, he lowered his revolver. Taking the cigarette out of his mouth he said, "See, they can't be trusted. Never could. That's why I got out." He began to wave his revolver about as he talked, as if he were a conductor at an orchestra performance.

"How many times have I told you…you can't trust the government! Been takin' away our rights for too many years. Constant state of war for fifty years. Takin' away guns. Hunt down moonshiners. It's wrong, wrong, wrong!"

"Bottoms," Matt said slowly. "We need to find out where they're takin' the boy. Do you know how to track em' down?"

Bottoms stood silently for a moment, rubbing his cigarette between two fingers. Scratching his chin, he asked, "Is the boy chipped?"

"If you mean a RFID chip, then yes," Kirk replied. "They were already required when he was born, so it was implanted at the hospital the day of his birth."

Bottoms took a couple of puffs on his cigarette and then said, "Damn things are the mark of the beast. Hate 'em. It's like a trackin' device under your skin. Let's the government track every move you make. Might as well shove a leech up your ass." He took another long, drawn out drag on the cigarette. "We can make it work to our advantage…use it to track him down. Follow me out to my tool shed."

Kirk and Matt followed the hunched over old man as he hobbled out the back door of the house. Not far from the house was a small building about the size of a single car garage. Like the house, the shed was sided with weathered board and batten siding. Bottoms opened the battered wooden door to the building, and motioned for Matt and Kirk to follow him inside. The interior of the building was dark, and filled with old garden tools, lumber, lanterns, and ancient farm machinery.

Standing near a wooden pallet loaded with bricks, Bottoms reached down and lifted one edge of the pallet. Surprisingly, it lifted easily, as you would open the lid to a cedar chest. Under the pallet was a dark hole three feet in diameter. Kirk could just make out the rails of a ladder peaking from out of the hole. "Down here's my shop. Do all my tinkerin' down here. That's where I got my ham set up."

"Your what?" Matt asked.

"Ham radio," Bottoms replied. He pulled a small flashlight out of his pocket, turned it on and said, "Follow me."

Kirk glanced at Matt with a puzzled look on his face. Matt just shrugged his shoulders and followed Bottoms down the ladder. Kirk waited until Matt was down several rungs on the ladder, and then he began his decent down the ladder. The hole was deep, perhaps fifteen feet down. When Kirk arrived at the bottom, Matt was holding the flashlight as Bottoms flipped a switch on the wall of the hole. What Kirk saw next blew his mind away.

The three men were standing in an underground room that was approximately twelve feet by twenty feet. Rows of overhead fluorescent lights lit the entire area. Along one wall were various milling and metal working machines. Along another wall was a large work table holding rifles and pistols in various stages of manufacture. To the left of where the men were standing was a table holding an old computer.

Bottoms pulled a chair over to the computer desk and sat down. He flipped the switches on several power strips, and then pointed to a large switch on the wall. "Flip that one; it raises my radio antenna. Works like a periscope."

Matt flipped the switch, and the hum of an electric motor could be heard. After about fifteen seconds, the hum stopped with a thud. Turning to Kirk, Bottoms handed him a pad of paper and pencil. "I need the boys full name, birth date, social, where he was born, high school name. That should be enough to track him down."

As Kirk wrote down the requested information, Bottoms lit another cigarette. After taking a several puffs, Bottoms began typing at the computer. As he typed, he began mumbling; neither Kirk nor Matt could understand what he was saying.

Kirk handed the pad of paper to Bottoms and said, "Here's everything you asked for." As Bottoms looked over the paper, Kirk said, "I thought you said this was ham radio; where's the microphone?"

Bottoms looked up at Kirk and said, "Not all ham radio is voice. You can send data just as well as voice. We use this setup to send encrypted messages and data."

Matt looked at Bottoms and said, "Who's we?"

"All of us," Bottoms replied.

"Well, who is *us*?" Kirk asked.

Bottoms looked back and forth between the two men and then took several small puffs on his cigarette. Tossing it onto the ground, he began to roll up his left sleeve. On his upper arm was a faded tattoo of a coiled rattlesnake. Under the snake were the words "Don't tread on me." Bottoms looked Kirk directly in the eyes and said, "The Sons of Liberty."

"You're a member of the Sons of Liberty?" Kirk asked.

Bottoms grinned. "You're lookin' at the Southwest Ohio branch."

"Are there many of you?" Kirk asked.

"Not around these parts," Bottoms replied. "Lots more down South."

"The US government says ya'll are terrorists," Matt said.

Bottoms nodded and said, "British said the same about the original Sons. Government is afraid of men who are willing to stand up for their rights. Freedom to do what I want, when I want, how I want…that's worth fightin' for. If all I end up with is the six feet of dirt they throw on me…it's worth it." Bottoms rolled his sleeve back down, and turning to the computer said, "Now let's see if I can put these guys to work findin' your boy."

As Bottoms plugged away at the keyboard, Kirk and Matt began looking at the rifles and handguns on the work table. Most of the handguns appeared to be variants of the colt 1911, but the frames and slides seemed to be different from the versions Kirk had seen in the past. The edges were sharper, and the general shape tended to be more angular.

"I just realized what he's doin'," Matt whispered.

"What?" Kirk asked.

"He's buildin' these from scratch. Look over there at that

milling machine; that's a half done 1911 receiver." Matt then pointed to a rifle part. "And that looks like an M-16 lower receiver."

Kirk pointed to a small machine sitting on the work table. "And is that a loading press?"

"Sure is," Matt replied. "He's makin' weapons and ammo. Look…no serial numbers. None of this stuff can be tracked."

"If the feds found out what he was doing here, he would go away for life," Kirk said. "He would be labeled a terrorist, wouldn't be given a trial, and then sent to Gitmo until he croaks."

Matt nodded. "Yep. One thing's for sure; crazy or not, he's one hell of a machinist." He picked up one of the handguns that was completely assembled. "Look at this thing; it's a work of art. Stainless steel, long slide, three dot sights. Smooth action."

"Genuine craftsmanship alright," Kirk replied.

"We've got it!" Bottoms shouted from his computer table. "We've got it!"

Kirk and Matt ran over to Bottoms, who was still seated in front of the computer. "What did you find?" Kirk asked with excitement.

Speaking with a lit cigarette in the corner of his mouth, bottoms said, "I've got his RFID tag; we can track 'im. Even better, I got some information from a contact inside the Cincinnati Police. Your boy's bein' taken to the Reynoldsburg education camp."

"That's near Columbus," Matt said.

Bottoms nodded, and then continued. "They stopped off in Cincinnati to refuel and eat. They're on their way again, but it should be easy to cut them off."

"But how will we track them down?" Kirk asked.

"Gotcha covered," Bottoms replied. He opened a desk drawer and pulled out what looked like an antique GPS receiver. He began talking again as he ran a USB cord from the receiver to his computer. "This is a GPS receiver from the late 1990's. I'm setting it up so that you can use it to track your son's RFID signature."

"I don't get it," Matt said. "I thought these chips needed scannin' close up, like the barcode readers at the grocery."

Bottoms started typing on the computer, speaking as he typed. "Most are like that, but the ones planted in people's bodies are different than the ones used on merchandise. There are designed to go active from the energy picked up by radio and microwave transmissions. In most areas, the RFID tags are constantly active. And military satellites are designed to track every one of them."

"So you're sayin' that every person born in the US in the past twenty years is actively bein' tracked?" Matt gasped.

"Welcome to the land of the free," Bottoms replied between cigarette puffs.

"It is disgusting what this nation has come to," Kirk said. "When they started tagging everyone, the government said it was to combat terrorism."

Speaking with his cigarette dangling from the corner of his mouth, Bottoms said, "They who can give up essential liberty to obtain a little temporary safety deserve neither liberty nor safety. They will lose both."

"What?" Matt asked.

Bottoms took the cigarette out of his mouth and looked at Matt. "Benjamin Franklin, 1755. Used to be inscribed on the staircase of the Statue of Liberty. Taken down years ago."

Kirk shook his head, saying, "This is what we have come to…we track the every movement of our own citizens."

Bottoms unplugged the USB cord from the GPS and handed the receiver to Kirk. "The receiver is programmed with one waypoint; that is your son's RFID signal. Because of how old this unit is, I don't think the feds will be able to track back to your position. Just in case though, after you get your boy, destroy the receiver. You'll also need to kill his signal. Follow me."

Kirk and Matt followed Bottoms to a workbench that was covered with partially assembled handguns. Bottoms handed Kirk what looked like an old film camera. "It used to be a camera," Bottoms explained, "But I gutted it and turned it into a RFID killer. Found the plans years ago on the net…before it was censored. Place the camera near an RFID tag and press the shutter button. It'll spit out a small EMP an' fry the chip. Won't hurt the boy a bit."

"Thank you…for everything," Kirk said.

Without speaking, Bottoms handed Kirk a handgun from the workbench.

"I already have one in the truck," Kirk said.

Matt took the handgun out of Bottoms hand, saying, "I don't. Mind if I nab one of your M16's, too?"

"Go ahead," Bottoms replied. "There are a few mags on the bench. That paper bag has 5.56 ammo, and there are boxes of .45 below the bench." Bottoms looked at Kirk and said, "Where do you plan to go?"

"South," Kirk replied.

Bottoms nodded and raised a single cigarette-burnt finger to his weather beaten lips. After a long pause, he said, "After you get your boy, take the back roads to Aberdeen. Go to the Trail Hollow Inn and ask for Dottie Moore; she runs the Inn. Her husband will take you across the river on the ferry. I'll contact 'em and let them know you're comin'."

"The Aberdeen Ferry has been out of service for years," Kirk protested.

"That's what the Sons of Liberty like people to think," Bottoms replied with a sly grin.

Kirk extended his hand to Bottoms, who shook it with a warm smile. "I doubt we will meet again," Bottoms said. "But good luck, nonetheless."

"Thank you," Kirk said.

"We've gotta move," Matt said. "Bottoms, thanks for everything."

Bottoms nodded, and then said, "Good luck. Be on your guard; there's gonna be a lot of shit goin' down in the next few days."

"Whatta ya mean?" Matt asked.

"You'll see," Bottoms said with a grin.

CHAPTER EIGHT

Mavis Young was looking out the window of the small jet she and Jack Spearman had been riding in for the past few hours. They had just landed at a small, nearly deserted airport."Where exactly are we?"

Jack Spearman looked up from the tablet he was reading from and said, "All I know is that we're somewhere south of the Mason Dixon line. Levi wouldn't tell me where the meeting was; said it was for our safety. I guess that's why we changed planes so many times; so that if we were bein' tailed, we'd be harder to track."

"Who would want to track us…and why?" Mavis asked.

Jack Spearman set down his tablet and looked at Mavis in disbelief. "You're shittin' me, right? After what we just saw in DC? You know the president's goons are going to be watchin' us real close, and I mean *real* close."

"But we haven't done anything," Mavis protested.

"Doesn't matter," Jack replied. "I've been kicked out of Congress for running a business, and it's well known that you're against most of this administration's policies. The president may be a communist bastard, but I will give him this: he is extremely intelligent and doesn't do anything without a plan. And we all know that he's a master at coverin' his ass. I guarantee that he's got someone watchin' us."

"Maybe you're right," Mavis replied. "But why all the secrecy? Why wouldn't Levi tell us what this meeting is about?"

Jack rubbed his forehead and shook his head. "Don't know; all he said was there had been developments and there was a meeting we needed to attend. When I asked what developments, all he would say was that the meeting was important for the future of Texas and the nation."

"But what does that mean?" Mavis asked.

"I don't know, but Little Sister, I intend to find out."

The copilot of the plane emerged from the captain's cabin and said, "OK, this is it. Our instructions are to drop you off here. You are to proceed to the white building at the end of the tarmac." The copilot pointed out one of the plane's windows and continued to speak. "Once inside, there will be someone there to show you to the meeting."

"Who are we meeting?" Mavis asked.

The copilot shook his head and said, "Ma'am, you know everything I know. The governor told us we would only be given the information essential for our mission…which was to transport you and the Senator here. He said it was for our own safety, as well as yours."

Jack picked up his tablet from his seat and said, "Son, thanks for the ride. Get the door open and we'll get this show on the road. Little Sister, let's get a move on."

Exiting the plane, Jack and Mavis were hit by a wall of heat and humidity; there was currently a heat wave in the Deep South, and it was unusually hot for this late in the year. Squinting in the bright sunlight of mid-afternoon, Jack raised a hand to his forehead to shade his eyes as he looked down the desolate runway. Shimmering heat waves distorted the view, making the runway look like something from a low budget horror movie. The airstrip was badly in need of maintenance; there were weeds growing through cracks in the asphalt, and debris was scattered everywhere. Not a soul was around…very unusual for an airport, even a small community airport. Approaching the white building, he spied a small, battered sign that read "Terminal Four."

As they entered the white building, Jack and Mavis found the building to be in shambles. Tables and chairs were turned over on their sides, trash scattered about on the floor, and vending machines with the glass broken out. It looked as if the place had been looted years ago and left to rot.

"What is this place?" Mavis asked.

"Don't know," Jack replied. "And what the hell happened here?"

"Abandoned eight years ago," a deep voice answered.

Jack and Mavis turned around to see a tall, dark skinned man walking toward them. He wore a dark blue suit that was stained with sweat from the oppressive heat. In his left hand he was carrying a pump action shotgun, and a shoulder holster was visible from under his suit jacket.

"Why?" Mavis asked.

The man looked at Mavis and said, "The airport was abandoned eight years ago when federal regulations made it too expensive for private aircraft to fly in and out of here. Since then, this place has been vandalized and burglarized countless times."

"Who are you?" Jack asked.

"And where are we?" Mavis added.

"Louis Parker," the man replied. "You are in Aliceville, Alabama. I am one of Levi Walker's…associates. He and the others are waiting downstairs for you; I am here to show you the way."

"What others?" Mavis asked.

"And why are we here?" Jack demanded.

"Representatives of thirteen states…governors, senators, congressmen, state assemblymen…all here to discuss the problems facing our nation."

"Let's go then," Jack said.

Louis Parker led Jack and Mavis through the remains of the airport terminal, occasionally telling them to watch their step, or to duck below a low hanging light. After descending several flights of litter-strewn stairs, they arrived at a narrow hallway. At the end of the hallway were two men wearing military fatigues. Louis pointed toward the two men and said, "Those guys are Alabama National Guard; just tell them your names, and they will let you into the meeting. I have to get back upstairs to keep an eye out; good luck."

"What does he mean by good luck," Mavis whispered.

Jack shook his head and said, "I don't know, but I have a feeling that we are about to find out. Come on, Little Sister. Let's see what this hubbub is all about."

Jack and Mavis walked down the litter-strewn hallway toward the National Guardsmen. As they drew near, one of the men picked up a small computer tablet from a nearby table and said, "Sir, Ma'am, can you show me some identification, please? I have to make sure you're on the list."

"Certainly," Mavis replied. Both she and Jack handed over their national ID cards.

After scanning the barcodes on the ID cards, the guardsman looked up, nodded and said, "Sir, Ma'am, thank you for your identification. Please enter through this door; Governor Levi Jackson is waiting to speak with you."

"Thank you, son," Jack replied as he and Mavis walked through the door.

Once through the door, Mavis and Jack found a large conference room populated by approximately fifty people. Many were former acquaintances from time spent in Washington DC…senators, congressmen and the like. Various conversations were taking place throughout the conference room, brining the sound level of the room to a low roar.

"Glad to see you made it," a voice said from behind the duo. They turned to see Levi Jackson, smiling as usual, drinking a cup of coffee. They couldn't help but notice the bags under his eyes; he looked exhausted.

"No problem, Levi," Jack replied.

"Except for the lack of information," Mavis added. "What's all this about? And why are we here?"

"This meeting is about the future of our nation, he replied. "The state of our nation is in shambles, and this president is leading us down the path to self destruction. I was in contact with the governors of a few other states, and we were talking about setting up a meeting such as this. However, after the recent events in D.C., we knew we couldn't wait any longer. That's when I decided to throw this meeting together…with the help of a few of the other governors, of course. Sorry about keeping you in the dark, but we felt it was best if as few people knew about the purpose of this meeting as possible…for safety."

"Whose safety?" Mavis asked.

"Everyone who's here," Levi responded.

Just then, a tall, gray haired man approached Jack, Levi, and Mavis. "Jack Spearman, good to see you well after all these years."

"Michael Duncan!" Jack exclaimed. "Haven't seen you in a coon's age. How have you been?"

"Not bad, other than the sorry state of our nation," he replied. "Haven't seen you since my oil drilling days."

"Governor of Louisiana now," Jack added. "How's that working out for you?"

"Wish I were back on the rigs now," he replied. "Been tryin' to fix the economic woes of Louisiana, but every idea I've had has gotten blocked by the Federal Government."

"Everything I want to do is illegal," Mavis mused. "Seems to be a common theme these days."

Michael nodded. "Yes, Ma'am. That's exactly why we are here…and what we intend to fix."

Turning to Levi, Michael continued, "My hat is off to you for settin' this thing up."

Levi shook his head and said, "This was not my idea alone; this was a group effort and a lot of trust and cooperation was needed to pull it off."

"I still don't know what this meeting is about," Mavis said. "Why are we here?"

"She doesn't know yet?" Michael asked Levi.

"No."

Michael cleared his throat. "It's pretty simple, ma'am. What just happened in DC forced our hand. We can no longer allow the Federal Government to take this nation down the toilet, and we are here to come up with a plan to take our nation back."

Mavis noticed that Levi was no longer paying attention to Michael, but was intently reading a message on his cell phone. "Everything all right, Levi?" she asked.

Levi hesitated and then said, "Yeah. I just got a message from Jason Stratton."

"Speaker of the House, Texas State Legislature?" Mavis asked

"Yeah," Levi replied. "There's just been a…development back home. Excuse me while I respond to him."

As Levi walked away, Mavis turned her attention back to Michael. "So, how are we going to take our nation back?"

"That's what we'll talk about at this gathering," Michael replied. "Lots of ideas are floating around. Some say the states just refuse to do the feds bidding…they are overstepping their Constitutional authority. Some say we go to the Supreme Court and fight it out there."

"That'd be a waste of time," Jack interjected. "The courts are all in the president's pocket ever since he loaded them with 9 new Justices…all handpicked by none other than the president himself and his closest advisors."

"And confirmed by paid off senators," Mavis added.

Michael nodded and said, "I agree, and I think most would agree as well, but maybe it's a starting point. Hell, at this point I am willing to entertain nearly *any* idea. Do you know that my state lost all representation in DC? We might as well be ruled by some European monarch."

Just then, the door to the conference room opened, and a short, stout man walked through the door.

"John!" Michael exclaimed. "Good to see you here. We've been waiting for you."

"You have any idea how long it takes to get from Juneau to Alabama?" the man replied as he wiped sweat from his brow.

Michael laughed. "I know, it's not a short trip. John, this is Congresswoman Mavis Young and *Former* Senator Jack Spearman, both from the great state of Texas. Mavis, Jack…this is John Amaruq, the governor of Alaska."

Mavis studied the Alaskan governor. His russet colored skin and facial features betrayed his Native American decent. "*Probably Inuit*," she thought. He had gray hair and looked to be in his early fifties. He wore a black suit, and around his neck there was a necklace of some type of animal tooth.

"Pleased to meet you," Mavis said to the governor. "Welcome to Alabama."

"Thank you," John replied. "Although there is nothing welcoming about this heat and humidity. Even in fall it's this hot? We've had snow in Juneau for some time already. I do not know how people can live like this."

Mavis laughed and said, "There's actually a heat wave going through the Deep South at the moment. It's normally about ten to fifteen degrees cooler this time of year."

"Ten…I wouldn't call that cooler," John replied. He then turned toward Jack Spearman and said, "Mr. Spearman, I have heard of you from my senators...or my former senators, I should say. They both spoke highly of you. The Texas oil man who invented his own drilling rig. Perhaps my state can soon use the technology you've developed."

"Glad to meet you Governor," Jack replied. "But Alaska is off limits to oil drilling."

"Things change," John replied.

About this time, Levi returned and said, "John, good to see you here. We were waiting to start until you got here…should we get this show under way?"

"By all means," John replied. "There is much to be done and time is short."

Levi, followed by John, walked to the front of the conference room, and stepped up onto the podium that had been erected. He raised his hands over his head and began to speak loudly. "Everyone, may I have your attention, please. If you can kindly take your seats, we would like to get started."

The congregation began to find their way to the folding chairs that filled most of the room. Mavis and Jack managed to get seats in the front row; to their left sat Michael Duncan. When everyone had taken their seats, Levi looked at John and nodded. John stepped to the front of the podium and began to speak.

"Many of you know me; some do not. My name is John Amaruq, and I am the governor of Alaska. As you may have guessed by my appearance, I am of Inuit decent."

"Alaska is a land of great national resources. There are massive oil and natural gas deposits; veins of silver, gold, nickel and copper run through our mountains. Our forests are vast with huge herds of game animals. Off our coasts, it is a fisherman's paradise."

"Beginning in the latter part of the twentieth century, Washington began telling Alaskans that they could not use their natural resources. We were told that certain animals could not be hunted; some were traditional Inuit game that have been hunted for centuries. The oil and gas were off limits; digging for minerals required permits from endless federal agencies, effectively making mining off limits, as well. The trees in our forest cannot be cut down for lumber, and fishing boats no longer work our coasts."

"Were this the will of the Alaskan people, it would be our cross to bear, as we would have brought it upon ourselves. Alas, that is not the case. Politicians and bureaucrats in Washington, D.C. have decided this. It is 3,700 miles from Juneau to Washington, D.C. I ask you, what do Washington bureaucrats know about Alaska? How many have even visited my state? So how is it that they can decide what's best for Alaskans?"

"It has been said that we must protect our environment; that mining our minerals, cutting our trees, and drilling for our oil will destroy our state. And who wants to breathe dirty air or drink polluted water? But I tell you, it should be Alaskans who decide what can and can't be done in my state, not the EPA in Washington. I believe the EPA will not be satisfied until we're living like Paleolithic people. Just because I am Inuit does not mean I wish to go back to the way my ancestors did in order to protect the environment."

"Some may argue that we Alaskans are as much to blame for the situation, as we had congressmen and senators in Washington. However, what can our few representatives do against so many when each has only one vote? And now, after the passage of the American Prosperity Act, we have no representation in either the house or senate."

"Nearly three hundred years ago, this nation was founded by men who would not be ruled by a foreign king. Now, we have our own foreign king, but we call him a president. We have our own foreign parliament, but we call it congress. Is this progress? Has our nation become what was once our greatest enemy? Have the oppressed become the oppressors?"

"My friends, I cannot tell you what your state must do as my duty is to my fellow Alaskans, but I can tell you what we Alaskans believe, and what we will do. I have just left a special session of our state's legislature where this very issue was discussed at great length. It has been decided that Alaska will no longer be ruled by foreign politicians; it will be ruled by Alaskans. In a unanimous vote, the state legislature has declared Alaska's independence; effective at noon tomorrow, we will secede from the United States."

There was absolute silence in the room. Looking around the room, Mavis could see looks of shock on some faces; disgust and contempt on others. Still others had blank expressions, as if they were still trying to comprehend what had just been said. Finally, Wilson Dodge, the Governor of Georgia looked toward Levi Walker and said, "So this is your big plan, Levi? We abandon our country, our heritage?"

"This meeting was set up to consider all options," Levi responded. "And yes, secession is on the table."

"That's been tried before," a voice from the back of the room said. "And we all know how well it worked in 1860."

John shook his head and said, "Things are very different today. The people in this room right now represent the most productive states in the nation. Once free of the burden of federal taxes and regulations, the economies of those states will grow and expand at a rate the world has not seen in over one hundred and fifty years. We will have the economic might to dictate terms."

"And you don't think Conrad White will march the army down on us?" another voice cried.

"I have considered that," John replied. But consider this. Most of the US military is scattered around the world, engaged in so-called peace-keeping missions. Those who are here in the United States are ill equipped, as most of the well maintained equipment is in use by deployed combat units. National Guard units actually outnumber regular military by two to one in most states."

"I am more concerned with the National Police," Levi said. "While they don't have the firepower of the military, they outnumber the military two to one."

"Three to one is a bit closer," Jack added. "Remember, CIA, FBI, IRS enforcement…all federal law enforcement was merged into the national police force."

"I agree that the police are more of a concern," John said.

"There is another thing in our favor," Levi added. "There are many Generals and Admirals who are in agreement with us. Should secession be the road we go down, I have assurance of the loyalty of a large percentage of the military that is stationed here in the US."

Jack Spearman looked at Levi Walker and said, "It sounds like you've been planning this for a while, Levi. Does that mean Texas will secede as well?"

Levi looked at Jack and said, "I received a message from the Texas Speaker of the House just before this meeting started. The Texas State Legislature will vote on that very issue tomorrow morning. They have been debating the issue for some time, and the Speaker wanted to send the delegates home to sleep on it before the vote."

"Thanks for keeping me in the loop," Jack replied.

"Sorry," Levi said. "Considering how sensitive this issue is, I've been concerned about everyone's safety."

Wilson Dodge looked at Jack and said, "What say you, oil man? Most here know you, and all know your reputation as a no nonsense guy. What do you think of this talk of secession?"

Jack took off his Stetson and ran his hand through his thick, graying hair. Holding his hat over his chest, he said, "I'm not sure. Will it work…could it work? I don't know. Here is what I do know. They days of debate and trying to do what is right through Congress and the courts are over. We play by the rules set forth in the US Constitution; the president and his allies do not. There is no way to win a war like that."

"That is exactly what secession will bring on us," a voice called out. "War."

Jack put his Stetson back on and adjusted it slightly. "We're already at war," he said finally. "Granted, it's not a shooting war yet, but it's war all the same. It is a war of ideas; free enterprise verses big government. Government taxes, spending, regulation… those are the things that are destroying our economy and our nation. As long as the current situation exists, there is no way our nation will be prosperous."

Mavis stood up and said, "I think you are all missing the bigger point."

All eyes in the room locked onto her.

"How is that?" Levi asked.

Mavis' eyes grew wide and she began to speak. "We hold these truths to be self-evident, that all men are created equal, that they are endowed by their Creator with certain unalienable Rights; that among these are Life, Liberty, and the pursuit of Happiness."

"The Declaration of Independence," said Michael Duncan.

"Yes," Mavis replied. "Everyone at this meeting has been talking from an economic standpoint, but there is more to this than economics. This is not just about money. This is about your God-given right to lead the life you want…to pursue the dreams that you want…all without the approval or disapproval of the government. I have heard people say that everything I want to do is illegal…is that any way to live? No gentlemen, this is not just about money; this is an issue of basic freedoms…freedoms which have been eroded to the point that I can no longer recognize our nation."

"The founding fathers formed this nation not just for economic prosperity, but as a place where liberty would reign supreme. That is why the United States Constitution places so many limitations on the powers of the Federal Government…to preserve liberty. What would the founders think of our nation today? The socialist movement which began in the early part of the twentieth century has festered for the past one hundred and fifty years, creating a top to bottom, cradle to grave welfare society, where government controls everything. Is this liberty?"

"The Declaration of Independence went further than saying we have the right to life, liberty, and the pursuit of happiness. It says that the government derives just powers from the consent of those governed, and whenever a government no longer has the consent of the governed, the people have the right to rise up and alter or institute a new government. Isn't that really what we're talking about here?"

Levi smiled; he looked around the room and saw nods of approval from all corners of the room. His smile broadened to the corners of his mustache; Mavis had a gift for inspiring speeches, and this one was no different.

"Does this mean you like the idea of secession from the United States?" Wilson Dodge asked Mavis.

"Absolutely not!" Mavis replied. "The idea of Texas, or any other state, leaving the United States saddens and sickens me. But I see no practical alternative. This is our last, best hope to fight for what we hold dear."

"I am in agreement with Miss Young," John Amaruq added. "I love my country, just as I am sure everyone here does."

"But," Mavis interjected, "you must ask yourself this. Why do you love your country? Is it because that is where you were born? Or is it something more? Is it because of the ideas of the ideas your country is founded on…the heritage of fighting for freedom and liberty? Because, in reality, if you love the United States because it stands for freedom and liberty…that nation no longer exists."

Just then, a senator from Georgia stood and said, "I think we have reached a point where the only way we can save our country is by leaving it."

"Agreed," Levi said. "I know there was a lot of ground covered here, and I'm sure everyone will need to take this back to their respective states. I say we call this meeting closed, and everyone returns home to meet with your state legislatures."

"I agree," Michael Duncan replied. "I can't say what the people of my state will say, but I agree with Miss Young…I see no better way."

Levi watched as people began leaving the room with the hope he could get everyone out of the meeting and transported home without detection by the Federal Government. He was on an emotional rollercoaster right now; part of him was excited by the possibility of freedom in Texas while part of him was dealing with thc invasive feeling of impending doom. He became lost in thought as his mind worked through the implications of what was done here today…and what would be done in the upcoming days. Once secession takes place, he thought, there *will* be civil war…he could see now way around it. Would the movement receive the support of the people? How would they finance such a war? Would he, along with all of the other members of the meeting, be sentenced to death as traitors?

The vibration of Levi's cell phone brought him back to reality. Pulling it out of his pocket, he looked at the screen; it was his assistant, Sarah. He pressed the talk button and said, "Sarah, we just finished up. Are you holding things together at the office?"

"Don't I always?" was Sarah's reply. "Sir, I have a message from the Son's of Liberty that you might be interested in."

"I told you to never mention that group on the cell phone!" Levi exclaimed. "You know we may be monitored."

"I'm sorry, but I thought this was important enough to take

the risk. It looks like the…the organization is helping move someone from up North."

"Send me all the details by secured data transmission," Levi said. "I want to know everything."

CHAPTER NINE

"How do you plan to pull this off, Colonel?"

Kirk Dillon and Matt Pickett had been driving for some time and they were now heading North on Interstate 275. Traffic was light, as was typical at this time of the day.

Kirk began to speak without taking his eyes off the road. "My hope is to get to the 275/I-71 interchange before they do. It looks like we'll beat them there because of their stop in Cincinnati. Plus, by the looks of the GPS, they are moving awful slow…must be an electric vehicle. When we catch up to them, I want you to put a bullet through the battery core; that'll kill their power and stop them dead. Once they're stopped, I'll get Sebastian."

"What'll I be doin' then?" Matt asked.

Kirk glanced at Matt and said, "Keep me covered. I'd rather not see anyone hurt, but if the police can't be persuaded…do what you do best."

Matt nodded, and then said, "Piece of cake."

As the Bronco merged onto the exit ramp to put them on Interstate 71, Matt picked up the GPS unit and looked at the screen. "Looks like they're still up ahead," he said.

"We'll catch them," Kirk replied as he stepped on the gas pedal.

The turbo-diesel roared as they accelerated. First seventy-five, then eighty-five…ninety-five. The needle of the speedometer began to quiver as they passed one hundred miles per hour. The other cars on the highway were a blur as the Kirk raced past them at nearly twice their speed.

"I guess you're not worried about a ticket," Matt said with a grin.

"Nope," was Kirk's reply.

"Must be from all that NASCAR you used to watch back in the day," Matt said. He leaned to his left to take a glimpse at the speedometer. Looking at Kirk, he said, "Good thing you put in that aftermarket speedo…otherwise, you'd never know you're runnin' one-ten."

"Yeah," Kirk said. "The great American joke of the 1980's…the eighty-five mile per hour speedometer and the 55 speed limit. I can't believe they brought back that stupid federal speed limit!"

Matt began to laugh, but then he pointed through the windshield and shouted, "There at your twelve! Black police van!"

"I see it!" Kirk exclaimed."Damn it, it's not an electric vehicle…that's got a regular combustion engine. Must have switched vehicles because of the long haul north."

Matt put the GPS unit on the dash and grabbed his M16 from the back seat. He slapped a magazine into the rifle and pulled back the charging handle, then let the handle fly. As a round loaded and the bolt of the rifle flew forward, it made a "click-clack" sound. Matt looked at Kirk and said, "Change of plans, Colonel. Bring me alongside the van and I'll put a round through the engine block."

"Alright." Kirk replied.

The Bronco was approaching the black van quickly, and Kirk expertly guided the SUV into the left hand lane. It was impossible to see inside the van, as the windows had a dark, reflective tint. Kirk slowed as he pulled up alongside the other vehicle. Matt raised the rifle to his shoulder, and took careful aim through the passenger's side window. There was a loud "crack" as the report of the rifle pierced Kirk's ears. He hit the brakes to back off a bit; he didn't want to be driving beside the van if it started to swerve.

Black smoke began to billow from under the hood of the van, and Kirk could see the brake lights come on. As the van quickly slowed, Kirk slowed as well, keeping pace but not getting too close. In seconds, both vehicles had come to a complete stop, with the Bronco being just behind and to the left of the van.

Looking at Matt, Kirk said, "We better do this fast. I'm sure this is already called in and we are going to have a lot of cops here very soon."

Matt was already opening the door of the Bronco, rifle in hand."Then we'd better get it done!" he replied.

Kirk's pistol was in hand by the time his feet hit the pavement. He pulled the pistol's slide back to chamber a round, and holding it in a combat grip with both hands, approached the driver's side door. "Open the door and come out with your hands on your head." He shouted. Nothing happened. He began to shout again. "I don't want to shoot through the door, but I will if I have to."

Kirk heard Matt's M-16 fire; looking over the hood of the van, he could see Matt shooting at the front tire. Matt began to shout."My friend may hesitate to shoot, but I guarantee I will shoot through the window if you don't get this van open now!"

Both the passenger and driver's side doors unlatched and began to open slowly. Both Matt and Kirk had their weapons ready and pointed in the direction of the opening doors. A voice was heard from within, saying, "Don't shoot, we are coming out!"

Two men, dressed in the typical black uniform of the national police, stepped out of the van. After exiting the van, the driver looked at Kirk and said, "You two are going to be in big trouble for this. And for what? We are carrying nothing of value."

Kirk had his pistol pointed at the man's head."All we want is your prisoner," he replied.

"Prisoner?" the man said somewhat perplexed."We aren't carrying any prisoners. All we have is a troubled teen who is being transported to Reynoldsburg for rehabilitation."

"You mean brainwashin'," Matt shouted.

Kirk looked the man in the eyes and said, "Everyone has heard stories about what they do to kids at Reynoldsburg, as well as the other camps. The kids come out a shell of their former selves…state controlled robots."

"We teach the children the errors of their former ways," the man replied.

"And not the meaning of the Hitler youth?" Kirk replied.

"I can't believe you are comparing the US government to the Nazi party!" the man exclaimed" Do you realize…."

Matt cut the man off. "Too much talkin'," he said. Looking at the other officer, he said, "Get the back door open, or I'll blow your damn head off."

"I don't have a key," the man replied.

Matt sighed, and then quickly pointed his rifle at the man's foot, and pulled the trigger. The man fell to the ground, grabbing his foot and screaming in pain."You shot me, you old son of a bitch!" he shouted. Kirk motioned for his prisoner to move to the passenger side of the van.

Matt pointed his rifle at the man's crotch."I'm only gettin' started, kid," Matt replied."Tell me no again, and you'll never father a child."

The man quickly reached in his pocket and pulled out a key fob. He pressed a button and the large sliding door on the side of the van began to open. Kirk and Matt could see Sebastian sitting in the back seat of the van as the door opened. "Good to see you boy," Matt said.

"You all right, son?" Kirk asked.

Eyes wide as saucers, Sebastian's eyebrows raised as he said, "You two are crazy! What do you think you're doing?" he asked.

"We're rescuing you and then heading south," Kirk replied.

"Helluva way to say thanks, kid," Matt added gruffly.

"All three of us are going to end up in prison!" Sebastian exclaimed.

"The boy is right," one of the officers said. "Why not just give yourselves up now, and maybe the judge will go easy on you."

"Shut up," Kirk said.

"I'm feelin' better than I have in years," Matt said. "Feels good to do what's right."

"Yes it does," Kirk said. "Sebastian, get in the truck; we need to get moving." Turning toward Matt, he said, "What should we do with these two?"

"Leave 'em with the van," Matt replied. "Back-up will be here soon anyway."

"You'll never get away with this," one of the officers said.

"We shall see," Kirk said. "Let's go."

Sebastian was already in the Bronco, and Kirk was close behind. Matt raised his rifle to his shoulder, aimed at the engine compartment of the van, and fired five shots. He looked at the two officers as he walked away and said, "Just in case. Better get a bandage on that foot." As Matt climbed into the front passenger seat, he said to Kirk, "What's the plan, Colonel?"

Kirk started the engine, and as he began to accelerate, he said, "We get off the highway at Mason-Montgomery, and get out of Mason as fast as possible."

"I think that's Kenwood, Dad," Sebastian added.

"Well," Kirk continued, "no matter if this is considered Mason or Kenwood, we need to get out of the heavily populated areas ASAP. We're meeting someone in Aberdeen who will help us escape to freedom. We also need to fry that RFID chip in your arm." Kirk looked at Matt and said, "Can you get that done while I drive?"

"Yes, sir," Matt replied. Reaching into his shirt pocket, Matt pulled out the modified camera and said to Kirk, "You know where the bug is?"

"Right arm, just below the elbow," Kirk replied.

"You sure?" Matt asked.

"I remember the doctors injecting it like it was yesterday," Kirk responded.

"What are you two talking about?" Sebastian asked.

"There is an RFID chip in your arm that relays your position to GPS satellites," Kirk said. "They started tagging babies at birth a few years before you were born."

Matt held up the modified camera and said, "I'm gonna fry that thing with this."

"Looks like a camera," Sebastian said.

"Used to be," Matt replied. "Now hold out your arm."

"Is this gonna hurt?" Sebastian asked.

Matt shook his head and said, "Nope." Holding the camera about an inch away from Sebastian's arm, Matt pressed the exposure button. There was a loud click, followed by a momentary buzzing sound.

"That's it?" Sebastian asked. I didn't feel anything. How do we know it worked?"

"Check the GPS," Kirk said.

Matt picked up the antique GPS receiver, looked at the screen, and smiled. "Got an error message; can't find waypoint. Looks like we done it."

Kirk grinned and said, "Excellent." Reaching into his waistband, Kirk pulled out his pistol and set it on the center console."We're about to get off the highway, so be ready. There's a good chance they'll try to stop us here…assuming we were reported."

Matt replaced the magazine in his rifle with a fresh one. "Ready, Colonel," he said.

As Kirk pulled off the highway onto the exit ramp, he could see the black vans of the national police blocking the end of the ramp. The red and yellow emergency lights on top of the vans were flashing, and several officers were standing near the vans. "We've got company!" Kirk shouted.

Matt nodded and said, "I see 'em. All national police…I don't see any state boys. I guess they weren't invited to the party."

"The national police probably didn't see us as that big of a threat, or they might have asked for local assistance," Kirk replied. "I'm going to go around them and drive through that grassy area to the left. Hopefully, we can pull this off without getting shot. Sebastian, lay down on the floor so you don't get hit."

Looking back at Sebastian, Matt said, "If they take out the truck, run like hell for the woods. I'll keep 'em busy as long as I'm still breathin'."

Kirk shifted out of overdrive into a lower gear and pressed the accelerator to the floor. The low rumble of the diesel was instantly replaced by the loud roar of the engine and the high pitched scream of the turbochargers. Kirk veered off the exit ramp into the scrubby grass near the exit ramp.

The ride was rough; the Bronco bounced up and down on its soft suspension, making it difficult for Kirk to steer. Looking to his left, Kirk could see the police officers yelling and motioning for him to stop, but Kirk kept on driving. He held his breath as they bounded out of the grass and onto the pavement of the local road, narrowly avoiding the traffic.

"Too many people around!" Matt shouted. "Gotta get us out of here before someone gets hurt!"

"Hold on!" Kirk said.

Kirk began to weave through the traffic; several times he narrowly avoided hitting other cars as he plotted his escape route through them.

"Sebastian! Are there any police vans following us?" he shouted.

"None!" Sebastian exclaimed. "I guess we're in the clear."

"Boy, this show is just gettin' started," Matt said.

As they drove, the homes along the road became less numerous and the suburban sprawl gave way to semi-rural suburbs. Kirk was sure he had lost the police when Matt said, "Look up ahead; another roadblock. And it looks like they've got weapons drawn. I guess they're serious about stoppin' us this time."

"They can't be too serious," Sebastian said. "There's an open field along one side of the roadblock. After what you just did back there, I can't believe they are going to let you do it again."

"Well, let's push our luck and try the same thing," Kirk replied. "When we get close I going to pull into that field and go around them. Sebastian, you stay down."

"Ok," Sebastian replied.

As they approached the roadblock, Kirk could see the police officers with weapons aimed at the Bronco. *"This may not go well,"* he thought. Kirk heard the first shot fired from a police officer's weapon; he automatically jerked the steering wheel to the left, and the large SUV bounded into the open field along the side of the road.

Matt leaned out the passenger's window with his rifle to his shoulder and pulled the trigger. A stream of bullets sprayed from the weapon, impacting one of the police vehicles at the front of the roadblock. Several of the police officers dove for the ground, dropping their weapons as they made the jump. Matt quickly pulled the rifle back into the truck and immediately replaced the empty magazine with a fresh one. Kirk turned hard to the right and pressed the accelerator to the floor, causing them to swerve back onto the pavement and continued away from the roadblock.

"Do you think this is the last we'll see of them?" Sebastian asked as the roadblock shrank in the distance.

"I don't know," Kirk replied. "I hope it is, but we need to keep our eyes open all the way to Aberdeen."

"How do you think it went, James?"

President Conrad White leaned back in his chair in the Oval Office, using his hands to form a triangle. His eyes were wide as he waited intently to hear what his advisers thought of the speech.

"Mr. President," James Duncan began, "the speech was magnificent, as always. It was energetic, decisive, and direct to the point."

The slightest hint of a smile tugged at the left corner of the president's lips. "I can always count on you to blow smoke up my ass, James. You are the number one ass-kisser in this administration. However, I am more interested in an objective opinion."

The president cocked his head to the left, raised his eyebrows slightly, and said, "OK, Ralph…let's have it. What did you think of the speech?"

As usual, Ralph Marco was standing with his hands in his pockets, rocking back and forth, heel to toe, and with a blank expression on his face. "Well," he began, "You were pretty good. Could have been a bit more fired up, but we weren't broadcasting…no big deal. Now, Samantha Ravana…she's a different story. She sucks. I hate writing speeches for her. I don't know if she doesn't practice before she gives the speech or what, but she sounds like a seven year old learning to read; she has the personality of a dead fish. Don't see how she keeps getting reelected year after year."

The president's eyes grew wide, and a smile appeared from under his gray flecked mustache. He began to laugh softly, and said, "I can always count on you to be a straight shooter, Ralph. Fine then; I'll try to be more energetic when I give speeches to Congress in the future. You're quite right about Ravana; she is terrible when it comes to giving speeches. By the way, she gets elected by buying votes…she and her husband are major stockholders in a tuna corporation, and they spread plenty of favors with tuna money to get her elected."

"I guess that explains the sweet deals for the tuna industry," Ralph said with a smile.

The president nodded and said, "Of course; do you think she would have lobbied for those deals if she wasn't a major stockholder in tuna?" President White picked up a hand-written note from his desktop and handed it to James as he said, "Here is a list of people I need dirt on. I need this as soon as possible."

James took the note and began to mumble, "John Wilder, Thomas Froycamp, Matt Manning, Jessica Benson…sir, these are some of your biggest supporters in Congress!"

The president raised one eyebrow and said, "They also have ambition. I don't know if they support me for my good or their own. I want to be sure that I have exactly what I need to keep them in line. Manning should be easy; it's well known that he likes the ladies…at least ladies other than his wife."

"Yes, Mr. President," James replied.

The president swiveled his office chair slightly to the right to face his assistant. "Theresa, what is the status of the gun collections?"

The young assistant cleared her throat and looked at her computer tablet. "In the Northeast, the national police have begun their door to door searches. They have turned up some illegal weapons, but counts have been very minimal. Of course, the Northeast and the west coast are where voluntary turn-ins were at their highest."

"That's because the people in those areas are spineless lemmings," Ralph said. "They would jump off a cliff if the president told them to do it."

The president's eyes narrowed and deep frown lines appeared between his eyebrows. "Ralph, sometimes you can be a royal pain in the ass. For once, I wish you would keep your mouth shut when nobody is talking to you."

Turning his attention back to his assistant, the president continued. "Have the police reported any problems or resistance?"

"That also has been very minimal, Mr. President," the assistant replied.

"Good; I think we can move up our timetable," the president replied.

"James, I want you to give the order to the national police to begin gun collections all along the west coast and the upper

Midwest. As we clear those areas, we will gradually push to the southeastern states."

"Yes, Mr. President," James replied.

The president's assistant looked up from her computer tablet and said, "On that note, Mr. President, there is some good news out of Texas. I have a message from the FCC Secretary. The Governor of Texas is giving a televised speech tomorrow, and the subject is to urge Texans to comply with the law and turn in their guns."

"Well, that's good news," James said.

Ralph shook his head and said, "I don't buy it."

"Nor do I," the president said. "That goes against everything that man believes in."

"Perhaps he has realized the futility in trying to defy the most powerful man in the nation?" James replied.

"Possible but highly unlikely. That man was born to fight."

The president's eyes glazed over and he began to rub his upper lip with his forefinger, apparently deep in thought. After a few moments, he looked at his assistant and said, "Tell the FCC secretary to give the OK on the broadcast. Make sure she has a full transcript of the speech. If there is the slightest hint that he is about to do something out of line, shut down the broadcast ASAP. Understand?"

"Yes, Mr. President," the assistant replied.

President Conrad White leaned back in his chair and said, "Anything else of importance?"

His assistant began scrolling through her computer tablet again, and then after a moment looked up and said, "The Department of Homeland Security is reporting an increase in the cyber attacks attributed to the Sons of Liberty."

Shaking his head, the president said, "That group has been a pain in my ass since I was elected. Have DHS increase the number of people working on that case."

"Yes, Mr. President," the assistant obediently replied.

"What is it with that group, anyway?" James asked.

"They want the nation to return to the way it was two hundred and fifty years ago," Ralph replied.

The president frowned and stared directly at Ralph. "And you approve of that?" he said in a loud voice.

"I'm just stating the facts," Ralph replied. "For better or for worse, that's what they believe."

"They are a radical fringe group who wish to destroy everything I have worked so hard to create!" The president exclaimed. "Luckily, their numbers are extremely small, so they are of little consequence."

Ralph shook his head and said, "You may be a genius, but I seriously think you have underestimated them, and I think all of your changes to this nation are going to drive more people to groups like the Sons of Liberty."

"That is why we are collecting firearms," the president replied. "To keep them out of the hands of radicals like the Sons of Liberty. But other than cyber attacks, what have they accomplished other than make a lot of noise? They are too small, too insignificant to do much. They are like an annoying mosquito…just enough of an irritation to let you know they are there."

Ralph shrugged his shoulders. As usual, his blank expression and half shut eyelids gave the impression of someone who didn't care. "Whatever. I just hope your mosquito doesn't become a flying elephant."

CHAPTER TEN

It was well after sundown when Kirk's Bronco arrived in the village of Aberdeen. As they passed an old, weather-beaten sign that read "Welcome to Aberdeen," they entered a town that looked forgotten. Most of the homes were in disrepair; many looked as if a strong wind would bring them toppling down. There were many houses and businesses with the doors and windows boarded up.

"Would you look at this place!" Sebastian exclaimed. "It's a dump. How can they live like this?"

"When a town's this small, it ain't exactly a national concern," Matt replied.

"I think I see the Trail Hollow Inn up ahead," Kirk said. "Let's pull into that side street, and then we'll go in."

Kirk turned down an alley near the inn, and the three finished the trip to the inn on foot. Trail Hollow Inn was a large, two story colonial which must have originally been painted white, but years of neglect had left the paint weathered, chipped, and peeling. Leading up to the Inn was what looked to have once been a concrete sidewalk, but had been recently replaced with a path of compacted gravel. The sign at the front door was the only thing that looked new. It was a large wooden sign, with a white background and bold black lettering declaring this to be "Dorothy's Trail Hollow Inn." Looking at Matt and Sebastian, Kirk said, "I guess this is the place," and opened the front door.

They filed through the door and entered a room that could have been out of the nineteenth century. The lobby was fairly small, with arched doorways leading to the left and right. At the back of the entry area, was a set of stairs of well-worn oak which must have led to the second floor. Centered in the room was a large wooden reception desk with a woman seated behind it. The woman looked to be in her late sixties, possibly even early seventies, and was extremely overweight. Her long, pewter gray hair draped limp over her shoulders, and her wrinkled, parchment colored skin seemed to hang off her arms and face. As the trio walked toward the desk, she looked up from what she was reading, peering at them over the top of her reading glasses.

"Good evening gentlemen," she said. "I don't think I've ever met you before. Welcome to the Trail Hollow Inn."

"Hello," Kirk replied.

"Are you here for dinner?" She asked. "Or are you traveling and need a room for the night? We've got a few rooms available, and they're all priced just right."

"Dinner sounds pretty good right about now," Matt said.

"A friend told me to stop by tonight," Kirk added. "He told

me to ask for Dottie Moore."

The woman took off her reading glasses and said, "I see. I'm Dottie Moore. Only my best friends call me Dottie. Was it Dan Bottoms that told you to stop by?"

"Yes, it was," Kirk replied.

Dottie smiled and said, "Then you must be Mr. Dillon. I thought I recognized you from the picture in one of your books…my husband is a big fan of your work. Don't worry…we can safely talk in the Inn. No national police around. Where did you park?"

"The small side street, about a block away," Kirk replied.

Dottie nodded and said, "I'll have it refueled for you. Does it run on natural gas?"

"No," Kirk replied. "Diesel."

"No problem," Dottie replied. "But you stirred up a damn hornets' nest. There's a nationwide APB on the three of you. Kind of surprising."

"What's surprising?" Sebastian asked.

Dottie looked at Sebastian and said, "The national police want to bring you three in at all costs. Usually they don't go after people like that…unless it's a political matter. You must have really pissed off someone high up in government to get this kind of attention."

Kirk shrugged his shoulders and said, "I can't be certain, but I think all of this is because I got a union official ticked off at me. I refused to join the International Brotherhood of Writers."

“Hmmm,” Dottie said. “Let me guess. You refused to join, they got pissed, and in retribution had the feds pick up your boy and send him for indoctrination. You…and your friend…then bust him out and end up here.”

“That’s a pretty accurate summary of events thus far,” Kirk said.

Dottie shook her head and said, “Unions got a lot of pull these days. Most people work for unions…hell, this is the only non-union business in town…and their dues money goes to the union bosses who use it to bribe politicians. Back in the old days, it was only the Democrat politicians who were getting bribed, but ever since the political parties were merged by President White, the unions have been greasing the hands of all politicians. Anyway, go on in the dining room and get some dinner; all three of you look famished.” Dottie took a few lumbering steps toward the doorway on the right and then shouted, “Justin!”

A young man in his early twenties appeared through the doorway. He was of medium height and very wiry, with crew cut hair the color of tar and taupe colored skin. He wore well worn blue jeans and an extremely wrinkled khaki shirt.

“This is my grandson, Justin,” Dottie said. “Justin, these are the men I was telling you about. Take them to the dining room; get them a table and dinner.”

“Yes, ma’am,” he replied.

“My husband Howard is going to help you get across the river; I’ll have him come out and talk to you in a bit. He is down at the ferry right now…said he had to fix something. Now, we do family style dinner here…roast chicken and green beans tonight, apple pie for desert.”

"That sounds great," Kirk said.

"Especially the apple pie part," Sebastian added.

"Follow me, and I'll get you a table," Justin said.

Sebastian, Matt, and Kirk followed Justin through the doorway to the right, entering a large, open dining area. Like the entry, the walls of the room were painted in a blue color, but this room had the addition of an oak wainscoting that extended to about three feet in height. Widely spaced throughout the room (in what seemed to be no particular pattern) were large, round wooden tables. Five of the tables were occupied, but the occupants seemed to pay no attention to Justin or his followers.

"Grandpa said you might like a table in the corner," Justin said as he led the group to a table in the far eastern corner of the room.

"This is just fine," Kirk said to Justin.

As the three men sat down, Justin continued, "My grandfather should be here soon; said he had a few things to check on before he met with you. What can I get you to drink? Besides the usual stuff, we do have some locally brewed beers."

"Really?" Matt said. "I thought all of the small breweries got put out of business years ago."

"Oh, no sir," Justin said. "Not all of them. The brewery here in Aberdeen is not allowed to sell beer outside the town, and they can only sell in establishments that also carry beer by the major breweries. But we are quite proud of our town's brewery, and most beer drinkers around here buy from them."

"I'll have one," Matt said. "The darkest brew you have."

"I'll have the same," Sebastian said with a smile.

"He'll have a coke since he's under age," Kirk said. "Bring me an iced tea with lemon."

"Right away," Justin said as he walked away.

Drinks came out soon, quickly followed by dinner. Matt commented that the beer was the best he had tasted in years, and all three complimented the quality and flavor of the dinner. They were just finishing the apple pie desert when a short, overweight, balding man in his late sixties approached the table.

"Kirk Dillon," he began, "Wow, I have been reading your books for years, but I never thought I would meet you in person. I loved your last novel; I hear rumors that you have another one in the works?"

Kirk pushed away his plate of pie crumbs and leaned back in his chair. "I assume you are Howard?"

The man began to shake his head and said, "Oh, how rude and silly of me. Yes, I'm Howard Moore; Dottie is my wife."

"Pleased to meet you, Mr. Moore," Kirk said. "This is Matt Pickett on my left, and that's my son, Sebastian."

"Nice to meet you, nice to meet you," Howard said rapidly. "So what about you next book? I can't wait to download it."

"It should be out by Christmas," Kirk replied. "We were told that you can take us across the river to Maysville on your ferry?"

Howard took a deep breath and then said slowly, "Well, that's only half correct. You see, we have hit a little snag. Couldn't be avoided, but we hit a snag."

"What kinda snag?" Matt asked.

"Well," Howard began, "the engine is out on the ferry. Jack, that's my son, has been working with me most of the day to get it fixed. But we can't get the parts needed to fix that old diesel. Nobody makes the parts anymore…at least not in this country."

"So we're gonna have to cross the bridge?" Matt asked.

"Yes," Howard replied.

Sebastian shrugged his shoulders. "So let's go into Kentucky on the bridge. What's the big deal?"

"It's likely the national police will be watching the bridge," Kirk said.

Howard shook his head. "It's not likely; they *are* watching the bridge. There's a police checkpoint on the bridge and they're checking everyone crossing into Kentucky. The word is that all of the bridges up and down the Ohio River are monitored. They really want you bad."

Matt took a loud gulp of beer, and Kirk sat silently, picking at his pie crumbs with his fork. After a moment, Kirk looked up and said, "It doesn't matter. We will just have to cross the bridge, police or no police."

Howard smiled and said, "Crossing the bridge isn't the hard part. There is a police station in Maysville, and one word from the bridge checkpoint, and you'll have over a hundred cops on you in a matter of minutes."

"So we have to take out the checkpoint...quietly," Matt said.

"Then sneak through Maysville quietly without alerting police," Kirk added.

"Exactly," Howard said. "Luckily, I have a few friends who are going to help get you across the river."

"Sons of Liberty?" Matt asked.

Howard quickly raised two fingers to his lips and said, "SHHHHHH! Never mention them in public! It's not safe!" Howard looked slowly to the left and right, and when he was satisfied that nobody was paying attention to their conversation, he continued in a much quieter voice. "Forgive me. It is not safe to mention the...the group in public. Federal agencies have been after us for years. We stand against everything wrong with the country, and are willing to stand up for what we believe. They can't stand that, and want to squash anyone who disagrees with the Federal Government."

"So is there a plan?" Kirk asked quietly.

Howard nodded his head several times and then said, "At four in the morning, the group will provide a distraction in Maysville that should keep people occupied. There are several abandoned buildings in the heart of downtown; they will be set ablaze. The buildings are really deteriorated, and we will make sure that they go up like match sticks. Even though police aren't firemen, a blaze of this size will create enough confusion that you should be able to slip past the town unnoticed."

"That still leaves the cops on the bridge," Matt said.

"That's where you'll come in," Howard said. "The group doesn't have enough manpower to handle the fire and take down the police at the checkpoint, too. You'll have to handle the police, but I would think combat vets such as yourselves should have no problem with a few law officers."

"The issue is doing it silently so as to not raise the alarm," Kirk said.

"Yep," Matt said. "And with them sittin' in the middle of the bridge, they're gonna see us comin' from a long way off."

"That is why the fire will take place at four," Howard replied. "There should be a thick fog that drifts over the river, and visibility will be next to zero."

"That'll make it a might easier," Matt said.

"Assuming we get the fog like he is predicting," Kirk replied. "But since Aberdeen is right along the river, I would assume you get heavy fog on a regular basis…at least this time of year."

"Yes, we do," Howard replied.

"Sounds like a plan then," Matt added.

Howard reached into his pocket and pulled out a folded piece of paper. He handed it to Kirk, saying, "Take this. After you get past Maysville, head to Livingston, Tennessee. The contact from the organization will meet you at Kelley's Korner; it is a sports-bar type restaurant. Directions are on that paper."

Kirk took the note and placed it in his back pocket. "Thank

you," he said.

Howard nodded, and then said, "Dottie has a room for you so you can get a few hours rest. Just stop by the front desk and she'll give you the key. Room 204; go up the stairs, second door on the right. I'll come get you around three and show you the way to the bridge. Sorry I can't be much more help, but I wouldn't know the first thing about how to incapacitate someone."

"With the cover of night and the fog, we should be able to pull it off," Kirk replied. "I do appreciate the help from you and the other…group members."

"It is our hope that one day our nation can return to its former glory," Howard replied.

"You mean as the world superpower?" Sebastian asked.

"That is the least of our concerns," Howard replied. "At one time, this nation was the freest, most liberty conscious nation in the world. Today, it's like we're in cold war era Russia. The difference is we didn't get here by a violent revolution. This was a change that took over one hundred years to come about."

"Soft socialism," Kirk added.

"Now what the hell does that mean, Colonel?" Matt asked.

Kirk's eyes opened wide as he began to speak. "A long time ago, one of the Soviet leaders…and I can't remember which…said that Americans would never jump from capitalism to communism. However, if American leaders dished out small doses of socialism, then the American people would one day awaken to find they have communism. We didn't get here overnight, and if all of the socialist changes had taken place at once, the people would have had none of it. But a gradual change…most people didn't realize it was happening."

"You tryin' to say we live in a communist country?" Matt shot back quickly.

"Pretty close to it," Kirk replied.

"Exactly," Howard added. "And we aim to bring the nation back from the brink. I hear there may be some big changes coming soon…changes that may help you get to safety, and bring about a revolution in this country."

"What kind of revolution?" Kirk asked.

Howard smiled, took a deep breath, and said, "Freedom."

Mavis Young stared at the darkness through the window of the plane, her mind lost in a whirl of thought. Before today, she had never given the idea of secession from the United States any thought; it was something that Southerners had done in the 19th century when they thought Lincoln would abolish slavery. However, after hearing the Alaskan governor's speech, nothing made more sense to her. The idea that a person could live her life how she wanted had been lost, and in the current climate, could only be restored by a fresh start.

Levi sat down in the seat across from Mavis. He looked at her, and began to stroke his mustache. "What do you think?" he asked.

Mavis looked away from the window to glance at Levi. The stress and lack of sleep over the past few days were apparent in his face. There were heavy dark bags under his eyes, and the crow's feet at the corners of his eyes appeared to have tripled in size since the previous day.

"What do I think about what?" she asked.

"The meeting," Levi replied. "I didn't know if you would be on board with the idea of Texas secession."

Jack Spearman sat down in the seat next to Levi and said, "I still don't know if I'm on board with the idea, but I don't see any alternative."

"I agree with Blackjack," Mavis said. "I think we've been backed into a corner, and have exhausted every other option."

Levi nodded his head and said, "Believe me, I had to do a lot of soul searching before I was comfortable with the thought. And I keep telling myself that this is a bad dream, and I will wake up soon. But it's not. When I dig down deep and look at the values I hold dear, this is the only option. You know that saying that it's better to die on your feet than live on your knees? Well, that is what's going on right here and now...and I for one am tired of getting down on my knees."

"So what's the next move," Jack asked.

"I already put out the word that we'll be holding a press conference tomorrow," Levi said.

"You can't honestly think that the Federal Government is going to let you tell the world that Texas will secede from the United States," Mavis said.

"I don't," Levi replied."So I had my assistant tell the FCC that the press conference was to urge the people of Texas to comply with the gun ban."

"And you think they'll buy that?" Jack said.

"They did buy it," Levi replied. "Or at least they seemed to. But that part doesn't matter. Once the press conference starts and we are on the air, I have some friends who will make sure that we stay on the airwaves...no matter what I have to say."

"Exactly what kind of friends could do that?" Mavis asked.

"Well, I might as well tell the two of you," Levi said. "I am a member of the Sons of Liberty."

Mavis pressed her back into the seat."The terrorist group?" she asked.

"I wouldn't exactly call it a terrorist group, even though that *is* the official US Government position," Levi said.

"And what about the bombings, vandalism, and attacks?" Mavis said angrily.

"Most of what you hear about the organization is propaganda spread by the president and his administration," Levi replied.

"I've seen pictures of the destruction," Mavis protested.

Levi took a deep breath and then said, "Everything the organization does is in the name of freedom and liberty. We have gone out of our way to make sure nobody is hurt in our...activities. That is why the organization relies heavily on cyber-attacks, and when you do see physical destruction, it is to fulfill a specific goal, not just destruction for the sake of chaos."

"And what kinds of specific goals could there be?" Mavis asked.

"Usually, it's to prevent the government from exploiting the citizens of an area," Levi said. "Or sometimes, it's used to help someone escape government prosecution...that has happened many, many times. It's going on right now."

"What do you mean?" Mavis asked.

"I got a call today about a guy and his son that the organization is helping," Levi replied. "He refused to join a union, so in retribution, they had the national police pick up his son to take to one of those reeducation camps."

"That's awful," Mavis said.

Levi nodded, and then continued. "The organization helped him...and a friend of his...grab his son from the police. As we speak, they are trying to escape the police; the Sons of Liberty are helping him run south."

"Where are they headed?" Mavis asked.

"I think they had planned on the Mexican border, but after tomorrow's announcement, they might do better to head to Texas. If they make it, I will make sure they get asylum."

Mavis turned her head and looked at Jack, who was staring out the window. "Blackjack, you haven't said a word. What is with you tonight?"

"Just thinking about what happened today," Jack replied. He turned his head to look at Mavis and Levi. "And what Levi said about being a member of the Sons of Liberty. Why didn't you tell us before?"

"It's not safe for anyone to discuss the group openly," Levi replied. "The Federal Government wants us gone because we are not afraid to fight for what we believe in...Traditional American values."

"The president isn't exactly a fan of those ideas," Jack said, "and people who disagree with him tend to disappear."

Levi chuckled and said, "Like the two of you?"

"We fared a whole lot better than many of the people who have crossed him," Mavis said.

"What do you think his response will be?" Levi asked.

"He is a master of propaganda, and has gotten ahead by making the other guy out to be the bad guy," Mavis said.

"I agree," Jack said. "I would expect him to move the national police against us right away. The military is a different story; he has always had a shaky relationship with them, so he may hesitate till he knows who they are loyal to."

Levi nodded his head and said, "That was my thought, too. Well, let's not worry about that right now. We need to get this announcement speech together."

Mavis had a puzzled look on her face. "We?" she asked.

Levi smiled and said, "Yes, we. The two of you will be with me at the announcement."

Jack laughed and said, "Well then, let's get to work."

It was a little after three when Kirk heard a knock at the worn wooden door of the room. He quickly and quietly jumped out of bed and headed toward the door; looking to his left, he saw that Matt had done the same. As Kirk reached for the door lock, Matt pressed himself against the wall to the right of the door and then nodded. Kirk unlocked the door, and slowly opened it a few inches; when he saw that it was Howard, he opened the door fully.

"Get any rest?" Howard whispered.

"A bit," Kirk said quietly. He turned his head to look at Matt and said, "Let's wake Sebastian and get moving. "

Matt didn't say a word, but simply nodded his head, and went to the dilapidated bed Sebastian was sleeping in. He shook Sebastian lightly and then quickly placed a hand of Sebastian's mouth. Sebastian's eyes opened wide and fast, and a panicked look appeared on his face. Matt took his hand off Sebastian's mouth and then motioned for him to be quiet. Sebastian angrily mouthed the word "asshole," shook his head, and climbed out of bed. Both Matt and Kirk struggled to not laugh.

Howard handed Kirk a large brown paper bag. "Dottie fixed you a little something for the road," he whispered.

"Thank you," Kirk said as took the bag, immediately handing it off to Sebastian.

"What am I, the pack mule," Sebastian said angrily.

"Watch your mouth, boy," Matt snapped quickly.

"He's always like this before breakfast," Kirk said with a smile.

"We're wasting time," Howard said. "I need to get you to the bridge fast...before the fireworks start."

"Let's move," Matt said.

The men left the room and began their decent of the stairs toward the entry hall of the inn. It was very quiet; only the creaking of the old wooden steps could be heard. Dottie Moore was standing at the bottom of the stairs looking up at them. As they approached her, she smiled and began to speak in a soft, quiet voice.

"Good luck to the three of you," she said. "I pray that you make it South to safety."

Matt and Sebastian nodded; Kirk said, "Thank you for all the help you and your husband have given us. You could get in a lot of trouble for helping us."

"There are a lot of things that we do that could get us in trouble with the law," Howard said.

"We do them anyway because it is the right thing to do," Dottie added. "With luck, one day the government will get out of our lives so that we can go about our daily business without worrying about big brother watching over our shoulder."

Kirk led the group to the Bronco; Howard climbed into the front passenger's seat, while Matt and Sebastian sat in the rear seat. Howard looked at Kirk in the driver's seat and then said, "I'll guide you to within a few hundred feet of the bridge, and then we'll go the rest of the way on foot. I'm afraid that the noise of your diesel engine will give you away if we get too close to the bridge."

"OK," Kirk replied.

Kirk didn't really need for Howard to show the way to the bridge; it wasn't far, and the lights on the bridge made it stand out. However, Kirk was glad to have someone local with them. *"Local intel is always best,"* was one of his most common saying during his Middle Eastern tours of duty.

As promised, Howard asked Kirk to stop a few hundred feet from the bridge. As they departed the SUV to finish the trip on foot, Kirk turned to Sebastian and said in a whisper, "You wait here. As soon as we've taken out the police, you can bring the Bronco up to the bridge and we'll cross into Kentucky."

"But I want to help," Sebastian protested.

"You are helping," Kirk said. "You're the wheel man. You know...the getaway driver."

"OK," Sebastian said somewhat mollified.

Kirk continued, "If something goes wrong, you *do not* try to rescue us. You get away from this place as fast as you can. Understand?"

"Yeah, I got it," Sebastian said. "But where do I go if that happens?"

"I'll help you with that," Howard said.

"Good," Kirk said. "Matt, Howard, let's do this and get this thing done. Sebastian, keep quiet and listen for our signal to bring the Bronco onto the bridge."

"Okay, dad," Sebastian said.

Howard led Kirk and Matt up a set of stairs that brought them to a walkway that spanned the length of the bridge. Once they reached the walkway, Kirk could see a police van, as well as two officers, at the central point of the bridge. Traffic was very light; only an occasional car crossed the bridge. Kirk looked at his watch; it was ten minutes before four.

"What do you think, Colonel?" Matt asked.

"We low crawl from here toward the police," Kirk replied. "Once we get close, we wait for the distraction. My guess is that they will receive a call on the radio about the fire. When that distracts them, we take them out."

"How are you going to do that?" Howard asked.

"Choke hold," Matt said.

Kirk nodded and then continued. "Incapacitate with a choke hold, then bind and gag them. That will give us enough time to get out of here. And with traffic as light as it is, we should be able to do it without being noticed."

Matt looked at Howard and said, "Stay here and watch. If we get into trouble, get Sebastian out of here."

Howard nodded, extended his hand to Matt, and said, "Good luck to the both of you."

Matt and Howard shook hands, and then Kirk and Howard did the same. Their thank yous to Howard were short as they were focused on the task ahead of them. Kirk and Matt then lay down on their stomachs and began the slow crawl toward the police. The rough pavement ground at their clothes and exposed skin; Kirk could already feel his knees and elbows becoming raw from the abrasive asphalt.

"This was a whole lot easier thirty years ago," Kirk whispered.

"Even easier forty years ago," Matt huffed.

They crawled until they were just a few feet away from the police. Lying on the ground, just on the opposite side of the police van, they could see the officers' shoes from underneath the van. Kirk looked at his watch; it was 4:05. *"Where's the distraction,"* he thought?

Suddenly, there came the sound of a huge explosion from the Kentucky side of the river. The explosion was far more powerful than Kirk had expected; it was enough to shake the bridge, if only slightly. *"Must be our distraction,"* Kirk thought. *"Better late than never."*

"What the hell was that!" one of the officers exclaimed.

"I don't know," the other said. "It sounded like it came from downtown Maysville."

It was about this time that Kirk could hear the police radio come to life. "There's been an explosion in an old warehouse downtown...must have been a gas line. Fire department has been called, and local police are working crowd control."

Kirk looked at Matt, who mouthed the words, *"Get it done"*. Kirk nodded in reply. Both men slowly rose to their feet and began to stealthily make their way around the police van; Kirk to the left, Matt to the right. As Kirk came around the van, he saw that an officer was directly in front of him, with his back turned. Kirk crept closer and was just about to apply his sleeper hold to the officer, when the man suddenly turned around. Both he and Kirk were momentarily startled.

"Who the he....," the officer began.

Kirk didn't give him the chance to finish his sentence. He quickly drew back and punched the cop in the nose. The officer staggered backwards as a torrent of blood began to gush from his nose. He quickly covered his nose with both hands in an attempt to stem the bleeding.

"You just broke my nose you old son of a bitch!" he said in a muffled shout.

Before the officer could say or do anything more, he was grabbed from behind by Matt, who quickly put him in a sleeper hold. The man struggled wildly at first, but within seconds, lost consciousness and his body went limp like a wet noodle. Matt lowered him to the ground slowly, and then looked at Kirk with a painful look on his face.

"I thought we were supposed to do this quietly?" Matt said.

"Sorry," Kirk replied. "Guess I'm getting too old for this shit."

Matt winced in pain and said with a gasp, "Me too."

"What's your problem?" Kirk asked.

Matt turned and pointed to the other officer, a woman, who was also unconscious and laying on the ground. "The bitch kicked me in the nuts."

Kirk began to laugh uncontrollably.

"Glad you think it's funny," Matt growled.

Kirk fought to regain his composure. When he thought he had control, he began to speak, but then burst out laughing again. Matt began to laugh, as well.

Just about this time, the two men heard the squeal of tires and the loud roar of a diesel engine.

"Got to be Sebastian," Kirk said.

"I thought you told him to wait for our signal," Matt said.

"I did," Kirk said with a sigh.

"I'm glad there hasn't been any traffic to see our little show...or his," Matt said.

"Me, too," Kirk replied.

In less than a minute, the Bronco roared onto the bridge, squealing to a halt within a few feet of Kirk and Matt; Kirk could see Sebastian in the driver's seat and Howard in the front passenger's seat. The engine stopped, and Sebastian leapt out. Howard followed, but at a much slower pace.

"I got Sebastian as soon as it looked like you had the cops taken care of," Howard said.

Kirk nodded, and then looked at Sebastian. "Do you know the meaning of the words low profile?"

Sebastian's nose wrinkled as he snarled, "I'm supposed to be the getaway driver, remember?"

"And the goal of the getaway driver is to not get caught," Kirk said. "That means don't do things that draw attention...like driving my Bronco like it's an Indy car."

Sebastian crossed his arms and frowned. "Maybe I was just worried about two old guys getting their asses kicked."

"Watch your mouth when you talk to your old man, boy," Matt scolded. "There's a roll of duct tape in the back of the truck. Get it so we can bind the cops' hands."

Sebastian stormed off with a huff and soon returned with the roll of tape. As Matt began to bind the hands of the cops together, Kirk turned to Howard and held out his hand.

"Howard, thanks for all of the help," Kirk said as he shook hands with Howard. "You should leave right away, before the police regain consciousness. I wouldn't want you to be identified as someone who helped us...who knows what the repercussions might be."

Howard nodded and said, "Good luck; I hope you make it."

As Howard walked away, Kirk turned toward Matt, who had just finished his task.

"That oughta hold 'em for a bit," Matt said. "I made it loose enough that they should be able to get free, and the bloody nose stopped bleedin'...shouldn't be a problem."

"Good," Kirk said. "Let's get out of here before someone comes along."

"You worried about drivin' through Maysville?" Matt asked.

Kirk shook his head and said, "No; the directions Howard gave me will bypass the downtown area, and looking at the town from here, it looks as if the fire has put out half of the lights. But we should get moving anyway."

Kirk, Matt, and Sebastian climbed into the Bronco. Kirk looked back at Sebastian in the back seat and said, "After we get past Maysville, I want you to get some sleep; we may need you to take a driving shift soon, and I can't have you nodding off behind the wheel."

"OK," Sebastian replied.

Kirk looked at Matt, who said, "On to Livingston?"

"Yes," Kirk replied. "That's not far from your hometown, is it?"

"Pretty close," Matt replied, "but I don't think we have time for a sightseeing tour."

Kirk turned the ignition key, and then shifted into first gear. He looked at Matt and said, "No. Let's head south and hope we aren't spotted."

CHAPTER ELEVEN

The sun was a low red ball of flame on the western horizon by the time Kirk's Bronco entered the town of Livingston. The trip from Maysville to Livingston would have ordinarily taken four to five hours to drive, but the winding, back road route that Howard provided took over twelve hours. Sebastian had even complained about how long the trip was taking. However, they encountered no police, and the few stops they made to refuel were uneventful.

Kirk found Kelley's Korner pretty quickly. As the name would suggest, the restaurant was found on a street corner. It was an old building, dating to possibly the 1920's, built of red brick with large, white framed windows in front. From the street, it was easy to hear the noise of loud music and people talking inside. A large, red and white sign advertised beer, chicken wings, and nostalgic music from the 1980's through 2010's.

"I'm going to pull back into that side street to find a place to park," Kirk said as he turned down a narrow alley near the restaurant. A suitable spot was found not far from the rear service door of the restaurant; Kirk made note of it in case they had to make a quick exit.

"I haven't been in a place like this for years," Kirk said excitedly as the trio entered Kelley's Korner. The restaurant was dimly lit, except for the yellow lamps hanging over the tall round tables. Most of the tables were filled with people of all ages, and there was a large crowd of men at the bar along the north wall. All of the walls held large viewing monitors, each showing a different sports program. The music was loud Southern rock; Kirk recognized the song, but had not heard it since his youth.

"It looks like this is the place to be!" Matt exclaimed.

"I wish they could do something about that noise," Sebastian said with a frown.

Matt quickly turned his head to look at Sebastian and said, "Watch your tongue boy, that's good stompin' music."

Kirk laughed and then said, "Let's find us a table to sit at. I have no idea who our contact is or what he looks like. I just hope that he finds us quick."

Kirk, Matt, and Sebastian sat down at a table near the east wall of the restaurant. Kirk was just reaching for one of the menus in the center of the table when a young woman who looked to be perhaps eighteen or nineteen years old, ran up to the table and put her arms around Sebastian in a big bear hug. "I knew you wouldn't stand me up tonight, Drake!" she exclaimed in a strong southern accent as she kissed him on the cheek. "I'm so glad you and your Dad and Uncle were able to make it so we can watch the game together!"

Sebastian had a puzzled look on his face; Kirk raised a single eyebrow and Matt chuckled. Before anyone could say anything, the woman began to whisper swiftly. "Just play along, Mr. Dillon…don't know who to trust. I'm here to help; I'm a friend of Howard Moore."

"Well don't just stand there; pull up a chair and sit your ass down," Matt said loudly. "How's your Dad doin'?"

"He's doing just fine," the young woman said as she reached for a stool. She pulled it close…extremely close…to Sebastian. Hopping onto the stool she scooted as close as she could to Sebastian, almost to the point that she was sitting on top of him. She wrapped her left arm around him and pulled him close, laying her head on his shoulder.

Kirk was having trouble not laughing at the situation. The girl's cover was brilliant; to the casual observer, Sebastian and the girl were boyfriend and girlfriend. And it was easy to tell that Sebastian was enjoying himself, as the young woman was definitely attractive. She was of average height and build, with shoulder length, russet colored hair that was pulled back in a ponytail. She had the golden-brown skin of someone who spent much of their time outdoors, and the tan line visible from her v-neck t-shirt proved her skin color was from working outdoors and not from sun bathing. Her most remarkable feature, however, was her eyes. Set off by thin eyebrows and extremely long eyelashes, her ice-blue eyes with flared pupils created a piercing gaze that seemed to both intimidate and intoxicate at the same time.

Looking at Kirk with a half-smile, she said in almost a whisper, "I'm Viviana, by the way. Something is about to happen that you will want to see."

Kirk looked around the room and then looked back at

Viviana before saying, "What?"

Her coy, half smile turned into a full grin before saying, "Something wonderful."

Kirk looked puzzled; he turned his head to look at Matt. Matt simply shrugged his shoulders and said, "I'm starvin'. We gonna order or what?"

"I already ordered us some food," Viviana said in her once again loud voice. "I hope nachos and wings are ok?"

"Fine with me," Matt replied.

A waitress soon arrived with their food, as well as drinks for everyone. Viviana continued her charade and began talking about her new job, and how her father was looking for new work since the local auto dealership had been closed by the government. She had just begun to describe how good her mother's sweet potato pie tasted, when all of the television screens in the restaurant flashed the same message: "We interrupt our regularly scheduled broadcast for an important government message."

Kirk looked at Viviana, who smiled and then nodded her head. "*This must be what she was talking about,*" Kirk thought. He leaned back in his chair to watch the announcement that was about to take place on the big screen. The loud noise of the restaurant dulled to that of a low whisper, as everyone in the restaurant gathered around the viewing screens.

The announcement was taking place at an outdoor location; the bottom of the screen told that it was the north lawn of the Texas State Capitol in Austin. Kirk recognized the man at the podium as Levi Walker, the Governor of Texas. There were two men standing to the right of the Governor; one was tall and thin, wearing a Stetson hat, and the other a short, stout gray haired man. To the Governor's left was a thin, blond haired woman of perhaps forty-five. The Governor seemed to be on edge and looked as if he had not slept in days. "*I can sympathize with that,*" Kirk thought. On screen, the Governor nodded, and then began to speak.

"Good afternoon and welcome to Austin, Texas. I'm sure that you all know about the Federal Government's effort to collect all firearms in civilian hands. A few days ago, I contacted the FCC to get permission to make this broadcast about how the state of Texas will assist the Federal Government in this effort; they agreed. I will now make a confession to you; I lied to the FCC so that I could make this broadcast about the true intentions of the Texas state government. Had I been honest about my intentions, the FCC would have never allowed this broadcast to take place. For this deception, I am sorry."

"Ever since the nineteenth century, we have allowed the Federal Government to take more and more power away from the states. At the same time, we have seen the power of the Federal Government grow almost exponentially. Beginning in the early twentieth century, we saw the quickening of the pace of the centralization of power in Washington. We also began to see the Federal Government get more and more involved in our daily lives. By the beginning of the twenty-first century, the Federal Government regulated nearly every aspect of our lives and every aspect of business. But that was not enough for the politicians in Washington. Hungry for more power, they cozied up to big political donors as well as every special interest group under the sun. Our natural resources were no longer ours to use, even if we owned the land that held those resources. More and more things were outlawed; businesses were regulated to the point that it was impossible to make a profit. Businesses moved overseas and unemployment skyrocketed."

"The president would have you believe that all of the government regulation and control is done for your benefit; it is to protect you, the citizen. I am here to tell you this is a lie; a fantasy created to get the people of this country to facilitate his quest for power. As you may know, he and his allies in Congress recently passed a bill that cast out senators and representatives who were business owners. This was done not for your benefit or the benefit of the nation, but for the benefit of the president and his cronies."

"There were some who fought to prevent the centralization of power in Washington; true servants of the people. God knows we have fought long and hard in Texas to keep government out of people's daily lives. However, I fear that it was too little, too late. Washington is nothing but a pit of angry vipers that strike out at anything that threatens their power."

"This nation was founded on the idea that a person should have the right to live his life how he wants and pursue his dreams as he sees fit. It is not government that gives us these rights, as human beings in a state of nature already have these rights. No; on the contrary, government can only take away these rights, and we have watched this government take away one right after another until we are all in a state of serfdom. Well, for the State of Texas, this is about to end."

"The Texas State Legislature has been in near constant session for the past few weeks, debating the issue of what to do about the Federal Government. After exhausting all other options, the legislature came to a final decision a few days ago. It is not lightly that this decision has been made, nor were the implications of this decision ignored. It has been decided that, effective immediately, the State of Texas will secede from the United States."

Kirk looked around the room; it was deadly silent except for the hum of the ventilation system. Looking at people's faces, he could see looks of bewilderment, shock, and excitement. There was also the occasional look of disgust or even disinterest. Matt had a look of surprise that Kirk had not seen in years, and it was easy to see that Viviana was almost giddy with excitement over the news.

The Texas Governor stepped aside as the short man stepped up to the Podium. "Citizens of the United States," he began, "Many of you know me; some do not. My name is John Amaruq, and I am the governor of Alaska. I must first thank Levi James Walker and all of the people of Texas for their hospitality."

"The people of Alaska have long had the same issues with the Federal Government as the State of Texas. I feel no need to repeat what Governor Walker has just said, so I will be short and to the point. The State of Alaska has come to the same conclusion as the State of Texas; effective immediately, Alaska is separated from the United States and is its own free nation."

"In both Alaska and Texas, we will no longer collect any federal taxes, and all federal laws and regulations will no longer apply. State laws and regulations will remain. However, Alaska will begin to look over the books and eliminate those laws that were imposed by federal authority; Governor Walker has informed me that Texas will begin to do the same. To all business owners: in both Alaska and

Texas, we welcome and encourage business, both big and small. All of the federal regulations that hampered your business no longer apply. Reopen the long abandoned oil wells and coal mines, tap the natural gas pockets that we have known about but have not been permitted to touch in twenty years. Likewise, if you have long dreamed of starting your own business but did not due to the burdensome regulations, please consider doing so now…you have the blessings of our respective states. If you wish to invest in a business, both Alaska and Texas will embrace both foreign and domestic investment with open arms."

"To the people of Texas and Alaska: we will respect your beliefs and if you wish to leave our borders for that of the United States, you are free to do so. Likewise, to the people of the United States who live in states other than Alaska and Texas, if you wish to come to our respective states to live free, our borders are open to you."

All at once, all of the television screens flashed to the image of a waving American flag. An announcement was heard that said, "In the interest of national security, the Federal Communications Commission has interrupted this broadcast. Please stay tuned as the service provider selects an alternative broadcast program."

For a few moments, the room remained silent. Finally, someone said, "So when's Tennessee gonna stand up to the feds?" Excited conversations erupted throughout the room, and the noise level began to increase. Soon the music began to play.

Kirk looked at Matt and said, "Did that really just happen?"

Matt raised his eyebrows, shook his head, and said, "I didn't think I would ever see that."

Kirk noticed that Viviana was franticly scrolling through a message on her cell phone. She looked up from the phone; her icy blue eyes opened wide. Quickly shoving her cell phone in her back pocket, she said with a worried voice, "We have to get out of here...they know where you are."

All four began to get up from their seats. Viviana said to Kirk, "I saw where your truck is parked when I came in. Follow me; I'll take you out the back."

"Anywhere we can get diesel fuel?" Kirk asked.

"Are you out?" Viviana asked frantically.

"No, but we won't make it to the next town," Kirk replied.

Viviana nodded and then said, "There is someone in the organization that can help us."

Viviana led the group through a set of double doors that read "Employees only." Once through the doors, Kirk realized they were in the kitchen of the restaurant. Employees in blue jeans and t-shirts were working diligently on various tasks in the kitchen, and most seem to pay no attention to the visitors. As they began to make their way through to the back, they were stopped by a large, overweight man who sported a handlebar mustache.

"Uncle Larry!" Viviana exclaimed, "They know they're here!"

"Sumbitch!" the man exclaimed in a strong Southern accent. "Git 'em outta here! Head out back; if they come in the store, I'll stall 'em as long as I can."

"Thank you," Viviana said.

Looking at Kirk, the man said, "My niece will git you outta here. Hurry up now!" The man then looked at Viviana and said, "You packin', girl?"

Viviana half smiled and then lifted her shirt a few inches at the waist to display a small pistol. "You know it," she said.

"That's my girl," the man said with a smile. "Now y'all git out of here quick!"

Viviana led the way to a steel door at the back of the restaurant kitchen. She opened the door just slightly and then looked through the narrow gap. "Looks like we're clear," she said as she threw the door wide open and rushed out. Kirk and the others followed close on her heels.

Running toward the Bronco, the group could hear the sirens of approaching police vans. Kirk pulled out his keys and began to unlock the driver's side; as he did so, he look at Sebastian and Viviana, saying, "The two of you climb in the back through the rear window!" The two obeyed, with Sebastian climbing in first. As Viviana began to climb through the rear window, Sebastian attempted to help her, and in the process managed to pull Viviana on top of himself. The two came crashing to the floor of the cargo area.

"I didn't think we were close enough at Kelley's, either," Viviana said with a giggle.

"I thought that was an act," Sebastian said with a smile.

Viviana smiled with her coy smile and said, "A little."

By this time, Kirk was in the driver's seat and Matt was climbing into the front passenger's seat. As soon as he had closed the door, Matt grabbed his M16, inserted a fresh magazine, and pulled back the charging handle. "Just in case," he said.

Kirk turned his head to look at Viviana and said, "Which way?"

Pointing through the front windshield, Viviana said, "Keep going down this street until we get to Adamson Street; take a left there."

"OK," Kirk said. "Sebastian, fold up the back seat to get it out of the way. We may need to have an open area to shoot from."

"Got it," Sebastian replied.

Smoke poured from the rears tires as they squalled, and the Bronco fishtailed slightly as Kirk floored the accelerator. Pretty soon, he driving far faster than the posted speed limit. Sebastian and Viviana worked to fold the rear seat…no small task at the speed Kirk was driving. When finished, the two sat on the floor of the now open and expanded cargo area.

Matt pointed ahead and said, "Right there...Adamson Street."

Sebastian and Viviana were thrown to the right side of the cargo area as Kirk took the turn onto Adamson Street far faster than he should have. Everyone could feel the center of gravity shift as the vehicle nearly tipped over in the high speed turn.

"You ain't no NASCAR driver!" Matt shouted. You're gonna get us killed!"

Kirk didn't reply to Matt's outburst. Seconds later, he shouted, "How much farther!"

"About six miles," Viviana replied as she tried to sit up while being rolled across the cargo area. "It's an old farm. Watch for a big white barn with a beat up silo next to it." Pulling her cell phone from her back pocket, she began reading a text message. "We got out of there just in time; police are there now. My uncle is trying to delay them as long as possible." She began typing on the phone, and then looked up. "They're expecting us at the farm. Go to the back side of the barn and there is a diesel storage tank that we can use to fill up your truck."

"Sounds good," Kirk replied.

They soon arrived at the farm. Kirk turned back down the long gravel driveway toward the white barn. As they approached the barn, a thin man carrying a shotgun ran out and franticly waved for them to follow him. He led them around to the north side of the barn, where they found a large red diesel fuel tank. The man was already inserting the fuel nozzle into the Bronco's fuel tank when Kirk got out.

"You Kirk Dillon?" the man asked in a worried voice.

"That's me," Kirk said.

The man nodded and then said, "Name's Jason Brewer. I got Viviana's message about fuel and got out here as soon as I could. I've also got directions to get you farther south."

By this time, Matt Pickett was standing next to Kirk Dillon."You a member of..." Matt began.

"I am," Jason interrupted. "No time to talk; the police may

be here soon. It is the opinion of the organization that you head for Texas. The Governor of Texas knows about your situation and will give you asylum if you make it to Texas."

"Sounds like your best option," Viviana said as she and Sebastian joined the group.

"Agreed," Kirk said.

Jason nodded his head and said, "The secession of Texas and Alaska is only the beginning; the revolution for freedom has begun."

"I don't think the US government is gonna take secession lightly," Matt said.

"It hasn't," Jason said. The national police have been put on alert and told to prepare for action. In response, Texas has mobilized its National Guard to protect its borders. It's also using the Guard to force the national police out of Texas."

"What about the US military?"Kirk asked.

"All military units in both Texas and Alaska have sided with the respective states," Jason replied. "A majority of the service members have decided to stay as well."

"At least we know what side Michael is on," Sebastian said.

"What's that?" Jason said.

"Michael is my older son," Kirk replied. "He's stationed at Ft. Sam Houston."

"With any luck, you will see him soon," Jason said. As soon as the refueling was complete, Jason screwed the fuel cap back on and said, "There. That should keep you going for a while."

Kirk handed Jason a wad of cash."I hope this will cover your expense."

"I couldn't accept it," Jason replied.

"Please do," Kirk pleaded. "Who knows how rough things are going to be...it looks like we're headed for war.

Jason shrugged and took the cash. As he shoved it in his pocket, he noticed Viviana reading her cell phone again.

"What is it, girl," Jason said.

She looked up from the phone, eyes as wide as saucers. "Police are on the way here!"

Kirk looked at Sebastian and said, "Get in; we need to get moving fast." Kirk turned to Jason and said, "Will you be OK?

"We know where to hide," Jason responded. "As soon as you are under way, we're out of here, too. Another thing; it may be harder going now. President White has issued an Executive Order that all people wanted by the US Government for political matters are to be apprehended at all costs. While that was targeted at the Sons of Liberty...I think he knows the group was involved in the states' secession...it will apply to you as well."

"You're welcome to come to Texas with us," Kirk said. Glancing at Viviana, he added, "That goes for both of you."

"Plenty of room, and we could always use a guy who knows how to use a shotgun," Matt added.

Jason shook his head and said, "I can't speak for Viviana, but my place is here. This is where I was born and raised; this is where I will stand and fight."

"I understand," Kirk said.

Sebastian looked Viviana in the eyes and said, "I'd love it if you came to Texas with us."

Viviana had the look of pain in her eyes when she said, "I can't. I couldn't leave my uncle." Looking at Jason, she said, "Or my brother." She reached into her pocket and pulled out a small piece of paper. Handing it to Sebastian, she said, "Here is my cell number and email. Promise me you'll text me when you get to Texas."

"It's a promise," Sebastian said with a smile.

Viviana returned his smile and then she leaned forward and kissed Sebastian on the cheek, and whispered into his ear, "You know, I think you're kind of sexy."

Kirk and Matt were already in the Bronco. Matt leaned out the passenger's window and said, "Hey, Doctor Lovejoy, we need to get out of here before the bad guys show up."

"I'm coming," Sebastian said with a huff.

"I almost forgot," Jason said as reached into his pocket. Pulling out several folded pages, he handed them to Kirk. "Here are directions to get you closer to Texas. They laid out a route that takes you through the Tennessee backwoods. They have a destination for you in south Tennessee where you will meet up with another member of the organization…the town's called Whitefield. They'll have instructions to get you across the Texas border."

"Thanks Jason," Kirk said as he took the documents. Kirk turned his head to look at Matt Pickett and said, "Ready Sergeant?"

Matt smiled and said, "Lead the way, Colonel."

CHAPTER TWELVE

James Duncan was running toward the Oval Office as fast as his overweight, out of shape body would carry him. When Jessica Wolfgang, the president's assistant, had called him to the Oval Office, he could hear the president cursing in the background. He was sure that this was due to the Texas press conference which had just aired; he was just as sure that he would receive a serious tongue lashing for the broadcast not getting cut off. James had been watching the broadcast from his office, and had made a frantic call to the FCC Director as soon as Levi Walker had announced to the world that he had lied to the FCC.

However, all communications in and out of Washington DC had been disrupted by a computer virus, and by the time the problem had been resolved, the press conference was nearly over.

Arriving at the doors to the Oval Office, James found two national police officers and Ralph Marco. Even though the doors to the Oval Office were made of thick oak, you could hear the president cursing a up a storm inside. As usual,

Ralph was standing with his hands in his wrinkled pants pockets, swaying back and forth as if he didn't have a care in the world. The officers were telling Ralph about what had happened at the Oval Office during the press conference.

"Yep," one said, "I've seen him pissed before, but this one takes the cake."

"Pretty ticked?" Ralph asked with a half-smile.

"Like you wouldn't believe," the other officer said. "Jessica was in the Oval Office when he lost his temper. He actually flipped the Resolute Desk over when he lost his temper."

"That's a pretty damn big desk," Ralph replied.

"Then he started cursing up a storm," the first officer added.

"What is going on?" James said between huffs.

"Just waiting for you to get here," Ralph said. Then with a grin, he added, "James, you really need to get in shape if you're going to run these halls."

"Shut up," James exclaimed. "In a time of national crisis, you should be more serious."

Ralph shrugged his shoulders and said, "You need to chill out. Just trying to lighten the moment."

"Let's go in," James said with a sigh.

James pushed his way through the doors of the Oval Office to see President White shouting at his assistant, Jessica. The president's eyes were narrow slits, and deep valleys lined his forehead, all of which displayed more prominently due to the ruddy color of his skin.

"…And when I say something is to be done a certain way, it is to be done that way!" he shouted. "I don't want excuses, or people telling me why it couldn't be done. Get it done or I'll replace that person with one who can get that job done! Is that understood?"

"Yes, Mr. President," Jessica replied.

"Get out of here!" the president shouted at her.

Jessica turned and hurried to the door. Her face was red, her eyelids were a bit swollen, and her lips were trembling slightly. As she walked past Ralph, she mumbled, "I've quit better jobs than this."

The president noticed James and Ralph. "Oh, I see, now the two of you show up!" he exclaimed. He pointed a stubby finger at James and said, "You spend most of your time crawling up my ass and tonight, when you are needed, nobody can find you. I should fire your asses!"

James nervously cleared his throat and said, "Mr. President, there were reasons why things went so wrong today…."

"I am sick of hearing excuses! That's all I have heard for the past few hours!"

"Maybe the great communicator should listen for once," Ralph said.

The president quickly turned to face Ralph and said, "What did you just say to me?"

"You heard me just fine," Ralph said calmly. "James was just trying to explain to you what happened today and you, as usual, are not listening."

The red color of the president's face intensified, and he took two steps towards Ralph; they were now only inches from each other. Peering into Ralph's eyes, the president said, "Are you forgetting who you are talking to!"

Ralph didn't move and began to speak in his usual, easy going tone. "No, but I know that your brain turns off when you get mad. And yeah, I know that people who cross you tend to disappear. I also know you back down when you face someone who isn't intimidated by you."

The president seemed to calm down slightly. He continued to stare Ralph in the eyes and said, "Alright James, let's have it. Why weren't the cameras shut off as soon as Walker's speech got ugly?"

"All communications in and out of D.C. were interrupted," James replied nervously. "I couldn't reach the FCC director, but that didn't matter; she already knew what was going on. Nobody at FCC headquarters could contact the broadcasters to stop the broadcast."

President White quickly turned and walked to the overturned desk in the middle of the room. "I can't believe in this age of technology that all communications would go down at the same time and at such a crucial moment."

"It was a computer virus," James said. "Or, more accurately, multiple viruses. Investigators are not 100% sure, but they firmly believe this is the work of the Sons of Liberty."

"Remember that flying elephant I warned you about," Ralph added.

Taking a deep breath, the president began to speak slowly and deliberately. "Contact the base commanders of all military bases in Alaska and Texas. I am declaring martial law in those states, and the military is to seize and control the capitals. I want the Joint Chiefs in session ASAP to come up with a plan to take back those two states."

"Sir, we can't do that," James protested.

The president sat at the chair behind his overturned desk, crossed his arms and said, "And why is that?"

James loosened his tie and swallowed hard. "In both states, the military has defected to the seceding state."

The president's eyes opened wide, "Every military member in those states?" he said.

"A large percentage," James replied. "Almost all staff officers went, and they gave their men the choice to go or stay. Most decided to stay; I don't have an official count, but estimates are in the eighty to ninety percent range."

"Damn traitors!" the president shouted. He took a deep breath, and began to rub his thumb and forefinger in a circular motion. "What kind of public support do they have in Texas and Alaska?"

"It is hard to determine in Alaska since the population is so sparse," James replied. "However, Texas has very strong public support."

"Strong public support is an understatement," Ralph said. "From what I heard, there was dancing in the streets, and church bells all over the state were ringing. People were shouting 'we are a free people once again.'"

"You approve?" the president said with a snarl.

Ralph looked the president in the eyes and said, "I'm just telling you the way it is. The people of Texas are fully behind this movement. My guess is the same for Alaska. The only way to get public support in your corner is to paint the leaders of the secession movement as the bad guy...and how you will do that, I have no idea."

"Well I do," the president replied. Turning to face James, he said, "James, I want every drop of federal monies cut off to Alaska and Texas. And I'm not talking just about state funds; I mean to the people, too. Welfare and food stamps are gone. Social Security cut off. All government loans...gone. No more healthcare payments. Any company in those states that has a federal contract...the contract is canceled. They want to leave the United States? Fine. We will take away everything. I want the peasants of those states begging to come back to the United States."

Cocking his head to the right, the president looked at Ralph and said, "I need a speech that is over the top. All of the stuff I have just taken away...we are going to blame the Texas and Alaska governments. We will tell the people that we are so sorry, but it was not our doing."

"I can do that," Ralph said.

"Good," the president replied. "But there's more. We need to make these secessionists out to be a bunch of rich, white racists who left the country because they wanted to lord over the poor minorities like masters over slaves. Add any extra details you need to make the story believable. I want the people rioting in the streets of Austin and Juneau. Those two states will be begging to return to this nation."

Ralph nodded; James began to scratch the back of his head. "Mr. President," James began, "the only problem with the racist part of your idea is that many of the leaders of this movement are people of color."

President White looked at James and squinted slightly as he said, "What's your point?"

James opened his eyes wide and his jaw dropped. "Besides not reflecting the truth, I don't think it's believable."

The president sighed and looked at the floor as he rubbed the deep valleys in his forehead. "You are one simple son of a bitch, James," he said. "This is politics .Since when have I been interested in the truth? I am the President of the United States of America; if I say it is, then it is. Besides, Ralph can write a speech like no other. I'm sure he can come up with something that will give the people exactly what I want them to have."

"Absolutely," Ralph added.

Leaning back in his chair, the president continued. "James, you are a great administrator and the biggest ass kisser in Washington, but there is a great deal that you don't know or understand about politics. The average citizen is not very bright, and also very gullible. As long as you keep the feeding trough of government handouts full, the American people will believe everything you say."

"But the American people are a hardworking and industrious people," James stammered.

The president chuckled and said, "Maybe at one time, but for the past hundred or so years, those people have been replaced by something that is much more like their European counterpart. Lazy, slothful, and absent any real ambition. They complain about a seven hour workday, and want the government to provide every want and need."

Ralph nodded his head and said, "Definitely not the nation it used to be."

"No," the president said. "But politicians have been using the same tricks for years. Social Security was initially signed into law in 1935 by Franklin D. Roosevelt as part of his New Deal plan. The program initially withheld 1% of wages, and paid out retirement income beginning at age 65. During the 1950's and 60's, social security ran huge surpluses, so it was popular to expand benefits. Not surprisingly, most benefit expansions took place in election years. In the early part of this century, Social Security default was looming and the Republican Party made reforms part of its platform. The Democrats crucified them, even though the Republican plan was financially sound and Democrats had no plan of their own. The mere thought of a reduced benefit was enough to kill them at the polls."

"I guess that's why the program is in the shape it is now," Ralph added.

"Absolutely," the president said. Leaning forward in his chair, he added, "Give the masses what they want, and you can have power…unlimited power."

Standing, President White adjusted his tie and pulled his suit jacket straight. Stroking his mustache, he began speaking again. "James, I do need to send a message…a message that this traitorous behavior will not be tolerated. This means dealing with the Sons of Liberty is a top priority."

"Yes, Mr. President," James said. "Do you want them to focus only on the Sons of Liberty?"

"No," the president said. "Anyone wanted for defying the Federal Government. Tell them not to worry about traffic laws, tax evasion, and petty crime…let the local police handle that. I want the nation to know that defying the Federal Government will be dealt with swiftly and with extreme prejudice. Understood?"

"Yes, Mr. President," James said.

"And speaking of defying the Federal Government," the president continued, "I want to send a message to the military that treason will not be tolerated. First of all, Ralph, I want you to change the oaths that all officers and enlisted personnel take. In the new oaths, they are to be pledging their loyalty to me, not the nation. Get rid of that defense of the constitution crap."

"Can do," Ralph replied.

President White turned to look at James and said, "James, I want military law changed so that anyone even suspected of treason is put to death…no trial, no appeal. I want all military members to know that the behavior in Texas and Alaska is not acceptable and will not be tolerated. Is that clear?"

"Perfectly, Mr. President," James replied.

The president was about to continue, when there was a knock at the door. All three men tuned toward the door, which opened slowly to reveal Jessica. Behind her stood a large, heavyset man leaning on a cane. He wore a pleated gray suit, and his wrinkled, leathery face reflected his advanced years.

"I'm sorry to disturb you, Mr. President," she began, "but

the chairman of the Freedom Party, Adolph Brooks, is here to see you."

At the sight of Adolph Brooks, the president's face turned slightly pale; once again he adjusted his tie. "That's fine; we're all finished here. James, Ralph...leave us while we talk. Stand this desk up before you leave."

Ralph nodded, and James said, "Yes, Mr. President." He and Ralph stood the Resolute Desk back on its feet, and then walked out the door. As they left, Adolph Brooks walked into the room and began to look around.

"I see you still have the occasional temper tantrum," Adolph said in a gravelly voice.

The president stood behind the Resolute Desk, still pale, with an emotionless look on his face. "It's my one true character flaw," he said. Extending his hand toward the chair across from the Resolute Desk, the president motioned for Adolph Brooks to have a seat. "Won't you sit down?"

Adolph Brooks smiled, which caused his weather-beaten face to look like a roadmap. Taking a seat in the chair, he leaned back and said, "You need to learn to control that temper of yours. It will be your undoing."

A thin smile appeared on the president's face momentarily, followed by an arched eyebrow. "Are you here to talk about my character flaw or something else?"

Adolph laughed and then said, "That's something you have never understood, Conrad. The power of small talk to lighten the mood. It works in both business and politics. I guess that's why you were a teacher for so long…you didn't have the head for business"

President White's face turned from a smile to a frown as he said, "Professor."

"What's that?" Adolph said.

"Professor," the president repeated.

Adolph laughed again and began to adjust his suit. "Oh yes, that's right; you're insulted when someone refers to you as a 'teacher' instead of 'professor'. Must have slipped my mind." Adolph rubbed his upper lip with his forefinger, and then continued, "It must have slipped my mind because I don't see one damn difference between the two."

Deep fissures began to appear on the president's forehead. "Did you come here to try and anger me, or is there something of importance that you want to talk about?"

Leaning forward on his cane, Adolph said, "Oh, you know why I am here. That little fiasco today."

The president's eyes widened and he looked Adolph directly in the eyes. "It's just a delay, and I already have a plan in place to take care of the situation."

"Do you now," Adolph said with a smile as he leaned back in his chair. "That's interesting. Is your plan going to use the same half-assed, I don't give a shit about the people methods that end up alienating the people of this country? Because you are pissing off a lot of people. And not just the business owners or the politicians you just kicked out of Washington. Things are getting to the point that the average Joe on the street hates your guts…and that is something that we can't have."

The president's face turned red again, and sweat began to

bead in the deep furrows of his forehead. He slowly rose to his feet and said, "Are you forgetting who you are talking to?"

Adolph stood and peered into the president's eyes. "No, but I should be saying the same to you. I am the Chairman of the Freedom Party, which means I control the purse strings for all politicians who want to play. That means you have to play by my rules, not yours. And do you remember how this came to be? It was all you. You, who campaigned on the idea of ending the fighting between the Republican and Democrat parties."

President White stood silent and crossed his arms.

"And if you remember," Adolph continued, "both parties were happy to merge, as there was very little difference between the two. Oh sure, there may have been differences at one time, but not in the past twenty years. Both had come to believe that big government was the key to real power, and both were right. You were smart to join the parties because you could control who got into politics, and this was something the people could get behind. They were tired of the billions spent on campaigns while the nation went further into debt. I was more than happy to become the Chairman of the Freedom Party; after all, it was the least you could do after I funded your campaign. But I will not allow you to blow this."

The president was silent for a moment, and then he began to speak quietly. "You're right, Adolph. There is a better way."

"Exactly," Adolph said. "Never forget that the president derives his power from the people. That means you have to keep them happy. Knocking the businessmen down a notch was not a bad thing; they were a threat. However, you have to keep the people happy. Remember, there are four hundred and fifty million people in this country, and only one of you. You have to keep them on your side."

A broad smile emerged from under the president's mustache. "Adolph, I'm glad we had this talk. You have given me some ideas that I think will set things right."

Adolph smiled and said, "Good. Now I have to be off, as I am expected for dinner at Bernardo's."

"Expensive," the president commented.

Adolph smiled and said, "Don't worry, I can afford it."

"Take care," President White said with a smile.

"You too, Conrad." Adolph smiled, and then turned to leave. After he had left the room, the president pulled a cell phone from his desk drawer. He pressed a few buttons, and then put the phone to his ear.

"Teddy," he said, "it's Conrad. Adolph Brooks just left my office and is on his way to Bernardo's for dinner. Make sure he has an accident…one that he doesn't walk away from."

"So, what did you think of my speech?"

Mavis Young looked at Levi, who was standing with her, Jack Spearman, and John Amaruq near the north entrance to the Texas Capitol building.

"I think it went well," Mavis said. Looking at John, she

continued, "Both of you were great; honest and right to the point. It's not often that the people get to see a politician speak honestly."

"Thank you, Miss Young," John said with a genuine smile. "And it appears the people in Austin are happy. I hear church bells ringing in the distance; it looks as if there will be celebrations tonight. However, what I am now concerned with is how soon the President of the United States will respond."

"I think we can expect a response any time now," Jack said. "In fact, I'm kinda surprised that we haven't seen or heard anything yet."

"I agree," John said. "That's why I should return to Juneau as soon as possible."

Levi nodded his head and said, "That's probably for the best. All of us are going to have a lot to do." He looked at Jack and grinned, saying, "There might even be a bit of work for an ex-senator."

Jack laughed, and said, "Just because I'm an ex-senator doesn't mean I've got nothing to do. I still own a business, and now that the feds are out of the way, I'm sure there's going to be wells to be drilled here in Texas."

"Alaska as well," John added. "I know many who may be interested in your company's services."

"Send 'em my way," Jack said. "Some of my boys have been working on some new techniques for natural gas extraction…I might have the time to get involved."

"I didn't know your company was involved in natural gas…I

thought it was just oil," John said.

Jack shook his head and said, "Oil is the major part of our business, but we're also into natural gas. Most of my natural gas operations are in Russia and the Middle East...you know, nations where it's still legal to extract natural gas. Guess that's gonna change around here."

"I'm sure it will," Mavis said. "The whole natural gas thing is a shame, too. The environmentalists were always going on about a clean energy source...that we had to get away from oil based technology. Natural gas could have been it, but they were dead set on having their electric cars."

"Absolutely," John said. "I can remember as a young man the beginning of a natural gas boom. Ohio and Pennsylvania were leading the charge...until the government caved to the environmentalists. "

"That was a bit before my time," Mavis said with a smirk.

"Some of us are a bit more seasoned than you, little sister," Jack said with a smile. "But I remember the boom, as well. Natural gas can be used as a fuel source or as a raw material to convert to methanol. While methanol vehicles don't get the miles per gallon that gasoline does, emissions are nearly nonexistent. But like you said, the environmentalists were dead set on their electric cars. So today we have high priced gas, high priced methanol, high priced natural gas, and high priced electric vehicles that don't run worth a shit."

"Getting back to you having more time on your hands," Levi said to Jack. "Just because you're not in the Senate doesn't mean that you can't be of service to your state."

Jack squinted his eyes slightly and said, "And what do you

mean by that?"

Levi put his hands in his pockets and said, "If other states leave the US…and it looks like most who were at the meeting will…then there will be a convention to form a new government. The Texas State legislature would like both you and Miss Young to represent us at that convention."

"I'm flattered," Mavis said.

Jack sighed, and rubbed his hand over the smooth granite column of the capitol building's entrance. "I never wanted to be a senator," Jack said, looking skyward. "All I wanted to do was to get politicians out of the way of business…to stop the government from destroying industry. All I want to do is get back to running my company."

John put his hands behind his back, leaned forward, and began to speak. "Mr., Spearman, it is not my place to tell you what to do. But it seems to me that is the exact reason you should represent Texas. You are not in politics for power; you are here for the right reason. And your record for not accepting gifts from lobbyists is exceptional. A person like you is exactly the kind of person who should be at that convention."

"I don't know," Jack replied. "Washington has soured my stomach against politics."

"I can understand that," Levi said. "Plenty of time to think about it; there is no date or location set for such a convention as of yet. Hell, we don't even know if such an event will occur. In the meantime, you and Mavis could help me out by bringing yourselves and your staff to the state capital. Now that we are independent of the US, there are hundreds of things to work out…and we were short staffed as it was."

Jack stroked his handlebar mustache in thought, and then said, "That's doable for the time being. I don't mind lending a hand to get things worked out. No promises about going to a convention, though."

Levi smiled and said, "Well, I'll take what I can get."

"As much as I enjoy the present company, I must get back to Alaska," John said. "As you said, there is much work to be done."

Levi held out his hand to John, and they shook hands; John then shook hands with Jack and Mavis.

"Great meeting you," Jack said.

"I look forward to seeing you and Miss Young again," John said.

"Sarah has arranged transportation to a small airport," Levi said. "A charter plane will be waiting. They have a route laid out that will not take you over the continental US."

John smiled and said, "Thank you, Levi. Goodbye."

As John walked away, Levi turned to Mavis and said, "I want to get you and Jack moved into the capitol as soon as we can. Luckily, both of you only have a single office here in Texas, so the move should be a simple affair. The capitol building is a bit cramped, but there is some office space in the expansion wing."

Mavis nodded and said, "There is nothing I need from my office in Washington. I'll just recall the staff back to Austin."

"I already cleared out the Washington Office…back when I was kicked out of the Senate," Jack added.

"Good," Levi said. "I guess the two of you will be working for me for a while. There should be some room in the budget to get you on the payroll."

"Don't," Jack said.

"Don't what?" Levi asked.

"Don't put me on the payroll," Jack said. "I could retire wealthy right now, so the money means little to me. Hell, I've been donating my Senate pay to charity ever since I was elected."

"The same for me," Mavis added. "While I may not be loaded like Jack, I can afford to go without pay for a while, and I have a feeling that Texas may need the money."

"OK, then. I guess the two of you are working for free," Levi said with a smile.

"Speaking of money," Jack said, "no matter if we form a new nation or remain an independent state, one of the first things that will need to be done is set an economic policy. The nation will need a stable money supply, and I don't like the idea of depending on a foreign currency. The US dollar is fine for now while we get things started, but since it is only worth what the US says it's worth, I think we need our own system as soon as possible. Something like the gold standard."

"That's smart," Mavis said.

Levi opened his mouth and was just about to speak, but

stopped as his assistant rushed out of the doors of the capitol. Her face was pale and she looked to be in shock. "Mr. Walker! I think it has started. President White is broadcasting a speech about what has happened in Texas and Alaska!"

Jack, Mavis, and Levi followed Sarah through the north entrance of the capitol building and into the lobby, where a crowd of the capitol staffers had gathered around a large viewing screen. On the screen was a view of the Oval Office, with the president seated behind the Resolute Desk. The president nodded and then began to speak.

"My fellow Americans and citizens of the world…it is with a heavy heart that I must address you today. As you know, it has always been my goal to make the United States a place where everyone gets a chance, a place where everyone's needs are take care of. Social and economic justice to all is my slogan…after all, is it not a good thing to share the wealth? There is plenty for all not only in this nation but in the world. All we need to do is share the wealth. And if we share the wealth, then every man and woman can live like a king…nobility or title is not required."

"However, there are those who do not agree with me. Greedy men; capitalists who just want more, more, more. To them, there is no limit to how much wealth they can acquire. Wealth acquired, mind you, on the backs of the working people like you. These greedy business owners put profits above all else, and do not care about the well being of the average man or woman. To them, you are just a disposable asset."

"Do you know why these people seek to have and control so much more than you? The answer is simple: racism. They see those of anything other than Anglo-Saxon white as inferior. And while slavery no longer exists, they wish to expand the gulf between you and them so you are in a virtual state of slavery. Their racism is so extreme and deep that they are willing to allow other whites to suffer along with the minority races…just so they can be the masters."

"As you know, I have fought these people all my life, and it has been my policy as president to reign in these corrupt capitalists. I have fought long and hard, and have won many victories. Today, only the wealthiest must pay for health services and education, and we have routinely seized land and property from the billionaires for use in projects that are in the public interest. Our latest attempt to reign in the businessmen was to kick them and their allies out of Washington, but it seems our work has pushed them farther than they were willing to go."

"Earlier today, I was informed that both the states of Texas and Alaska were leaving the United States so they could be free of the rule of the United States law. Even then I knew what this meant…this was the code to say they were forming new nations where slavery would be the rule for those of non-white ancestry. Much like post World War II Berlin, both states are building massive walls between us and them, and I have been informed that they have employed sharpshooters to stop civilians from trying to cross the border."

"I have also been informed that all forms of US government aid have been cut off by the governments of Texas and Alaska. This includes social security, Medicare, Medicaid, food stamps and government pensions. We believe this was done to bring the population to its knees, so that they would do whatever the state government wants. My administration has reached out to the governors of both states, but I am afraid the plea has fallen on deaf ears, as I have heard nothing from either governor."

"I would like to say to the people of Texas and Alaska: be strong! Do not allow the racist dictators of your states to take away what is rightfully yours. Protest to your government; take to the street if need be. Remember that you have paid into the system all of your life; you are owed social security, you are owed Medicare. To the rest of the world: avoid the borders of Texas and Alaska, as the border sharpshooters are killing people in droves."

"In response to the threat of hostilities with these two states, I have ordered the mobilization of the national police, who will begin an aggressive policing policy. As we must protect against terrorism, the national police are adopting a zero tolerance policy against acts of questionable patriotism. I am also asking the citizens of this nation to report anyone who seems to be engaging in questionable behavior. I once again reach out to the governors of these two states. Stop the madness and stop the killing of innocents trying to cross the border! Give back to the people what is rightly theirs. Thank you for your time."

Jack stood with his arms crossed and mouth open as he watched the president's broadcast. When it had finished, he looked at Mavis and said, "Will you get a load of that lump of shit."

One of the capitol staff looked at Levi and said, "Mr. Walker, you didn't end Social Security and Medicare, did you? My mother is retired; she paid into those programs for forty years and depends on them as part of her income."

Another shouted, "The same goes for my parents."

Levi raised his hands and said, "Everyone, this is the first I have heard about these programs getting cut off. If they have been cut off, I assure you that it was not my doing."

From the back of the crowd was heard, "That doesn't change the fact that our elderly, poor and disabled need to be taken care of. What are we going to do?"

"Not panic for starters," Jack said.

"Right now we don't even know if that is true or just one of the president's lies," Mavis added.

"Congresswoman Young has a good point everyone," Levi said. "We don't know if this is true or not. Let's all get back to work; I need someone to find out for me if those things have been cut off or not. If so, I think a special session of the state legislature is needed so we can act."

As the crowd dispersed, Mavis walked over to Levi and said quietly, "Do you think the president has cut off all of those services?"

Levi shook his head and said, "I wouldn't be surprised if he did. Probably wants to use it to divide the people."

"Hindsight being twenty-twenty, we should have expected that and prepared for it," Jack added.

Levi and Mavis nodded in agreement.

"On a more positive note," Levi began, "There are several German firms who wish to begin manufacturing in Texas. They are importers to North America, and now that we are free from the US, they are very interested in setting up businesses in Texas."

"Something else that we may want to start looking for outside of our borders is food," Mavis said. "Yes, we are a major producer of cattle, and to a lesser extent poultry, but we don't produce everything people want in terms of food. And I have a suspicion that Conrad White is not going to allow trade across the US border."

"That's a good point, Mavis," Levi said. "Something I had not considered."

"Mexico," Jack said.

"What?" Levi asked.

"The United States imports more than twenty percent of its fruits and vegetables," Jack said. "Most comes from Central and South America. We can do the same; bring that stuff across the Mexican border; Conrad White can't stop that."

Levi nodded his head and said, "Good idea; I'll get some people on it right away."

At that moment, Levi's assistant, Sarah, ran up to the three of them.

"Mr. Walker," she said in between breaths, "It's true; the United States has blocked all Social Service payments to residents of Texas. It also looks like all monies to medical practices have been cut off, too."

"Damn socialized medicine," Jack said.

"Let's not panic," Levi said. "Sarah, call the legislature into emergency session. We've got work to do."

CHAPTER THIRTEEN

"Colonel, you had best wake up; I think we're gettin' close."

Kirk Dillon opened his eyes slowly. It was early morning, and the landscape was just beginning to brighten up. Looking to the East, he could see the faintest streaks of red and orange as the sun forced its way onto the horizon. They had driven through the night, and had rarely encountered another car along the Tennessee back roads. Around four am, Matt had taken over driving so that Kirk could get some sleep.

"Let me take a look at the directions," Kirk said groggily. He read over the notes given to him by Jason, and then looked at Matt and said, "Looks like we're not going into the town. The meeting place is an old abandoned farm to the north of the town. We need to watch for Willow Street."

"Alright," Matt replied. "Think we should wake Sebastian?"

Kirk twisted around to look behind him. The rear seat was still folded up, and he could see Sebastian asleep on the floor. "No, let him sleep a while longer," Kirk replied.

Kirk and Matt soon found Willow Street, and after a few minutes of twisting gravel roads, they arrived at the farm described in their notes. Situated near the road, the house must have at one time been a grand Victorian farmhouse, but years of neglect, abandonment and vandalism had left the home a mere shell of its former self.

"Not much to it," Matt mumbled.

Kirk looked up from his directions and said, "Follow the driveway; we are to meet at a barn at the back side of the property." Kirk turned his head toward Sebastian. "Sebastian! Wake up!" he said loudly.

Matt turned the Bronco onto the pothole strewn dirt driveway and began the slow trek toward the back of the property. After cresting a gradual rise in the landscape, they saw the barn at the bottom of a shallow valley. Matt piloted the Bronco toward the barn, going slowly to lessen the impact of the bone-jarring potholes.

Kirk turned to look in the cargo area of the Bronco; he could see that Sebastian was still asleep and had not moved. "Sebastian wake up!" he shouted.

"OK, OK…don't have to be so loud," Sebastian said

groggily.

"Circle around the barn before you stop," Kirk said. "I want to take a look around...make sure we don't get ambushed."

Matt nodded, and drove the Bronco around the barn. Other than a rusted out tractor and broken farm tools, there was nothing to be seen.

Satisfied, Kirk said, "Park on the back side of the barn; I want to make sure that if someone comes back down the driveway, they don't see the Bronco.

"Will do," Matt replied.

Matt parked, and the three men exited the Bronco. Kirk made sure his Colt .45 was still tucked in his waistband. He noticed that Matt was carrying his M16. He also noticed that Matt was limping as he walked.

"What's with the limp?" Kirk asked.

"The arthritis in my knees," Matt said painfully. "I'll be fine once I get movin' and get some meds in me."

Kirk smiled and said, "The wear and tear of Army life on the body."

Matt nodded and said, "You ain't kiddin'. After almost forty years of jumpin' out of airplanes and fightin' in the Middles East this body is plumb wore out. Can't read without my glasses, my knees are crippled, and the rest is personal."

Sebastian giggled and said, "I hope I never get as old as the two of you."

"Your time will come kid," Matt said dryly.

The three men entered the barn through a large sliding door at the rear of the Bronco. Inside, they found dozens of old farm tools…rakes, shovels, hoes, sickles…as well as a rusty plow. There was also an enormous hay baler, which at one time must have been painted green, but was now mostly rust covered.

Along the west wall of the barn, they found an old gas cook stove with a small table nearby. The table held cups, bowls, plates, and other kitchen items, while the stove held several pots and pans.

"Someone's been here recently," Matt said.

"How can you tell?" Sebastian asked.

Matt pointed to a small table. "See that cup? It's got fresh water in it." Matt reached down and put his finger in the cup. Looking at Kirk, he said, "still kinda cold. Whoever was here hasn't been gone long."

"I'm right up here," a voice called from in the loft of the barn.

Looking up toward the loft, Kirk could see a man and a woman with rifles pointed at Kirk, Matt and Sebastian.

"I'm guessing you're Kirk Dillon," the man said.

"That would be correct," Kirk said. "And you are?"

The man smiled and motioned for the woman to follow him down a ladder. Both slung their rifles over their shoulders and began down the ladder. Upon reaching the bottom, the man extended his hand to Kirk.

"I'm Timmy Robinson," he said and offered his hand to

Kirk. "This is my wife Jenna. Didn't expect to see you so soon."

"We drove through the night," Kirk said.

Timmy nodded and looked at Sebastian while saying, "And you must be Sebastian."

"That's me," Sebastian said with a grin.

Matt stepped forward and extended his hand toward Timmy. "Matt Pickett," is all he said.

Timmy smiled and said, "We heard about you through the organization. They say you don't take shit off anyone."

"Boy, that's the truth," Sebastian said with a grin.

"I especially like the story about you clubbing the union thug over the head with a shovel," Jenna said. "That takes guts what with how much pull the unions have and all."

"I didn't see any way out of it," Matt replied.

Timmy looked at Kirk and said, "We're using this place as a rally point for people heading to Texas. We'll be going with you as well as several others. Not sure how many others; it depends on how many make it here by sunset. We'll use the cover of darkness to slip past the national police and cross the Texas border."

"Sounds like a good plan," Kirk replied.

"How's your fuel supply?" Timmy asked.

"Pretty low," Kirk replied. "We need diesel."

"No problem," Timmy answered. "The organization has been stockpiling gas, diesel, and natural gas at this site for some time. We'll get you filled up, and then grab some breakfast."

"Breakfast sounds pretty good right about now," Matt said.

Jenna leaned her rifle against the old plow and then said, "Sebastian, why don't you help me with this old cook stove? We'll see if we can't get some breakfast going while Timmy and your Dad get the truck gassed up."

"I don't know," Sebastian said as he pointed at Kirk, "He's the chef in the family."

Kirk looked at Sebastian and said, "Just follow directions and you'll be fine."

By the time Kirk and Timmy returned from refueling the Bronco, Jenna and Sebastian had a pot of water and a coffee pot simmering away on the cook stove. As Kirk approached, Jenna looked up and said, "I hope you like either grits or oatmeal."

"Beggars can't be choosers," Kirk said.

Jenna smiled and said, "Not my favorite breakfast either, but dry oatmeal stores a long time."

Matt was sitting on an old rocking chair, rubbing his knee. He looked up and asked, "Regular or instant grits?"

"Regular," Jenna replied quickly. "Nobody from the South with a shred of decency would consider eating instant grits."

"Good." Matt smiled and leaned back in his chair.

Sebastian looked at Kirk and said, "What's a grit?"

"Think of it as corn based oatmeal," Kirk answered. Sebastian rolled his eyes and made a groaning sound.

"Watch it boy," Matt said. "Grits are a good Southern breakfast. Only thing better is a bowl of hominy."

Kirk wrinkled his nose slightly and said, "I draw the line at hominy. It's like eating wet, greasy popcorn."

Timmy laughed and said, "You're not from the South, are you?"

"Born and raised in a little town called New Richmond...about twenty five miles east of downtown Cincinnati," Kirk replied.

"He's a damn river rat," Matt said with a grin.

Jenna laughed and said, "Don't let them be too hard on you, Mr. Dillon. I was born in Chicago...but I moved here when I was a little girl. Dad came down here to start a business after the death of Detroit auto manufacturing."

"How did that work out for him?" Kirk asked.

"He managed to earn a living," Jenna said. "But finally, government regulations and taxes killed the business. Moved job to job after that. Anyway, that doesn't matter now. We're headed to Texas for a fresh start. Timmy and I are going to fulfill our dream of opening a roadside diner."

Matt leaned back in his chair and said, "I hear the restaurant business can be brutal."

Jenna smiled and said, "It is. But I think people will warm up to the idea of a diner that isn't owned by a big corporation...like the roadside diners of the early twentieth century."

"Well, I wish you all the luck in the world," Kirk said.

"Hey," Sebastian said loudly, "Reality check, here. We have to make it to Texas first, and who knows how many national police are between us and the Texas border."

Take it easy," Timmy said. "We've got a good plan, and the organization keeps me up to date with the movements of the national police."

"Don't pay him any mind," Matt said with a smile. "He's still pissed because we had to leave his little girlfriend back in Livingston." Matt and Kirk both began to laugh.

Sebastian's face began to turn red. "Well, I'm going to go back there one day to see her." Sebastian turned to Kirk and said, "While I'm thinking of it, can I use your cell to send her a text? Mine was taken away by the police."

"You know," Kirk said, "now that you mention it, I haven't even looked at my cell phone in a few days. I bet I have a million messages and texts."

"Bet that publisher of yours is tryin' to get in touch with you," Matt added.

"I'm sure he is," Kirk said as he pulled his cell phone from his pocket. "I didn't even have the damn thing turned on."

Kirk turned on his cell phone and watched the screen for messages to load. After a few minutes, he looked up and said, "One hundred sixty five messages. Thirty two from my publisher. Here is one from the Veteran's Administration…it says my VA benefits have been suspended because I am wanted for a treason. Another one from the Social Security Administration that says the same thing."

"Good thing you're loaded," Matt said with a grin.

Kirk laughed. "Three from that Writer's Union…it says they can take care of all of my legal troubles if I join the union. And here's one from that dirt bag Richard Boyle."

"What does it say?" Matt asked.

"You thought you could make it without union protection. You thought it was a good idea to stand against the union. Let's see how you like it when the government has your son…I warned you not to cross me. Want him back? Just join the union and I will have this all swept away." Kirk looked up from the phone and shook his head while saying, "So much for looking out for the common man."

"Those days ended for unions long ago," Timmy said. "Long before any of us were born."

Jenna nodded and said, "I can remember as a little girl in Chicago when the teacher's went on strike. I remember my Dad explaining to me that the teachers were mad because they wanted a huge raise and didn't want student performance to be part of their evaluation."

"I remember that," Matt said. "I was overseas at the time, but I remember reading about it. If I remember right, Chicago had a new Mayor who was pushin' for education reform. Teachers were ticked because they had been workin' five hour days and then were workin' seven hour days...for the same pay."

“I’d be mad if I had work those extra hours for free,” Sebastian said.

“Anyone would,” Kirk said. “However, it should have never gotten to the point of the teachers only working five hour work days. And as far as the evaluations...why shouldn’t someone be graded on their performance?” Kirk put his cell phone in his pocket and began to walk toward the barn door.

“Hey!” Matt exclaimed. “Where you goin’?”

“I’m going to call my publisher,” Kirk replied.

“What about breakfast?” Matt asked.

Kirk looked at Matt and said, “Don’t worry about me...this shouldn’t take long.”

Kirk walked out of the barn and sat beneath a large oak tree as he dialed the number to Byron Reynolds office. As usual, Jenny Thelon answered the phone. Before Kirk could say anything, she told him that Byron had been anxiously waiting for his call and she would put him through at once. After waiting on hold for just a few seconds, Kirk was greeted by Byron’s gravelly voice.

“Kirk!” he exclaimed, “What the Hell is going on? I have had the national police crawling all over this place. They say you, your son and that friend of yours are wanted for felonies.”

“Calm down, Byron,” Kirk said. “You remember that guy from the union…Richard Boyle?”

“Of course,” Byron said.

"He had the police abduct Sebastian and take him to Reynoldsburg reeducation camp."

"Son of a bitch," Byron exclaimed. "That explains it!"

Kirk continued, "Matt Pickett and I tracked down the police while they were en route to Reynoldsburg. We stopped them, got Sebastian, and have been on the run ever since."

Byron began to speak more slowly and calmly. "You should have come to me, Kirk. My boys down in legal could have fixed this up right away."

"I wouldn't want to get you involved," Kirk said.

"It would be the least I could do," Byron replied. "I could still get my legal team involved…it would probably be harder for them to work their magic at this point, though."

"At this point I'm not interested," Kirk said. "We are on our way to Texas to start a new life…should be there by tomorrow."

Byron whistled through the phone. "Texas may be your safest place to be with what is going on now. Anything I can do for you?

"Yes, you can," Kirk replied. Remember you offered to put my royalties in an offshore account? Do it. I have what is with me and nothing else."

"Done," Byron said. "I will do one other thing to help you out. I think your story could be used not only to get public support for you, but also further the cause of liberty."

"And how will you do that?" Kirk asked.

"By beating the government at its own game," he replied. "I will use the media against them."

"Don't do anything that would jeopardize you or your company," Kirk said.

"Not to worry, my boy," Byron replied. "I'm a soul of caution. You take care…give me a call when you get to Texas."

"You can count on it," Kirk replied.

Kirk placed his cell phone in his pocket and walked back to the barn. He entered to find everyone eating. Matt looked at Kirk as he approached.

"Colonel," Matt said, "maybe you can explain GI espresso to everyone. Nobody seems to believe me."

Kirk smiled and said, "Take two sugar packets and one instant coffee packet from your MRE. Tear open the packets and dump them in your mouth, followed by a big swig of water."

"That's nasty," Sebastian said.

Matt chuckled and said, "It ain't supposed to taste good. It's an instant caffeine and sugar buzz. It'll keep you on your feet when you need a little somethin' to keep you goin'."

Kirk looked at Jenna and said, "Where's a good place around here to get some sleep? I can't speak for Sebastian or Matt, but I'm going to get some rest before we move out tonight."

Jenna pointed up to a loft area of the barn and said, "Up there. There are a few sleeping bags in the loft. You and your friends are welcome to use them."

"Thank you," Kirk said. He turned to Sebastian and said, "I'm going to get some sleep. It would be smart if you did the same."

"Okay," Sebastian replied with a mouth full of oatmeal.

Kirk began the climb up the ladder to the loft. He thought about how far they'd had to come…and how far yet to go to make it to the Texas border. Reaching the loft, he found several old sleeping bags laid out on the wooden floor. Laying down on one of the bags, he noticed the thin padding of the bag did little to soften the hard wooden floor. He ignored how uncomfortable it was; he was too exhausted to care.

Jack Spearman sat at his desk in his new office in the State Capitol. His staff had worked late into the night to get his office moved, and as always, they had come through for him. While they were still busily setting up the staff area, his office was complete. He rubbed his hand across the worn oak finish of the desk. This desk had been a gift from his parents when he started his own company, and he had refused to let it go even after all these years.

He thought back to all of the adversity he had faced trying to start his own business. The government regulations, bureaucrats who didn't want to see him compete with their favorite business, the mega oil corporations who wanted him to fail…at times, they had seemed impassable obstacles. He had vowed long ago that if it were in his power, he would make sure nobody had to go through what he had been through…starting and running the business were hard enough.

Like his staff, Jack had been working late into the night, but for different reasons. He had been trying to come up with solutions to the dual dilemmas of funding retirement plans and medical care. While Jack was sure that free market solutions were the best course of action, he was unsure of how to implement those solutions.

What had made the research especially difficult was the FCC banning of certain internet content. For over thirty years, the FCC had had the authority to ban web content. One of the earliest things to be banned was any discussions of free market solutions to rising health costs, as the government was pushing for socialized medicine. So Jack had to resort to sources outside of the United States for reference. Unfortunately, most of Europe and Asia had socialized medicine, so finding information in those countries was difficult, as well.

Finally, Jack found a few websites that had information about free market principals, and he found information on healthcare in the early twentieth century. This had given him the information he needed, and he was presently pouring over the historical text.

"Mr. Spearman..."

Jack looked up to see a man standing in the open doorway to his office. Appearing to be in his early thirties, the man was tall and lean with close cropped brown hair. He wore a gray and white pinstripe suit and carried a small briefcase.

"Mr. Spearman," the man continued with a smile, "My name is Tristan Schmidt, and I represent Energy International."

"I know who you are," Jack said quickly. "I remember you from some of my company's negotiations over drilling contracts. I'm kinda busy, so what can I do for you?"

Tristan continued smiling and said, "There are several states that are unhappy with the United States Federal Government. We know that a few days ago, you attended a meeting of those states, and while Texas and Alaska are the only states to leave the US so far, we know there will be, most likely, more to come."

Jack leaned back in his chair and put his hands behind his head. "You seem to know a lot," he said.

As he sat down in the chair across from Jack, Tristan continued to speak. "We also know that most or all of these states intend to form a new nation."

"That remains to be seen," Jack replied. "What's your point?"

"Energy," Tristan replied. "To be a productive nation, a plentiful, affordable supply of energy is needed. Without it, industry will struggle, services struggle…everything revolves around the supply of energy."

"I agree," Jack said.

"We know that you will, most likely, be the representative from the state of Texas to the convention to form the new nation. We believe this a smart move on the part of Texas government. You are well known not only in Texas but throughout the nation; because of this, your opinion will hold much weight when the new nation is formed. What we wish is for you to push for our corporation to become the exclusive energy supplier for the new nation. As we are invested in all types of energy production…wind, solar, oil, gas, nuclear…we can provide whatever works best for each region. And we can provide it at the best price. In exchange for you effort, we are prepared to offer you a great compensation package."

"Go on," Jack said slowly.

Tristan smiled again and continued. "We will use your company exclusively throughout North America for our drilling needs. You will also be given a seat on the board of directors."

"I can see where a man would be awfully tempted by that offer," Jack said.

"Then we have your support ?" Tristan said as he began to stand. "I knew we could count on you. You are, after all, a fellow oil man."

Jack quickly leapt to his feet. "HELL NO YOU CAN'T COUNT ON ME!" he bellowed. Pointing his index finger at Tristan, Jack continued in a loud, thunderous voice. "You are exactly what we are trying to get away from. This crony capitalism shit is givin' me a case of the redass and it has to stop!"

As Tristan's smile disappeared, his face became pale and gray. "I don't understand, Mr. Spearman. This is your opportunity to provide an endless supply of energy for not only Texas, but the whole of the new nation."

"I don't like puttin' all of my eggs in one basket," Jack said, "and giving you a monopoly on the energy market does just that. Not only do I believe that a free market can better provide all of the energy we will need, it will provide it at a much better price than you will."

"To that end, you are totally incorrect, Mr. Spearman," Tristan said. "Our company has the most state of the art equipment as well as the most highly trained employees, and by sheer economics of scale we can offer energy prices that nobody can compete with."

"Just because you can doesn't mean you will," Jack replied. "With no competition, you will have no reason to offer the lowest price. This is why monopolies don't work, and why it doesn't work when the government is the only rodeo in town. You say you can offer the best prices? Fine. If that's true, then you will have nothing to worry about from the competition. But I don't think that's the case or you wouldn't be here. You are just like every other crony capitalist…just lookin' for the government to give you a monopoly. Well, you won't get it from me. I have fought this shit my entire life, and I am not about to stop now."

Tristan stared Jack directly in the eyes and said, "You won't accept our offer? Not a problem. There are thirty one members of the Texas Senate and one hundred fifty in the House of Representatives. We will find those that we need within those bodies, and we will be sure that someone who fulfills our wishes will be the person from Texas who is the representative to the new government. You stupid cowboys and your sense of pride…we would have thought you of all people would understand the power of money."

"I understand fully the pride someone feels when they earn it themselves," Jack said. "And it doesn't matter if that person is poor or rich, you will respect it if you earn it. Your problem is that you have not earned the money so you don't have respect for it."

"Touching," Tristan said with a sneer.

Jack crossed his arms and said, "Mister, you are about as welcome as a skunk at a lawn party. Get out of my office and never show your damn face here again, if you know what's good for you."

Tristan turned and walked out of Jack's office without another word. Jack grabbed the computer tablet he had been working with and headed out of his office. As he entered the outer office, he encountered Mavis Young.

"Jack," she said, "I was just on my way to see you about the medical and retirement research."

"That will have to wait," Jack said. "Come take a walk with me; I've got to see Levi."

Mavis' eyes widened. "Why? What's wrong?"

Jack opened the door of the outer office and said "I'll explain on the way…something that may shape the future of Texas."

CHAPTER FOURTEEN

Kirk Dillon awoke to the smell of musty sleeping bags and the pain of a sore back. He sat up stiffly and looked around. On a nearby sleeping bag, Matt was fast asleep with his M-16 cradled in his right arm, just the way he used to sleep while in the field during the Middle East wars. "*Old habits die hard,*" Kirk thought.

Looking down from the loft, Kirk could see Sebastian talking with Jenna; Timmy was nowhere to be seen. Kirk straightened himself the best he could, and then proceeded down the ladder from the loft. Upon reaching ground level, Kirk once again tried to stretch his aching back; Jenna and

Sebastian both watched him with interest .

“Having problems?” Sebastian said with amusement.

“I’m getting to old for this shit,” Kirk said as he stretched. “The spirit is willing, but the body can’t take sleeping on the hard ground anymore.”

“You were in a sleeping bag,” Sebastian said.

“That sleeping bag didn’t offer a lot of protection from the wooden floor of that loft,” Kirk said. “Did you get any sleep?”

“Some,” Sebastian said. “But I slept most of the night last night.”

“Yeah, I know,” Kirk said. “From the front seat I could hear you snoring.”

“I don’t snore,” Sebastian protested.

“I’ve heard that before, too,” Kirk chuckled.

“Sebastian was just telling me about the girl he met in Livingston,” Jenna said.

“She helped us get through the town without getting caught by the National Police,” Kirk said.

“I think Sebastian was interested in her for reasons other than her helping,” Jenna said with a smile.

Kirk laughed and said, “Well, she was a hottie, no doubt about that. I can see why he would have been attracted.”

“I wish you wouldn’t use that word,” Sebastian said.

"What word?" Kirk asked.

"Hottie," Sebastian said. "They stopped using that word about five hundred years ago."

Jenna laughed; Kirk said, "Well, I guess I didn't get the memo on that one."

Just then, Timmy entered the barn. Looking at Kirk, he said, "Get any rest?"

"Some," Kirk replied. "My body just can't take sleeping on hard surfaces anymore."

"I've never been able to do it," Timmy said. Pointing at Jenna, he said, "That's the person who likes to sleep on hard ground. Hell, our bed back home was as hard as a rock."

"I've always liked a firm mattress," Jenna said and Timmy laughed.

"So when do we head for the border?" Kirk inquired.

"In a few hours," Timmy said. "I want to wait until after sundown; the dark should give us an edge. And if any more travelers show up between now and then, we can all go together."

"That's exactly what we wanted to hear," a voice said.

Kirk looked toward the sound of the voice and saw four national police officers, pistols drawn, rushing into the barn through the large door. Kirk began to reach for the pistol tucked in his belt.

"Don't even think about it old man," one of the officers said to Kirk.

"Everyone put their hands on top of their heads," another officer ordered.

One of the officers looked at Kirk and said," You're Kirk Dillon, aren't you?"

"Yes, I am," Kirk replied.

"The boy must be his son," an officer said. He looked to another officer and said, "Phone back to district HQ and let them know we not only captured people at the suspected Sons of Liberty hideout, but two of them are Kirk Dillon and his son."

"Yes, sir."

The officer looked back at Kirk and said, "You have created a major headache for the US Government but it looks like you're finally going to pay."

"*I* created a major headache!" Kirk exclaimed. "How about the government abducting my son because I refused to join a union?"

"Everything the government does is for our benefit," the officer said. "Otherwise, the government wouldn't do it. That's why the government does everything it does…it's all for our benefit. The president has said so himself."

"He got promoted because of loyalty, not brains," Timmy said.

"Keep your mouth shut," an officer said to Timmy.

"I guess the truth hurts," Timmy said with a grin.

"What I want to know," Kirk said, "is how you managed to

track us here?"

"Your son is carrying an RFID chip in his body," one of the officers said.

"We thought we destroyed it," Kirk said.

'No," the officer replied."You must have destroyed the one he was implanted with at birth. Starting a few weeks ago, the police department began tagging everyone it incarcerates with RFID chips; your son was carrying two chips."

Kirk looked at Sebastian and said, "Why didn't you tell me?"

"I didn't know," Sebastian said.

"He wouldn't have known," the officer said. "The doctor knocks people out before he implants, and he does it in the middle of the back so it's difficult to reach the area."

"I see," Kirk said.

"What I want to know," the officer said, "is why you did what you did? I have read all of your books…you were an American hero. Why would you turn your back on your country?"

"Nobody loves the idea of America more than me," Kirk said. "But that idea…that dream of the founders…it has been lost. The founding fathers created a nation of the people, by the people, and for the people. A place where a man could succeed or fail on his own. That nation no longer exists; it has been replaced by a tyranny."

"You lie!" the officer bellowed. "Every law President White has created has been for us, the people."

Kirk shook his head and said, "If things were working the way they should, the president wouldn't be creating laws…that's the job of Congress."

"No!" the officer shouted. "The president had to do things…Congress wouldn't act to help the people…the president had to help us."

Kirk looked the young officer in the eyes and said, "Our Federal Government was intended to be very limited. It is there for national defense, to settle disputes between the states, and not much else. The United States made it for over one hundred years by doing just that. In fact, until 1913, we didn't have a federal income tax, and yet we still had roads, schools, railroads, and a military. You need to ask yourself why the Federal Government needs to take so much out of the pockets of its citizens and be involved in every aspect of their daily lives."

"Enough talking," another officer said. "Handcuff these detainees, and take them to the van. We will set up an outpost here to try to nab as many of the traitors as possible."

An officer walked toward Timmy and ordered him to place his hands behind his back. The order was obeyed quickly, but as the officer reached for his handcuffs, Timmy pulled a short knife from the small of his back. Timmy lunged and slashed and the left side of the officer's neck. The blade must have struck an artery, as blood began to spurt vigorously with every beat of the officer's heart. The officer, stunned at what had just happened, tried to reach for the wound, but instead fell to the ground.

One of the other officers fired his pistol at Timmy, striking him in the center of the chest. Jenna screamed as blood began to well from the hole in Timmy's chest. His face turned an eerie blueish-white, and his body began to tremble. As he collapsed to his knees, he reached for the wound in his chest, feebly trying to cover the gaping hole. Jenna tried to run to Timmy, but was held back by a pale faced officer.

Kirk took advantage of the moment of confusion and took a swing at the officer closest to him. As fist impacted nose, the officer fell back, momentarily stunned. Pressing his advantage, Kirk kicked the man in the crotch and watched as he fell to the floor. Kirk was just about to reach for his pistol when heard two gunshots ring out from the loft of the barn. Looking up, he could see Matt with his M-16 at his shoulder. Kirk then turned to look at the officers; two of them were lying dead on the floor, each with a single bullet hole through the head. The officer who had been slashed by Timmy was now motionless and lying in a pool of crimson blood; most likely he had bled to death. Only the officer who Kirk had hit and kicked remained alive.

Both Kirk and Jenna rushed forward toward Timmy. Kirk rolled him over on his back and checked for a pulse on his neck; there was none

"He's gone, Jenna," Kirk said. "There's nothing that we can do."

Jenna nodded her head as tears rolled down her cheeks. She began to cry in earnest, and leaned over Timmy's body. Kirk pulled his pistol from his belt and turned to the one remaining officer, who was lying on his backside, clutching his crotch.

"Get up," Kirk ordered.

Kirk held his pistol at the ready as the officer slowly stood.

By this time, Matt had made his way down the loft ladder and was standing at Kirk's side.

"The gunshot woke me up," Matt said. He walked over to Jenna, who was still crying over Timmy's body. He knelt down on one knee and said, "Ma'am, I'm sorry I couldn't have saved Timmy. Had I been awake a bit sooner, I might have been able to save him."

Jenna turned and faced Matt. Her chin trembled as tears ran down her cheeks from swollen, bloodshot eyes."It wasn't your fault. Timmy always said that he would go out with his boots on; that he would rather die for what he believed in than live as a slave to the government. I always thought they were nice words…never thought about what that really meant."

"Ma'am," Matt said, "I served in and out of combat for over thirty years and have seen few who had a passion for their beliefs like Timmy. I am proud to have known him, even for the short time that it was."

"Thank you," Jenna said. She wiped the tears from her face with the sleeve of her shirt, and then reached into her pocket and pulled out her cell phone. "Need to let the Sons of Liberty know that they need a new rally point. It's not safe here anymore."

Matt stood and looked toward Kirk. While Matt had been talking to Jenna, Kirk had stripped the remaining officer of his body armor and ammunition belt, as well as his weapon. Kirk was now handcuffing the officer to one of the posts supporting the barn.

"You will just leave me here like this," the wide eyed officer said.

"I heard you radio your division HQ for backup," Kirk responded. "My guess is they will be here in a short while. You can hook up with them when they show up."

"Right or wrong, it's my duty to follow orders," the officer said.

"Maybe that's the problem," Kirk replied. "You and too many people in this country have stopped thinking about what is right and wrong."

Jenna walked up to Kirk and said, "Sons of Liberty know this place has been discovered. They will find a new rally point. A group is on its way here now; some will go with you to Texas, the others will help me with Timmy."

"Are you giving up on going to Texas?" Kirk asked.

"I don't know," Jenna said. "There will be a delay at least. I will see to it that Timmy is buried, and I must talk with his family. After that…I don't know. It's too soon."

Kirk nodded. He was about to speak when he heard the sound of vehicles outside of the barn. Sebastian was already running toward the barn door.

"An old car and truck," Sebastian said. "Neither is a police van."

Matt checked the magazine in his rifle and then looked at Sebastian and said, "Can't be too careful; let them come to us."

Sebastian backed up from the barn door as Matt knelt down on one knee and aimed his M-16 at the barn door. Kirk flicked off the pistol's safety and took aim at the barn door.

From outside of the barn, you could hear the sound of engines shutting off, and of car doors opening and closing.

"Jenna!" a voice call from outside.

"Inside the barn," Jenna shouted nervously.

Through the barn door strode six individuals who were certainly not police. There were four men and two women; all had a ragged look, and all were armed. Kirk and Matt remained with their weapons at the ready, but Jenna rushed forward toward one of the women.

"Jessica," Jenna said, "I'm so glad to see you."

The two women embraced as Jessica said, "We just heard about Timmy. Can't tell you how sorry I am, Jen."

"Thank you," Jenna replied.

Kirk lowered his pistol and said to Jenna, "These are friends of yours?"

"Yes," she replied. "For many years."

Kirk looked at Matt, who nodded and then lowered his weapon. Walking toward the closest of the group, Kirk held out his hand and said, "I'm Kirk Dillon."

"We know who you are, Mr. Dillon," one of the men said in a strong southern accent as he shook hands with Kirk. "I'm Elliot Rayburn. Your story's been all over the internet, radio, and TV; you're getting to be somethin' of a national hero."

"I can't believe the government is allowing my story to be told," Kirk replied somewhat astonished. "I would have thought that some spin would be put on it to make it sound like I'm some cruel, heartless terrorist."

"Sons of Liberty must have hacked the FCC again," Elliot said, "because all of the sources are saying they got the OK from the FCC to run the story, and it looks like your book publisher is pushing the story, too."

Kirk smiled and said, "That would be Byron Reynolds' doing. He said he would use the media against the government."

"Looks like he's doin' a good job of it," Elliot said. "More important is we gots to move quick." With this, he pointed to another of the group. "Danny and I will be goin' with you to Texas; the rest of 'em 'll be helpin' Jenna take care a' Timmy. You fueled up?"

"Yes," Kirk replied. "Timmy helped me fuel this morning."

"Then we had best get movin'," Elliot said.

As Kirk, Matt and Sebastian headed toward the barn door, each stopped to say goodbye to Jenna, who in turn told them not to worry about her, and that they should hurry. When they emerged from the barn, Kirk noticed the sun far in the west. He pulled his cell phone from his pocket to check the time. It was nearly six in the evening; much later than he'd thought. At this time of the year, it wouldn't be much longer before the sun set.

Elliot ran his hand over the hood of the Bronco and said, "What year is that Bronco?"

"1985," Kirk replied. "It took me seven years to restore it."

"Very nice," Elliot said as he rubbed his hand over the

Bronco's fender. "What's under the hood?"

"Five liter Cummins," Kirk replied. "Not sure of the year, but I know it is earlier than 2025."

"Nice," Elliot said. He pointed to an old, rusty Mustang sitting near Kirk's Bronco. "We call her the rustang. She looks old and beat up…just the way we like it. But under the hood, she's a beast."

"What year is it?" Kirk asked.

Elliot smiled and said, "2013 boss Mustang. Four hundred forty four horsepower from the factory."

"Sweet ride," Kirk said.

"Hey!" Matt yelled."You two can drool over cars some other time. We've got to move."

"He's right," Elliot said. "Danny and I will be in the rustang, you three in the Bronco. Here is an ol' time walkie-talkie so we can talk back and forth when drivin'. The rustang will take the lead, you all follow. "

"Sounds like a plan," Kirk said as he climbed into the driver's seat of the Bronco. He looked at Matt, who was already in the passenger's seat, and then back at Sebastian, who was sitting on the floor in the back.

"Where's the back seat?" Sebastian asked.

"Timmy and I took it out when we fueled up," Kirk replied. "We thought it would give more room in the back in case we need an area to shoot from."

"I guess you guys didn't care that I have no place to sit,"

Sebastian said angrily.

"You're tough," Kirk said with a smile.

Sebastian rolled his eyes and said, "Whatever."

"Enough talk," Matt said. "Let's get this bucket of bolts moving."

"Watch what you say, sergeant," Kirk said as he turned the ignition key. The engine roared to life, and Kirk shifted into first gear. "We're off," he said.

As the Bronco began to pull forward, the rustang's engine revved, and Elliot pulled out in front, leading the way down the driveway of the old farm. As they pulled onto the main road, Kirk couldn't help but feel a sense of relief. They were less than a day away from the Texas border, and it felt as if they couldn't be stopped.

"*Don't get cocky*," Kirk said to himself. "*That's when mistakes are made.*"

Levi James Walker was walking as fast as he could through the Texas Capitol extension building, on his way to the auditorium. Jack Spearman had come to him to tell the story of bribery from Energy International. After checking with his contacts within the Sons of Liberty, Levi had found that many members of both the Texas House and Senate had been approached, as well. Levi decided to try and put a stop to Energy International's bribery before it started, and had called for a meeting of the entire state legislature.

The lieutenant governor had protested, saying that there was not a precedent for the governor to address the legislature. Levi had ignored her arguments, saying that the governor had the right to address any group he wished.

Arriving at the entrance to the auditorium, Jack found both Mavis Young and Jack Spearman.

"Are we ready?" Levi asked.

"Yes, Levi," Mavis replied. "Even with such a short notice, we managed to get every member of the legislature here."

"And the media?" Levi asked.

"Like ticks on a hound," Jack said with a smile. "Believe me, the entire state of Texas is gonna know what you say here today...probably the rest of the world, too."

Levi smiled and said, "That's just what I want. Thanks for the help."

Jack put his hands in his pockets and said, "What that company is tryin' to do rubs me raw. A big company already has an advantage because of its size. No reason to legislate a monopoly."

Mavis placed her hands on her hips and said, "With the regulations of the United States Government out of the way, I'm sure they were looking at Texas as a potential goldmine, and they wanted it all for themselves."

"I'm sure of it, as well," Levi replied.

One of the doors to the auditorium opened, and out walked Jayden McCoy, the lieutenant governor. She looked at Levi and said, "Levi, I know your intentions are good, but I'm going to ask you again not to do this. Don't get involved in the legislature's business…let them do their work and you do yours. I am the President of the State Senate; I can push through your legislation without you overstepping you powers as governor."

Levi shook his head and said, "Jayden, I told you before I am just giving a speech, and I can give a speech to any group I like."

"But you're using your position as governor to force people to come to your speech," Jayden protested.

"If you look at the emails and text messages I sent out, they were requests, not demands," Levi replied. "Everyone here is attending by free will. Anyone who wants to leave can do so; I won't stop them."

"I still think you should call this off," Jayden replied.

"I'm not, so get over it," Levi said quickly.

Jayden sighed quickly and said, "Have it your way."

"I plan to," Levi replied. "Now, let's get in there and get this show on the road."

Levi pushed his way through the doors into the auditorium. The room was filled with the representatives and senators of the state of Texas; some were standing, talking to each other. Others were seated. As Levi entered the room, someone shouted, "Ladies and gentlemen, the governor of the great state of Texas!"

Everyone turned their attention to the rear of the room where Levi had just entered and began to applaud. Levi smiled, and without saying a word, walked quickly to the podium set up on the stage. Levi raised his hands above his head, and the deafening applause quickly subsided.

"Fellow Texans, thank you for coming today on a matter of great importance. So important, in fact, that I have asked members of the local media to come here today and broadcast what will be said. I believe that it is important not only for our fellow Texans to hear what will be said, but for the rest of the world to hear, as well.

"We have all witnessed the events of the past few days, and I believe all of us hope for a bright future for Texas. We are presented with a unique opportunity...the privilege of setting the course of Texas politics for generations to come. Now I must ask you...what will that course be?

"Both Texas and the United States were founded on a single, simple principle. That a man could live how he wants, where he wants, and succeed or fail of his own accord. That dream was lost long ago in the United States, when the forces of socialism decided to redistribute wealth, as well as create a nanny state that would cater to every special interest group. When we realized the dream had been lost, we left the United States; it is essential that we keep that dream alive here in Texas.

"How do we keep that dream alive? We must make sure that our laws do not inhibit business competition. Competition is a must; it keeps businesses, both big and small, lean and trim, while at the same time keeping prices low for the consumer. Without competition, business becomes bloated and slothful; prices rise, and the consumer pays the price.

"It has come to my attention that a certain energy corporation has petitioned many members of the Texas

Legislature to pass a law making it the only energy provider in the state. They claim they can provide all of the energy Texas will ever want, and all at the right price. Their claims may or may not be true, but that is beside the point. Do we want to legislate a monopoly? Have we learned nothing from history?

"It does not matter if we are talking about the East India Trading Company of the seventeenth and eighteenth centuries, the insurance industry of the late twentieth century, or Energy International today. When business and government get in bed together, it is not good. It is not good for the consumer; it is not good for other businesses. Without competition, the monopoly has no reason to keep prices low. Without competition, the monopoly has no reason to innovate. If they are barred from the marketplace, how will innovators create their new products? What would have happened in the twentieth century if IBM had a monopoly and had blocked all competition?

"There is only one thing that happens when you have a monopoly. Wealth is concentrated in the hands of a few, and with all government mandated monopolies, those few who hold the wealth do not hold it because they were smarter businessmen, or because they had a better product. No, they have all of the wealth because the government mandated it. Let me say that again...the government mandated it. No matter if the intentions were noble or not, the government authorized monopoly will concentrate wealth in the hands of the few because the government mandated it.

"There will be a bill introduced for debate in the Texas Legislature known as the Spearman-Young Bill. Named after the two individuals who wrote it, the bill makes some simple rules. It will be illegal for the legislature to pass laws that create a barrier to entry to a marketplace. Secondly, it requires the state to treat all businesses equally; there can be no favoritism, no special deals or carve outs for anyone's pet company, industry, or project. I am requesting that this bill be debated and voted on as soon as possible.

"Texans, it has been a privilege to be the governor of this great state through these times. We are witnessing a rebirth...a return to the Texas of old. Let us not make the same mistake that our forbearers made. Let us always choose the freedom to choose. Thank you."

As Levi put his hands back in his pocket, members of the audience began to applaud. The applause grew in strength and intensity, as members began to stand and applaud vigorously. Soon, the sound was deafening. Levi looked to the back of the room; Mavis and Jack were standing with beaming faces. Levi exited the podium, and intended to leave the room, but was stopped by a mob rushing forward to shake his hand.

"Well done."

"Just what we wanted to hear."

"This should have been done a long time ago."

"You have secured a great start for the new Texas."

Mavis turned to Jack and said, "What do you think, Blackjack? Will the bill get ratified by the house and senate?"

Jack looked at Mavis and said, "Little Sister, we've done all we can. Levi made a fine speech, and I hope the coverage of this will shame anyone who considered taking the bribe."

"I guess so," Mavis said.

Jack nodded his head and said, "Let's go; this is all in God's hands now."

CHAPTER FIFTEEN

Kirk was worried; the needle of the fuel gauge was sitting on E, and he had already used the extra can of diesel that he kept mounted to the spare tire carrier. While their drive time was less than an hour from the Texas border, it would be meaningless if they ran out of fuel. Kirk looked toward the passenger seat where Matt sat, rubbing his left knee.

"Arthritis bothering you again?" Kirk asked.

Matt grimaced as he rubbed his knee. "No, sir. The word is still. I ran out of my arthritis meds yesterday, and I'm tryin' to make do with ibuprofen. It just ain't cuttin' it."

"What do you take for the arthritis?" Kirk asked.

"Metho-somethin' or other…I can't say it," Matt replied. "All I know is I have to take folic acid with it, and it works. That's enough for me."

"It's hell getting old," Kirk said with a smile.

"It ain't the years," Matt said, "It's the wear and tear." Matt pointed to his knee and said, "This is the price I pay for thirty years on jump status."

"Jumping out of airplanes does take its toll on you," Kirk commented.

"You bet," Matt replied. He smiled and then said, "But I wouldn't have given it up for the world."

"Matt," Kirk said, "We are almost out of fuel. Call Elliot on the walkie-talkie and tell him we need to refuel ASAP."

"Yes, sir," Matt replied. He pressed the talk button on the walkie-talkie and began to speak. "Elliot, we need to refuel ASAP. Over."

The walkie-talkie crackled to life and Elliot's muffled voice replied, "We're low, too. Sit tight; there's a fuelin' station just a few miles up the road."

Matt looked at Kirk and said, "You hear that?"

"Yes," Kirk replied. "Hopefully, we don't encounter any police."

Through the course of the night, they had managed to avoid several police patrols, due in no small part to the messages Elliot received from the Sons of Liberty. Kirk was amazed at how they always seemed to know the whereabouts of the national police.

"No wonder they have never been caught," Kirk thought. He made a mental note to ask Elliot how the Sons of Liberty got their intelligence on the national police.

Gazing into his rear view mirror, Kirk could see Sebastian sleeping spread eagle on the floor in the rear cargo area of the Bronco. "Sebastian!" Kirk shouted, "Wake up; we're about to stop and refuel. I need you awake and alert."

Cracking open eyes still swollen with sleep, Sebastian began to groggily fumble around, finally rolling onto his belly. "Five more minutes," he mumbled as his eyes once again went closed.

Matt picked up a rifle magazine and threw it at Sebastian. The magazine hit him in the center of the forehead, causing him to scream and jump. His jump was a little to forceful, causing him to hit his head on the fiberglass ceiling of the Bronco. Falling back to the floor and clutching his head, Sebastian looked at Matt and shouted, "Son of a bitch! Why did you do that?"

Matt's eyes narrowed, and then he said, "When your Dad tells you to do somethin', he means now. Get your ass in gear, boy."

Kirk laughed and then returned his attention to the road. Peering into the distance through the hazy, early morning light, Kirk could just make out the glowing green sign of a gas station a mile ahead. "Looks like we have a gas station coming up," Kirk said with a sigh of relief.

"Let's hope they have diesel," Matt added.

"Hurry," Sebastian said, "I have to race like a piss horse."

Kirk looked at Matt and said, "You been teaching his stuff like that?"

"No, sir," Matt said as he struggled to suppress a laugh.

"Bullshit," Kirk said. "He even says it wrong…just like you."

The walkie talkie once again came to life with Elliot's voice. "Here's the fuelin' station. We'll circle around once to see if we got any police."

Matt pressed the talk button on the walkie-talkie and said, "Affirmative. We'll hold back and keep you covered in case of police. Over."

The Mustang, which up to this point had been only slightly ahead of the Bronco, pulled ahead toward the gas station. It was quiet for a few moments, and then the walkie-talkie came to life again.

"Can you make it another twenty miles?" Elliot's voice said.

Matt looked at Kirk, who shook his head no."Not a chance," Kirk said. "Five, maybe ten miles is it."

Matt pressed the button on walkie-talkie and then said, "We have to stop…can't make it. Over."

"That's a big ten-four," Elliot said. "We got two police here; both in the store. I say we get gas and hope they don't see us."

Matt looked at Kirk and said, "What do you think Colonel?"

"I don't see any alternative," Kirk replied. "We can't make it to another gas station or the border. We have to refuel."

Matt nodded and pressed the talk button. "Let's do this. Over."

"Pull in and start fuelin'," Elliot said. "The row on the far left has a diesel pump. We'll be right next to you. Danny's gonna keep an eye on the cops while I gas up."

"Affirmative. Over," Matt said into the handset. Matt placed the walkie-talkie on the dash and picked up his M-16. He pressed the magazine release, checked the ammo level, and then popped the magazine back into the rifle.

"Keep that out of site unless we're recognized," Kirk said. "If we're lucky, we won't be recognized."

"Yes, sir," Matt replied.

Kirk slowed as he approached the gas station, which was on the left hand side of the street. As the Bronco pulled off the street and into the gas station parking lot, Kirk could see Elliot fueling the Mustang, with Danny leaning on the passenger's side of the car, watching the station store. Kirk was just about to pull up next to the Mustang, when the two police officers rushed out of the store, guns drawn. One of the officers fired his pistol, hitting Danny in the abdominal area. Danny doubled over and collapsed next to the Mustang as Elliot let go of the gas pump handle and raised his hands over his head.

Before Kirk could say or do anything, Matt had his M-16 at his shoulder, and fired a series of shots. One of the officers hit the ground after two bullets struck him in the chest; the other officer was hit in the neck. Grasping the gash in his neck which was now spurting blood with every beat of his heart, the officer dropped his handgun and screamed in pain. The hand on his neck was not enough to stop or slow the pumping of blood and as the cop became bathed in red crimson fluid, he began to stagger and lurch about. In seconds, he too, dropped to the ground.

Kirk pulled the Bronco next to Elliot's Mustang; Matt, M-16 in his left hand, leapt out before the vehicle had come to a complete stop. Looking toward Elliot, he shouted, "You hit?"

"I'm fine," Elliot said. "But I think Danny's dead."

Matt walked towards Danny's body and knelt down on one knee. Pressing his middle and index fingers against Danny's neck, he felt for the faintest of heartbeats.

Looking up at Elliot, Matt said, "He's gone."

Matt then checked the two police officers as well. "They're dead, too."

While Matt was checking the bodies, Kirk had jumped out of the Bronco and drawn his pistol."Sebastian!" He shouted. "Start fueling the Bronco! Matt and I will cover you."

"Got it!" Sebastian yelled. He opened the rear of the Bronco and climbed out. He immediately began looking for the diesel pump. "Methanol, unleaded, super…where's the diesel?"

"To your right," Kirk shouted.

Sebastian looked to his right and found the diesel pump."Dad! It says pay before pumping!"

"Damn it!" Kirk shouted. He looked at Matt and said,

“Cover me. I’m going in to pay!”

Matt’s eyes grew wide and he shouted, “You’re gonna WHAT?”

Kirk ran into the store with his gun drawn. Customers inside the store backed away from Kirk, some gasped or screamed. At the checkout counter was a young man of perhaps twenty-two years of age. His eyes were wide, skin pale and sweat was running down his forehead.

Kirk walked up to him and tossed several bills down on the counter in front of him.“Turn on pump four,” Kirk said calmly. “Keep whatever change is left for yourself…sorry for the inconvenience.” Kirk then noticed the people in the store watching him. “My friends and I are being hunted by the government and are heading to Texas for freedom.”

An older woman stepped forward and said nervously, “Why are you wanted?”

Kirk looked at her and said, “Because I wouldn’t let them take my son when I refused to join a union.” Kirk began to back his way toward the door.

“Who are you mister?” a teenager asked.

“I’m Kirk Dillon,” Kirk said as he slid out the door of the store.

As he exited the store, Kirk could see Matt at the passenger door of the Bronco. He looked up; Kirk could see he had several rifle magazines in his hand.

“Colonel,” Matt said quickly, “We got two police vans comin’. We gotta slow ‘em down to give Sebastian and Elliot more time to refuel."

"Got it," Kirk said.

"Mr. Dillon," Elliot said, "Take Danny's rifle…it's on the front passenger seat."

Kirk leaned in the window of the rusty, weather-beaten Mustang. On the passenger seat, he found an AK-47. As he picked up the rifle, Kirk noticed three magazines lying beneath it; he took those, as well. Kirk stepped back from the Mustang and said to Elliot, "Thanks. Get out of here as soon as you're refueled." Elliot nodded, and Kirk ran to catch up with Matt.

Matt had knelt down behind one of the concrete barriers near the road. Kirk did the same, placing himself about fifteen feet away from Matt. Kirk pulled back the charging handle of the rifle, checking to make sure the magazine was full. Satisfied, Kirk let the charging handle go, which flew forward with a clicking sound. Looking down the road, Kirk could see the police vans about five hundred yards off.

"How did you know they were coming?" Kirk asked Matt.

"Elliot got a text," Matt replied. "Sons of Liberty always seem to know where the police are. How'd they miss the gas station?

"I don't know," Kirk said. As he laid out the spare rifle magazines, he said to Matt, "How you want to do this, sergeant?"

Matt looked toward the oncoming police vans, and began to speak. "Soon as they get out of those vans, we tell 'm to stay back. They won't, but at least we warned 'em. They'll likely have handguns, so the longer we keep 'em at a distance, the better. You take the left, I got the right. Call out when you change a mag."

Kirk smiled and said, "Sounds like you have this all figured out…except for the part where we don't get killed."

Matt looked at him and said, "When it's your time, it's your time. But I don't think the good Lord intended either of us to die today."

"That's good to know," Kirk replied.

When the police vans were about three hundred yards away, Matt said, "Fire into the engine compartment of the one on the left. I'll get the one on the right."

Kirk didn't say anything; he simply raised his rifle to his shoulder and fired in unison with Matt. Tires squealed as the vans came to a screeching halt. The vans sat, idle and silent for a moment, and then a voice was heard over a loudspeaker.

"We are the national police. Drop your weapons. You are wanted for the crimes of treason, assault, murder, resisting arrest, and destruction of national property. Put your weapons down and surrender. Your service to your country will grant you leniency in your sentencing."

"Kiss my ass!" Matt shouted and Kirk laughed out loud.

"This is your last warning!" the voice said.

"Bite me," Matt shouted.

The side doors of both vans opened, and six police officers jumped out of each van. The officers were dressed in the typical black uniforms of the national police, but they were also wearing bulletproof vests and Kevlar helmets. A few carried pistols, but most carried submachine guns. They all had their weapons raised and began to advance toward Matt and Kirk.

"Let them have it," Kirk said.

Both he and Matt opened up with a burst of automatic fire; Matt hit an officer in the upper thigh, and the officer fell to the ground, screaming in pain. Kirk's bullets peppered an officer's torso, knocking him to the ground. However, the armored vest the officer was wearing must have done its job, as a few seconds later, he stood back up and began to advance again.

"Damn body armor," Kirk scowled.

The officers began to return fire, and the combination of pistol and submachine gun fire rained a barrage of lead down on Matt and Kirk. They both ducked behind the concrete barriers as lead flew over their heads like a swarm of angry hornets. Matt rolled onto his stomach to the left of his concrete barrier and fired a few shots before rolling back behind the safety of the barrier.

Kirk poked his head around the barriers and fired, striking another officer in the chest. The officer staggered back, momentarily stunned. Kirk took advantage of the officer's disorientation and fired again, this time hitting the officer several times in the arm. This time, the cop clutched his arm and fell to his knees as he screamed in pain.

Matt rose up on his knees and fired a few short bursts before dropping back down behind the concrete barriers again. As he changed magazines, he shouted, "How many you got?"

"Two down," Kirk said as he fired another burst. "What about you?"

"Four," Matt replied.

Just then, Kirk heard a few bullets impact the ground to his right. Looking across the street, he saw two police officers standing in a forested area.

"This could be a problem," Kirk thought. Matt and Kirk were completely exposed to the officers in the trees, and the trees would provide excellent cover for the officers. *"Must have military training,"* Kirk thought.

"We have two in the trees to our nine o'clock!" Kirk shouted. "I've got them; you focus on the rest."

"Yes, sir," Matt replied.

Kirk lay on his stomach and began to fire at the officers in the trees. Luckily, the terrain allowed Kirk to fire from a prone position, while the officers would have to stand erect to return fire. One of the officers was hit in the shoulder with several bullets; he toppled to the ground and began shouting, "I'm hit! Damn it, I'm hit!"

Kirk could hear a slow, steady pop-pop-pop sound from Matt's rifle as Matt fired singles shots at the police officers. *"Matt always preferred single, aimed shots to full automatic fire,"* Kirk thought.

Returning his attention to the remaining officer in the trees, Kirk found him moving tree to tree, using the trees as cover in an attempt to avoid his partner's fate. Kirk was just about to fire again, when he heard the sound of an AK-47 firing in full automatic mode. He looked to the right to see Elliot, standing in the middle of the street, firing an AK-47 from the hip.

"This is how southern boys fight you socialist pig!" Elliot shouted.

"Elliot! Get down!" Matt and Kirk yelled in unison.

But the warning came too late. A hailstorm of gunfire erupted as every remaining officer opened fire on Elliot. As the bullets impacted every conceivable area of Elliot's body, he dropped his rifle and collapsed like a sack of wet cement. He began to groan in pain as the bullets continued to whiz over his body.

"Elliot!" Kirk shouted.

"Help me," Elliot cried weakly.

Kirk rolled onto his backside and inserted a fresh magazine into the rifle. He then shouted, "I'm going for Elliot!"

"Don't do it; you'll be hit," Matt said.

"I can't leave a fallen man in the path of fire," Kirk said. "Cover me."

Kirk rolled off his backside into a kneeling position and aimed in the direction of the remaining officers. He squeezed the trigger and held it down; over the next three seconds, his AK-47 spewed thirty bullets towards the officers. The cops dove for cover, and Kirk tossed his rifle to the ground as he ran toward where Elliot lay. When he got near him, Kirk dove to the ground, and then crawled up next to Elliot, who was lying motionless in the street.

"Elliot, can you move?" Kirk asked. There was no response.

Kirk check for a pulse on Elliot's neck; he could find none.

"He's dead," Kirk shouted.

Kirk leapt to his feet and ran for the cover of the concrete barriers. He could hear bullets flying past his head and torso, as well as feel the rush of wind the bullets created. Suddenly, Kirk felt as if an anvil hit him in the chest at one hundred miles per hour. A sudden weakness overcame his body. He couldn't get a breath; his running slowed to a walk, and everything seemed to move in slow motion. He looked down and saw the blood gushing from his chest. *"Oh my God, I've been hit,"* he thought.

He tried to put his hands over his chest to stop the bleeding, but his hands just didn't seem to work. Then Kirk felt another impact, this time to his abdomen. The impact sent a shockwave through his body that forced him to stop walking. His legs became shaky, and he fell to the ground, gasping for air.

"Colonel!" Matt shouted.

Kirk tried to respond, but he couldn't get enough air to speak.

"Colonel!" Matt shouted again. After there was no response a second time, Matt returned his attention to the two remaining police officers. Matt flipped the selector switch of his M-16 to full automatic and took aim at one of the officers. Matt pulled the trigger, and unleashed a hail of full automatic fire. The officer was hit several times in the chest, causing him to fall backward. The remaining officer, realizing he was alone, lost his courage and dropped his submachine gun and raised his hands over his head.

Matt inserted a fresh magazine into his M-16 and then stood, pointing the weapon at the officer."Go on, get out of here!" Matt shouted. The officer turned around and ran to one of the police vans. He wasted no time in climbing in the van and starting the engine. Tires squealed as the officers spun the van around and sped off.

Matt ran to Kirk, who was still lying in the street and having difficulty breathing. Kirk was covered in blood, and the blood around the chest wound looked like red foam. The chest wound was also making a sucking sound, the sign of a punctured lung. Matt slung his rifle over his shoulder, and then knelt down to pick up Kirk's body. The weight was heavy but manageable, and Matt began to walk toward the Bronco as fast as he could.

"I'm gettin' too old to keep savin' your ass," Matt said.

As he approached the Bronco, Matt could see Sebastian sitting on the tailgate of the SUV. "Sebastian! Get in and start the engine! We gotta go fast!"

Sebastian turned and saw Matt; a look of disbelief crossed his face.

"What happened?" Sebastian said with panic in his voice.

"He was hit two times," Matt said. "We got to get him to a hospital, fast. Get behind the wheel and drive!"

Sebastian nodded his head and climbed through the open cargo area towards the driver's seat; by the time Matt had Kirk in the rear of the Bronco, Sebastian had the engine started and was buckling his seatbelt. Matt then climbed in through the rear, pulling the tailgate closed as he did.

"What direction?" Sebastian asked.

"Same way we were goin'," Matt replied. "This here road leads to the Texas border. Don't worry about no stop signs or speed limits; you drive as fast as you can."

"Yes, sir," Sebastian replied.

Gravel sprayed as the Bronco peeled out of the station parking lot and onto the road. As the truck barreled down the street at speeds it was not designed for, Matt grabbed the first aid kit in hopes that he could do something for Kirk. He was relieved to find that the first aid kit was well stocked; he pulled several military bandages from the kit, as well as a square of plastic. Matt wiped the frothy blood away from the chest wound as best as he could, and then placed the plastic over the wound, pressing in into place. He then covered it with one of the military bandages and began apply as much pressure as he could.

"How's he doing?" Sebastian shouted.

"Circling the drain," Matt replied. "Just drive!"

"Sergeant," Kirk said weakly as he struggled for air.

""Don't talk; just breath," Matt said.

"Don't worry about me," Kirk said. He felt as if everything was going dark. "Just get Sebastian to Texas."

"You are not about to die on me!" Matt shouted. "You will pull through, you hear me!"

"Get Sebastian to Texas," were the last words out of Kirk's mouth before the darkness washed over him.

Levi Walker sat in his favorite chair, thinking about the events of the past few days. Looking out the window, he could see the setting sun paint the western horizon in shades of orange and red. "*What a day*," he said to himself. Levi felt the cell phone vibrate in his pocket; he pulled it out and found a text message of nonsense. He knew this was from the Sons of Liberty.

He booted up his ancient laptop's messenger program and found two messages waiting for him.

"Speech well received by legislature and people of Texas. Retransmitting speech to organization branches throughout US. Well done."

Levi knew that the speech had gone well, and that it had been very popular with the people of Texas. For far too long, big business had taken advantage of the citizenry. Nearly every industry was dominated by a single or few big businesses, making it nearly impossible for new businesses to compete. In most cases, the US government had simply made it illegal to start a new business in a particular sector. Other times, the sector was so heavily regulated that only the big businesses could afford to comply with the regulations. This new bill would cure that, at least in Texas.

The lieutenant governor had tried to stop the bill in the senate, but it had passed by a wide margin with minimal debate and no changes. The bill was set to be debated by the house the following day. It was expected to pass by a huge margin. Levi typed a response to the message.

"Thanks. Request: investigate Jayden McCoy. Can I trust her?"

"Understood. Consider it done."

Levi moved on to the second message. It read:

"Conrad White has taken clips from the speech and is spinning it to make Texas look bad."

Levi leaned back in his chair. The actions of the US President were not surprising; it would have been more surprising had he not tried to use Levi's words against him. Levi began to type on his laptop. *"Not surprised. What is the danger level?"*

"High. He is organizing, so the free states have time for a defense."

"What kind of defense?"

"A political prisoner in the North was working on a technology that could be used as a defense against invasion."

"Where is he being held?"

"She is at Marysville Ohio. She must be freed. We can provide support."

Levi sighed, and then typed his final message. *"Understood. Will be in touch for more details."*

CHAPTER SIXTEEN

"He's starting to come around. I'll take over from here."

"Yes, sir."

Kirk could hear voices and the opening and closing of doors as he tried to open his eyes. With considerable effort, he opened his eyes and tried to focus on his surroundings. At first, everything around him was blurry, but his eyes soon began to focus. He then realized that he was lying in bed in a hospital room. He noticed a dull pain in his chest as he tried to take a deep breath. Next to his bed was a young, dark haired man who was sitting on a stool and watching him intently.

"Easy, Mr. Dillon," the man said. "You've had a rough spell, but you are going to be just fine." The man slapped the name badge on his shirt and said in a loud voice, "Kirk Dillon has just woken up. Please show his family in." The man slapped the badge again and then said to Kirk, "Mr. Dillon, I am Lieutenant Callebs, and you are in a hospital room at Brooke Army Medical Center, Fort Sam Houston."

Kirk struggled to speak but found his mouth and throat extremely dry. Finally, he managed to say, "How long have I been here?"

"Two days," Lieutenant Callebs replied. "The surgeons removed one bullet from your left lung, one from your lower abdominal cavity. No organs other than the lungs were hit, but you lost a lot of blood. That's why you lost consciousness and why it took so long to come back around. On the bright side, it doesn't look like there will be any permanent damage, and you should make a full recovery."

The door of the room opened, and Sebastian rushed in, followed closely by Matt Pickett. Sebastian had a worried look on his face.

"How are you feeling," he said quickly.

Kirk swallowed hard and then said in a coarse voice, "Like fifty miles of bad road, but I'll pull through; I always do."

"I'm gettin' a bit too old to keep savin' your ass," Matt said sternly.

"I'm getting too old to get shot," Kirk said. "How's the arthritis?"

"Thank the Lord for ice," Matt replied.

Kirk nodded and then said, "What happened after I passed out?"

"Didn't think we'd make it," Matt said. "Sebastian was drivin'...damn good drivin' too...and I was tryin' to patch you up. After I got the field dressing on you, I was shootin' at the police comin' after us. I stopped a couple of the police vans in their tracks, but I was runnin' out of ammo. I was sure that we were done for when we got to the Texas state line and ran into a National Guard unit. They covered us and called in a dust-off."

Kirk smiled weakly. "Feds didn't want to mess with the Guardsmen?"

"Not after they saw they were outnumbered ten to one," Sebastian said with a grin.

Kirk heard the door to his room open again. Looking toward the door, he saw two men walk in; the first of which was his son Michael. The second was a tall, lean, silver haired man.

"Michael!" Kirk exclaimed weakly.

"How are you feeling, Dad?"

"I've been better," Kirk replied. "But I'll live."

Michael nodded, and then said, "Dad, you remember General McRain?"

Kirk nodded, and then said, "Excuse me if I don't salute, General."

They silver haired general smiled and said, "Welcome to the

Republic of Texas."

"What is a United States Army General doing in Texas?" Kirk asked.

General McRain smiled and began to speak. "All US military installations in the state of Texas have been handed over to the Republic of Texas."

Kirk looked startled. "All of them? I can't believe that Washington went along with that!"

Shaking his head, General McRain said, "Washington didn't go along with it, but they had no choice. Most of the senior officers here in Texas agreed to hand over the bases in exchange for political asylum. Asylum was also offered to all military personnel in Texas. Most have accepted; those that didn't are being sent north as we speak. The bases were handed over to assist in the formation of the new nation."

"The new nation? You mean the Republic of Texas?" Kirk asked.

"No," General McRain replied. "You missed out on a lot of events while you took your two day nap. In the past two days, Louisiana, Mississippi, Alabama, and Georgia have all left the United States, and it looks like Tennessee and the Carolinas will be leaving soon."

"I think I know where this is going," Kirk said. "Those states are going to band together to form a new nation?"

The General nodded and said, "Yes. There is delegate meeting in two weeks to begin the work to form a new nation. The nation will be founded on the same principles that the United States was founded on…individual liberty and personal freedom within a constitutional republic."

"I guess the great experiment failed," Kirk said.

"What do you mean," Sebastian asked.

"Thomas Jefferson called the United States Constitution the 'Great Experiment,'" Kirk said. I guess he was wrong; it didn't last."

"Not necessarily," the General said. "There is hope among many that the new nation will become an economic powerhouse. Once that happens, and the people of the United States see how a nation full of free, productive people can prosper, it may pressure the United States into reverting back to the old ways."

Kirk shook his head and said, "All those people hooked up to the government umbilical cord…I don't know that they would give that up."

General McRain sighed and said, "You may be right. In that case, the new nation becomes what the United States once was."

"Does it have a name yet?" Kirk asked.

"The new nation?" General McRain shook his head. "No. Some have suggested the American Republic. I've also heard The Federation of American States. A few hard core Southern pride types have suggested The Confederate States of America, but I doubt they will get enough support for that name."

"I would avoid that name altogether," Kirk said. "As well as any reference to the Confederacy or the Civil War. As it is, the president and his cronies are going to get the propaganda started about how this is a racist movement."

"But there wouldn't be any truth to that," Sebastian said.

"Little Brother," Michael said, "power hungry politicians will never let the truth stand in the way of their ultimate goal."

"And that ultimate goal is always more power…more control over people's lives," General McRain said.

Kirk stared at the ceiling for a second and then said, "Has everyone who voted for secession thought about the consequences of their actions? And I'm not talking about the formation of a new government."

"What are you talking about?" Matt asked.

"What Washington is going to do," Kirk replied. "Do you really think that President White is going to allow a secession movement to take place?

General McRain scratched his head and said, "I think the people who believe this will be a walk in the park are in the minority. "

Lieutenant Callebs looked at General McRain and said, "Do you think we are looking at another civil war, sir?"

"I can answer that for you," said an aged voice.

Everyone turned toward the sound of the voice. Standing in the doorway was Byron Reynolds, with Jenny Thelon standing directly behind him. Byron walked slowly into the room, using his eagle headed cane for assistance. Byron looked at Kirk and said, "You look like hell. At your age, you should be writing, not trying to relive your twenties."

“Good to see you, too,” Kirk said. “Why are you in Texas?”

“There are some great opportunities in Texas,” Byron said. A smile slowly formed as he stroked his goatee. “Former federal buildings are up for sale at a price I can’t pass up. I just struck a deal for my new center of operations in Dallas.”

“Aren’t you going to miss Cincinnati?” Kirk asked.

“I will miss Reds baseball and goetta,” Byron said.

“Don’t forget Skyline Chili,” Sebastian added.

Byron laughed and said, “The boy’s got a point. But joking aside, in my business, I need to be somewhere where free speech is permitted. Right now, that is Texas.” Byron took a few more steps into the room. “As to your question doctor, here is your answer. Jenny, put that broadcast on that screen, so everyone can see this.”

“Yes, sir,” Jenny replied. After typing on her computer tablet for a moment, Jenny looked up and said, “Watch the screen on that wall. This is a speech by the president, made less than an hour ago.”

Everyone looked to the viewing screen on the wall of the hospital room; the screen came to life, showing the President of the United States seated at his desk in the Oval Office.

“My fellow Americans and citizens of the world, I speak to you tonight with a heavy heart. As you know, racist businessmen have taken control of the state governments in Texas and Alaska, forcing the states to secede from the United States. Unfortunately, I have been informed that the states of Louisiana, Mississippi, Alabama, and Georgia have also fallen to the racists and have left this grand union that we call the United States. I have reached out to the leaders of all of the former states, but to no avail; they have severed all diplomatic ties with the United States, and are intent on creating a nation of white supremacists where people of all minorities are slaves."

"Yesterday, the chairman of the freedom party was killed when the brakes in his car gave out and he drove through an intersection here in Washington, D.C. While we initially thought that this was just an accident, investigators with the national police have determined this was no accident. It has been determined that this was an act of murder on the part of the terrorist group Sons of Liberty. The national police have also informed me that the terrorists have been working hand in hand with the governments of the states that have seceded. It is now apparent that this act of terrorism was planned many months ago, and was intended to disrupt our political process, allowing them to leave the union while we were distracted by the tragedy. I am here to tell you we will not stand for this injustice. We will bring his killers to justice, and we will prevail. Until the party can hold elections, I will act as the temporary party chair."

"Along the borders of the seceded states, there has been the senseless killing of innocents. This must stop, as these are simple people who are trying to rejoin their loved ones across the border. We have sent diplomats to these seceded states to ask that the killing stop, but to no avail."

"The United States has existed for nearly three hundred years. In the early 1800's, men spoke of Manifest Destiny…the vision of a nation which spanned coast to coast. Now, racists who wish to recreate the days of Confederate slavery have attempted to destroy that dream. Well, not on my watch. Because of this and the senseless killing along the border, I am asking the Congress for a Declaration of War against the states of Texas, Alaska, Louisiana, Mississippi, Alabama, and Georgia. My fellow Americans, have no doubts about it; we are at war."

"To ensure the safety of the citizens of this nation, border states will be placed under the control of the national police. We will also begin to recall military troops from around the globe. I am also asking the United Nations for an embargo against the seceded states, and the Coast Guard will set up a naval blockade of the southern coasts. More details will be release soon. Good day and thank you all."

As the screen went blank, General McRain shook his head and said, "I was kind of expecting something like this. We already had reports of military units from all around the world being recalled home. I think the only reason we haven't seen full scale battles yet, is because of how scattered the US military is. It will take some time to bring them home and get organized."

"You said full scale," Kirk said, puzzled.

"There have already been skirmishes between National Guard units and National Police," General McRain replied. "There have also been a lot of drone attacks. That is why you need to get rested and get healed."

"What do you mean?" Kirk asked.

The General looked Kirk directly in the eyes and said, "We are going to need every man we can get our hands on." General McRain smiled and then continued. "Even if that guy is a washed up old light colonel who doesn't know how to keep his mouth shut." Turning toward Matt Pickett, the General added, "And we could certainly use a man with over thirty years of combat experience."

"Don't you think that Matt and I are a bit old to lead an infantry platoon into the field?" Kirk protested.

"Not sure how much more poundin' this old body can take," Matt said.

"I'm more concerned with what's inside your heads, not the condition of your bodies," the General said. "I was just talking with the Governor. We both think you would be perfect for a little job he needs done…but it can wait until you've healed."

Kirk sighed and the stared at the ceiling. "This is far from over, isn't it?"

General McRain laughed and said, "Over? This is just getting started! We're looking at the rebirth of freedom!"

"Freedomredux," Kirk said.

"What?" General McRain asked.

"Freedomredux," Kirk repeated.

"What does that mean?" Sebastian asked.

"Redux is based on a Latin word; it means brought back or restored," Kirk said.

"See, I knew that big brain and big mouth of yours were good for something," General McRain said. "OK, Freedomredux it is."

EPILOGUE

"Don't worry, Mr. President. I will have the Mexicans eating out of my hands."

President Conrad White smiled, and then continued his phone conversation. "That is exactly what I wanted to hear, and I don't care what you have to tell the Mexican Government. You just do whatever it takes for them to halt all trade with the seceded states."

"Understood, Mr. President."

"Good," the president said. "Now get moving and have a safe flight."

The president hung up the phone and opened the top drawer to his desk. He pulled out a thick journal that was bound in well-worn brown leather and had a brass colored lock holding it closed. He also pulled an antique fountain pen from the drawer. Taking a key from his pocket, he unlocked the journal, and the pulled the cap from the fountain pen. Flipping the journal to first blank page, he began writing.

October 17, 2049

The events of the past few days have been unexpected, but can be used to my advantage. To date, six states have seceded from the nation. What they do not realize is that they have provided the leverage I will need to force changes upon this nation. I will have no trouble passing my legislation now. When you tell the American people that we are doing something to support the war effort, the dim-witted populace believes it.

But this will be different. This time, the war will be at home. Not since the attacks of September 11, 2001 has the country been attacked on its home soil. And if I can manipulate public opinion (a task which I am a master at), I can get the people of this country to give up freedoms that they would never dream of. Once those freedoms are gone, they will not be returned, as it will be necessary for the formation of my One World Government. The people of this country will come to realize that there is nothing special about them, and they are just one other nation among many. This idea of "American Exceptionalism" is foolishness.

The treason of the military was unfortunate. However, this setback will yield progress, as well. Loyalty to the President of the United States is of the upmost importance, and the selection of officers and enlisted men will be based on that loyalty. I will begin a purge of the military to get rid of even the slightest hint of disloyalty. The disloyalty of the military will also allow me to expand and strengthen the national police.

I have sent diplomats to Mexico to persuade them not to trade with the seceded states. In addition, my allies in Europe will work to prevent Germany from allying itself with the seceded states. Germany must be put in its place, so it may be prudent for all European Union nations to stop all trade with Germany until she rejoins the Union.

I can see the light at the end of the tunnel. One step closer to world domination.

ABOUT THE AUTHOR

AJ Reissig lives in New Richmond, Ohio with his lovely wife Christina and children. Born in 1973, he grew up in the small river town of Moscow, Ohio. He is a graduate of the University of Cincinnati with a background in chemistry. After spending several years as an analyst in manufacturing, he began to pursue writing as a part-time freelancer. His hobbies include gardening, woodworking, home improvement, and anything outdoors.

AJ has long followed politics. Over the years, AJ has become increasingly disturbed by the trend toward big government in the United States. His novel series, *FreedomRedux*, revolves around a United States of the future that is governed by a totalitarian regime that is bent on world domination, and those who wish to restore the United States to the nation that the founding fathers intended.

16302405R00173

Made in the USA
Charleston, SC
14 December 2012